Like her cousins, Sheila wears a Claddagh ring ......
Broun lineage with the MacLomain clan. Already having witnessed
the strife ravaging the medieval Scottish highlands she's eager to
once more be thrust back in time...even if it's into the arms of the
enemy.

Imprisoned fourteen winters and now first-in-command of the
enemy's army, Grant MacLomain must find a way to save all those
he cares for. Though under the watchful eye of his master and
chieftain, Keir Hamilton, he unleashes his plan the moment he
connects with a lass from the future.

Through hardship, forgiveness and even acceptance, Sheila and
Grant struggle to push past their abused hearts and the war that
divides them in, Faith of the Highlander.

1

Faith of the Highlander
By Sky Purington
COPYRIGHT © 2014

**Edited by *Cathy McElhaney*
Cover Art by *Tamra Westberry***

Published in the United States of America

Dedication

For my mother-in-law, Nancy.

Thank you for over thirty years of dedicated service to those who have been mentally abused or suffered otherwise. I can't imagine how many people you helped as a therapist and social worker.

God Bless.

Faith of the Highlander
The MacLomain Series-Next Generation
Book Four

By

Sky Purington

Prologue

Few could say they'd made a home out of a dungeon.

But then few could say they'd spent fourteen winters in captivity yet was first-in-command of one of the most powerful clans in Scotland. Now Grant's bars were inlaid not by Hamilton stone but by his own clan, the MacLomains. Though at first chained up, he was now in what was likely the largest cell in this dismal place.

"You dinnae complain much, aye?"

So at last his brother spoke from the shadows. Oh, he'd known Malcolm was there. Rather than respond, he had waited. After all, it was what he did best.

Eventually, Malcolm came forward, half his face revealed in the torchlight.

Now if he'd just come a little closer…

They eyed one another for some time before Malcolm finally spoke. "I want to know what happened to Iosbail MacLomain."

No doubt that was amongst many answers he sought.

But no answers could be given.

Not so long as Grant was mentally shackled to the MacLomain's enemy and his former master, Keir Hamilton. Only one person could help him at this point.

Sheila.

His one light in eternal darkness.

Even his kin held little appeal next to her. Now gone far into the future, he felt the loss of her as acutely as he would if his heartbeat crawled to a stop. She was the key to setting him free. Without her, communication with the MacLomain's was not an option.

And communication was vital.

This was the first time his brother had ventured down to 'visit' him and Grant needed to be sure he executed this transaction just right to accomplish his goal. Slow to stand, acting the part of a man unused to such confinement and dankness, he moved to the bars.

"I dinnae know the outcome of Iosbail MacLomain." Eyes locked on his brother, he shook his head and made a discreet come-hither motion with his hand, hoping that Malcolm understood the need for discretion. "I wasnae told a thing."

Malcolm's eyes narrowed. When he started to speak, Grant shook his head sharply then put a finger to his lips. Keir Hamilton could hear everything Grant said and heard.

Again he made a come-hither motion.

Clearly unsure but curious despite, his brother took another step forward.

That was all Grant needed.

Lightning fast, he grabbed his brother's wrist and started to murmur words Keir would *never* hear.

Words only heard between him and Sheila.

Her words to be precise.

"This ring's for me. Soon I'll be back for ye."

Malcolm tried to yank his hand away but it was too late.

Magic already stirred.

Grant's magic.

And it was far stronger than Malcolm's.

Fluctuating, powerful, Malcolm barely had a moment to react before the bars warped and twisted. Fast, with speed his brother never could have anticipated, Grant lunged out of his cage, wrapped a hand around Malcolm's throat and slammed him against the wall.

Within a breath of his kin, he whispered...

"*Now* we will see an end to this."

Chapter One

North Salem, New Hampshire
2014

"We really need to figure out how to end all of this," Sheila muttered and tossed her tea bag in the trash.

"I get that. I totally do." Seth sat on the counter and shook his head. "But I can't be the one to help this time."

"McKayla will be disappointed."

"McKayla will understand." He frowned. "You're making this hard, hon."

Sheila sat down at the kitchen table and eyed her cup of tea. She hadn't expected this to go so poorly. If anything she thought Seth would jump at the opportunity to travel back in time again to medieval Scotland. She figured he'd do anything to help out her cousin and his best friend, McKayla. But it seemed his wife was pregnant and he wasn't willing to leave her in such a state.

She didn't care if his priorities were in line. Sheila held up her ring finger. "*You* helped create these rings. *You* helped fight off Keir Hamilton and Colin MacLeod before. How will we manage without you?"

It was still hard to believe that she'd returned to the future to try to recruit three paranormal investigators, who also happened to be warlocks. The goal was to convince them to travel back to medieval Scotland to help defeat their enemies. Grant had been clear. They were needed. Okay, maybe he hadn't been *that* clear. He didn't say *exactly* how many of them were needed. Still.

"Your cousins always manage," Seth assured, sipping his coffee. "Besides, Devin and Leathan aren't off the table yet. I called them. It's safe to say Leathan would give anything to travel back in time to medieval Scotland and Devin would do anything to help out period."

"Yet neither gave you a definitive answer over the phone."

Sheila sifted through the novel McKayla had written. A novel that almost seemed to have started all this.

"Well, no, but that was just a few hours ago." He glanced out the window. "And look, they're already pulling into the driveway. You'll have your answer soon enough."

Sheila shook her head. A few hours amounted to several days in medieval Scotland. It was a side-effect of the *time-travel time exchange*. That's what she'd taken to calling it since time went by much faster here than there...almost as if it was trying to catch up with itself.

When she'd left that time period which dated back eight hundred years ago, all hell was breaking loose. A highland war unlike any other was well underway and not only were her cousins involved but the MacLomain men they'd fallen in love with. Her cousin McKayla had ended up with the chieftain, Colin, while Leslie wed his brother Bradon and Cadence found herself with their cousin Malcolm.

Malcolm, of course, was Grant's brother.

And Grant was the number one reason she needed to get back to medieval Scotland.

"Tell me again how this all started?"

Sheila looked up, startled, as a tall handsome man with dark auburn hair and smoky green eyes walked into the room.

Seth met him at the door and gave him a hug. "Devin, good to see you, cuz."

Sheila stood, smiled and held out her hand. "It's been a long time, Devin. Thanks for coming."

A charming grin curled his lips. "What's that then, lassie?" An Irish lilt was obvious when he spoke. "I seem to remember us competing as to who had less red in their hair when we were kids." Instead of shaking her hand, he pulled her in for a quick hug.

Warmed by his greeting, she nodded when he pulled away. "I'd forgotten about that."

No sooner had he walked in the door then someone else followed.

Just as tall and good looking as his cousins, the third man had blond streaked brown hair and dark brown eyes.

"Good to see you, Leathan." Seth said, as he embraced him. "It's been too long."

"Aye." Though his Scottish brogue was far different than the MacLomains, Sheila's heart clenched. God, she missed them so much.

Seth turned to Sheila. "Not sure if you two remember one another."

Barely. Sheila held out her hand. "Thanks for coming."

Leathan shook it. "Good to see you again. It's been a long time."

Had it ever! Too long ago and too briefly she supposed to be asking these men to put themselves in harm's way to help her and the MacLomains.

But she would.

Seth nodded at the table. "Please, sit. What do you want to drink?"

Leathan and Devin gave him a pointed look.

"Right." Seth poured a few glasses of whiskey and plunked them down alongside the bottle.

They nodded their thanks and Devin once more turned his warm regard her way. "Seth filled us in on some of your story but I'd like to hear your version, Sheila. Again, tell us how this all started."

Well, she supposed if they were sitting here listening that was a good start.

So she filled them in.

"Sorry if I repeat stuff you already know, but I'm really not sure what Seth has told you. So here we go… it all began when my cousin, McKayla traveled back in time to medieval Scotland with a friend who wasn't exactly who he pretended to be. Not by a long shot. He had abandoned his clan to become an assassin. The MacLomain's eventually welcomed him back and made him chieftain, as was his birthright." She took a sip of tea. "His name is Colin MacLomain."

Convinced they were paying attention, she continued.

"When McKayla and Colin came together everything happening now started to unfold. As it turned out, to save McKayla, Colin killed his mentor who was Keir Hamilton's son. Keir, if you didn't already know, is the mega nemesis in this particular tale. Furious, he declared war on the MacLomains. But as it turned out, he'd always had his eyes on the clan, specifically their best kept secret, Torra. Yet even they didn't know exactly why Keir wanted her so much."

Sheila shrugged. "Sure, Torra was the chieftain's sister but more importantly as they soon found out, she was part dragon." She shook her head. "When that came to light they also learned that they fought not only Keir but an allied enemy named Colin MacLeod." She looked skyward. "I know, confusing, two Colin's in this tired tale. One's the good guy, the other not so much."

Devin and Leathan downed half their whiskey and nodded for her to continue.

"Long story short, I've been back to medieval Scotland several times and can catch you up. The MacLomains are days away from full on war with their rivals, the MacLeod's and Hamilton's. And I'm talking like mere hours our time." She tried not to get too anxious. "Like in *time-travel time exchange* terms."

Leathan's brows lowered in question.

"Never mind." She shook her head. "As it turns out through much trial and tribulation, Keir Hamilton managed to trap half of Torra's soul at his castle. The other half is trapped in her dragon form which now lies in the loch beside the MacLomain castle."

"Half her soul?" Devin murmured, frowning.

Of course that part would interest a paranormal investigator. Sheila nodded. "Yeah, half." She swallowed her emotions. "And it's an incredibly sad sight to see."

"No doubt," Leathan acknowledged. "Tell me why you need us in this venture?"

He seemed to be the leader, so she nodded. "Getting to that." Sheila took another sip of tea, her throat way too dry. "Through all of this we learned that Malcolm's brother still lives."

"Who's Malcolm?"

"He's cousin to the current laird, Colin MacLomain."

"And last I knew, didn't you have a little thing for him?" Seth asked.

Sheila shook her head. "No." Then she nodded. "Okay, yes, for a bit. But I worked through all that and now he's all about Cadence."

Leathan cocked his brow. "Flaming red hair?"

Naturally they'd remember Cadence even if they hadn't seen her in over a decade. "Yep, that's her. As it turns out, she's in love with Malcolm."

"Sorry about that," Seth said.

"No need to be." Sheila shook her head. "He wasn't meant for me, anyway."

"I'm guessing you know that because of the ring?" Seth said.

"Right, the ring." Sheila didn't mean to sound so flighty but her mind was all wrapped up in Grant. Every second that passed was one more that she wasn't helping him. "As I'm sure Seth told you, he helped create the Claddagh rings my cousins and I now wear." She held up her ring finger to show them. "Created by Seth, a warlock, and both Colin MacLomain and his sister Torra the dragon, they're a means for us girls to travel through time."

"But that's not all," Seth prompted.

"No, that's not all," Sheila said. "These rings have other unique magical abilities. The stone, made from a piece of the original Highland Defiance, aids in time traveling. The other stuff," she glanced at Seth, "well you'd have to ask him how he managed it, but it seems the stone will only burn and glow for our one true love. A MacLomain. Mine happens to burn for Grant," she tossed Seth a look, "*not* Malcolm."

"And you and the other girls are witches, aye?" Leathan asked.

Sheila nodded. "As it turns out, we sure are."

Leathan and Devin downed their whiskey and refilled.

"If we hadn't gone through all we had and become warlocks in the process, I might think you were completely out of your mind," Leathan said. "But we did and so we believe you."

Sheila thought back to Grant's request that these men were the only means to release Torra from Keir Hamilton as they, like the dark overlord, were warlocks. "So I assume Seth told you why you're here."

"Aye," Devin said. "And you filled in some of the blanks."

"So while I know Seth won't...or can't...will either of you travel back in time and help the MacLomains?" she asked. *Please say yes.*

"You can't imagine how much I'd like to," Leathan began, heart in his eyes. "But as it turns out, I'm in the same predicament as Seth."

Seth's eyes widened. "No."

A small smile lit Leathan's face. "Aye, Dakota's pregnant."

The men again embraced, clapping one another on the back.

It seemed everyone was pregnant nowadays.

But she certainly wouldn't hold that against them.

"Congratulations," she said softly as Leathan sat.

So that left only one man who might be able to help.

Devin.

Sheila started to speak but garbled words came out of her mouth. What the heck? So she tried again. This time they were slightly clearer. "This ring's for me. Soon I'll be back for ye."

Mortified, she clamped her hand over her mouth.

That was *not* what she'd been trying to say.

Alert, Devin and Leathan's eyes narrowed.

"Magic. Someone pulls her," Leathan muttered. Hands instantly thrown in the air, he started to chant.

Oh shoot. Not yet.

But when she tried to speak again the same words poured from her mouth. They were the very words she used to travel through time. Only one person could possibly know what they were.

Grant.

Seth and his cousins clearly understood she was in trouble and started chanting. Yet whatever they said grew further and further away as the same words kept pouring from her mouth over and over.

Sheila clenched her fists and bent her head as the smell of burning sugar filled her nostrils.

Time travel.

Fast, precise, she was being yanked back.

Pain ripped through her seconds before the room spun away and everything fell. As soon as panic started to seize, she nearly thumped to the floor. Yet before she did, a strong hand came around her wrist and kept her on her feet.

Discombobulated, she blinked in the darkness.

Pulled against a hard body, she shuddered.

Grant.

Grasping the pentacle around her neck, his harsh words entered her mind. *"I can block my ears against Hamilton to what others say but never my own words. If you dinnae tell Malcolm that all is well and that he should stand down when I release him, he will soon die."*

Nothing like being thrust back into the thick of it!

"I'll say no such thing until I know he's okay," she said into his mind.

"Look then!" Grant said. *"I cannae tell him to keep his peace lest Keir hear."*

Vision slightly clearer, she blinked. Oh hell! Malcolm's eyes were narrowed on her and his face red as Grant squeezed his windpipe.

"Malcolm." She shook her head. "He can't speak to you or Keir will know. He means no harm." She nodded at her pentacle. "He speaks to me telepathically. You know it to be the truth. If he lets you go and you freak out it'll be real bad for us all."

Malcolm's eyes narrowed further.

So did Sheila's. "Seriously. I need this to go well. *Please.*"

It seemed Malcolm relaxed some because Grant slowly released. But Malcolm was Malcolm.

With a harsh thrust, he pushed his brother away then attacked.

"Damn," Sheila muttered and scrambled after them.

Malcolm had already punched Grant several times in the side. Ducking, Grant drove him against the far wall and unleashed several sharp jabs. Malcolm came right back. *Punch. Punch. Punch.* He slammed Grant against the opposite wall.

Horrified, she tried to step between them.

Of equal strength and size, the pure physical power exploding between them was formidable. Grant grabbed Malcolm around the waist and pushed then wrapped his arm around his brother's neck and whipped him to the hard stone floor. With a quick swipe of his foot, Malcolm brought Grant crashing down after him.

"Step aside, Sheila," she heard from just behind her.

She glanced over her shoulder, eyes rounded when Devin appeared and flung out his hands. Horrified, she watched as dark tendrils snaked out from his hands and wrapped around both MacLomains.

"Devin, what are you doing!"

Yanked apart and bound against the wall beside one another, Malcolm and Grant howled in rage. Not at Devin who had so clearly bound them with his black magic, but at one another. Then suddenly, Devin was flung aside, bound by a different sort of magic altogether.

Sheila turned.

Coira.

Malcolm and Grant's mother shook her head as she walked up beside her. "Welcome back, lass."

Powerful in her own right, Coira MacLomain was one of the four original MacLomain wizards. By the look on her face she was less than impressed by what was transpiring.

Sheila went to Devin, shook her head, and whispered, "Sorry, I'll get this worked out soon."

Bound by magic and unable to speak, his brows lowered in answer.

Sheila was about to explain to Coira what had happened but the older woman shook her head. "No need to explain, 'twas merely the prisoner trying to escape." Her narrowed eyes went to Devin. "Unbind Malcolm *now*."

Coira leaned close and whispered in her ear. "You need to tell Devin to listen to my orders so I can sort this out. Then mayhap Grant will at last be able to speak freely. But be discreet."

Trusting Coira explicably, Sheila did just that. Devin, however, wasn't so trusting, and still had narrowed eyes on Coira. He might for all appearances be a happy-go-lucky Irishman, but beneath all that was a warlock teeming with black magic.

And something more...but she couldn't quite figure out what that was.

"*Please*," she murmured in his ear. "Trust me if no one else."

But he had no real reason to trust her.

"Please," she said again. "Coira was only defending her sons."

Devin looked at Sheila long and hard before he finally managed to nod.

Coira must have seen it because she spoke harshly. "I will free you, then you will release Malcolm."

Malcolm only watched, still seething mad.

Grant now hung his head, eyes to the floor.

Coira again leaned close to Sheila, words soft. "When your warlock releases Malcolm, go to Grant. I will deal with the other two."

With a thrust of Coira's hand, Devin was released. After a quick chant and murmur he flung out his hands again and the black oily whips that held Malcolm shriveled away.

As he did this, Sheila sidled over next to Grant, grasping her pentacle so that she might speak to him through her mind. *Tell me what should happen next?*

"Free me," he whispered into her mind, the feel of his essence washing through in sharp, erotic waves. It always felt like this…incredibly intimate.

"Put the pentacle in my hand then wrap your hand around mine," he continued.

So she did.

Before she understood what was happening the air buckled around them. There was no other way to describe it. A low murmured chant came from his lips. *"Et posita abrumpat. Restitue animam meam a me.* Break the bonds laid by he. Give back my mind taken from me."

As if she watched through a fogged over window, Malcolm was flung away and the bars to the cell bent back into their original rigid form with her and Grant on the inside. Blurred, as if caught on a wave of air they couldn't fight, Coira, Malcolm and even Devin were pushed up the long winding stairs until they vanished from sight.

Cool air brushed by her face and she stumbled back against the wall, wide-eyed.

As Devin's black oily ties slithered away so too did something else…something only seen in the flexing of Grant's muscles and the sharp glow of his pale bluish gray eyes. *Sweet Jesus*, was he a beautiful man. Even within the throes of his powerful magic, her eyes wandered over his face. She'd never really had a chance to admire him before.

Though he had the same strong chin and high cheekbones as the other MacLomain men, there was a particular brand of fierceness about his well-formed lips and deep-set brows that not even his brother could rival. Even the scar that ran from beneath the corner of his right eye and up his temple couldn't take from his stark handsomeness. No, if anything the scar heightened his masculinity, his near untamed prowess. Add in the near black hair with dark mahogany streaks contrasting with his startlingly pale slate blue eyes and any woman would be hard pressed to look away, never mind gawk.

Sheila started to tremble when he broke free from the last of whatever or whoever had imprisoned him. A shiver raced through her and she knew.

Grant had just broken free from Keir Hamilton's mental hold over him.

He tore off his tunic and whipped it aside. With nothing but the Hamilton's plaid hung low on his waist, he was an impressive sight. Legs braced, arms by his side, fists clenched, he closed his eyes. Cast in the soft, flickering glow of a single sputtering torch, sweat slicked muscles rippled down his long warrior's body. Was he praying? Long moments passed. Every one of them a lifetime as her heart thundered. Then, as if replacing one swift divine moment with another, his eyes snapped open and met hers.

It felt like a freight train hit her.

"Och, my wee geal," he whispered.

Wee what?

Sheila made to speak but the words died on her lips when in two swift strides, he pulled her into his arms. The word 'wee' seemed a massive understatement when up against him. Though she was fairly tall at five foot seven, he had to be a foot taller. Lord, she felt tiny! What had been but a tremble became a harsh fiery heat that whiplashed through her body. Emotional state and sensory awareness in overdrive, she put her hands against his hard chest.

"Oh, I shouldn't have done that," she murmured. But she didn't pull her hands away.

No, if anything, she pressed tighter and curled her fingers slightly. It was one thing to meet a man in your mind, another thing entirely to feel him pressed up against your body. When he tilted up her chin, her eyes slid shut. Why, she'd never know. She supposed somewhere deep inside she wasn't ready to look too closely into his eyes.

But why?

Perhaps she was afraid of what she'd see there. Perhaps though he seemed so strong she'd see years of mental abuse flicker in his gaze. Mental abuse inflicted by Keir being twisted within his mind for so long. The very idea of it made her sick to her stomach.

But none of that mattered when she felt his warm breath whisper over her lips. Close, so very close. She could all but feel his mouth hovering over hers. Time slowed as her lips fell open. Sensation heightened. A slow burn covered her cheeks. An ever so slight throbbing began first on the sides of her neck as emotion welled. Her heart pounded so strongly that her lips pulsed, ready for the pressure, the weight of his mouth against hers.

"Nay, lad, she isnae yours until we know you're ours," came a soft voice.

Sheila opened her eyes at the sound of William's voice.

The former MacLomain chieftain stood on the other side of the bars. She was embarrassed to be caught in such a position. Especially in front of his father. It took everything she had to pull away from not only Grant but also the emotions pounding ruthlessly against both her mind and body. Regardless, she extracted herself from the highlander holding her.

"William, always good to see you," Sheila said. "The last I knew you'd stayed with Colin."

Just a few days ago they all thought this man was dead but because of ancient Viking magic he was once more alive. William squeezed her hand through the bars. "You dinnae belong in here, lass. I will let you out."

Sheila slowly shook her head, conviction in her voice. "I belong in here as long as your son is here."

"Really?" Leslie said, joining William.

She and her cousin had come a long way since this whole adventure began but they were by no means kindred spirits. Though she never took her eyes off William, she spoke to Leslie. "Good to see you, Les."

"Better I'd say if you were on this side of the bars."

Sheila didn't have to look at her cousin to know her eyes were on Grant.

William's gaze left Sheila and drifted over her shoulder to his son. "You've great magic about you now. 'Tis too dangerous to release you."

When Sheila glanced over her shoulder it was to see Grant sitting on the cot, back to the wall, legs crossed in front of him. His emotionless eyes met his father's, words hard. "I dinnae fear a dungeon. Keep me here but know this," he nodded at the wall, the direction in which the dragon lay in the loch, "only I know how to release Torra back into her human form and only I know how to save her from Keir Hamilton."

Before William could respond Grant continued, his eyes distant, seeing something only he could see. "He will not rest until he has

17

her. All of her. Body and soul. Caught as she is now, in dragon form she is helpless, defenseless, weighed down by a powerful body. But in human form her divided spirit will not feel the harshness as strongly." His narrowed gaze once more swung to his father. "You seal her fate if she stays as a dragon right now. The beast cannae be without a whole soul...a wee lass," his gaze flickered to Sheila then back to William, "well she can survive with only half a soul for a time."

Sheila clenched her jaw. Grant understood her better than anyone. Having merged mentally, he knew her from the inside out, the years with her ex-boyfriend, Jack, everything. Yet she realized while he might know her, *his* mind had all but been blocked from her. No doubt Keir Hamilton had something to do with that but she suspected Grant was a whole lot more reclusive and powerful than she ever could have imagined.

In fact, he was a complete stranger.

Not to mention the enemy.

She recalled the first time she'd seen him at the Hamilton castle. In vivid detail. Standing side by side with Keir's right-hand-man, Colin MacLeod, they'd rallied the enemy to war against the MacLomains. And who was in command of the armies? Who was a well-trained and unmistakably vicious warrior?

Grant.

Kidnapped by the MacLeod's at eleven years old he'd spent most of his life at the Hamilton castle. Yes he'd made a telepathic connection with her via the pentacle and yes he'd helped save her life but what if it was all a ploy? A means to infiltrate the MacLomain clan?

Sheila gripped the bar and shook her head. No, she wasn't going to start thinking like this. When he'd helped save her life he'd asked her to have faith in him. And she would. She'd been manipulated by men for far too long. No more. Now she would believe in one, trust that he wasn't warping her mind.

Her eyes flew to William. "You need to let us both out. I know Grant's considered the enemy so keep him hidden. Say he's still imprisoned, do whatever is necessary, but damn, give him a chamber with a bed and fire and," she shook her head and looked skyward, "anything but this."

William's eyes never left hers, his face so unbelievably similar to the man he kept imprisoned. At long last, his gaze once more swung to Grant, his voice harder than she'd ever heard it. "Sheila will be the only one to suffer if you dinnae follow peaceably. What think you of that, son?"

Grant's face continued to show no emotion when he looked at his father. "I think Sheila will be the *last* to suffer if I've anything to say about it." Then his voice grew softer, deeper, promising. "And I *will* have the last say."

Sheila wasn't surprised to see several others appear out of the shadows to join William.

Malcolm, Coira, Devin, even Torra's parents, Iain and Arianna.

"Ah, so now you're all here to keep my magic at bay," Grant murmured.

"*Or*," Sheila looked over her shoulder at him, unable to help herself, "you could say, thanks for coming down here to support me."

Leslie snorted. "Yeah right."

Grant's eyes stayed steady on the group rallied on the other side of the bars. "They all know I've the power to escape if I wanted to. This," he said softly, "is just curiosity."

"Be that as it may." Coira swung open the gated door. "I'd like to think your Da is right. You willnae do anything that will hurt Sheila."

Grant's jaw clenched as he stood, his eyes flickering to Devin. "The warlock is no longer needed. I but required his dark powers in combination with the pentacle so that I might free myself from Keir."

Surprised, Sheila narrowed her eyes at Grant. "Why didn't you tell me that before? Why did you lie to me?"

Maybe giving him the benefit of the doubt had been a bad idea after all.

Grant's eyes met hers. "I'm sorry, lass but 'twas not really a lie. I said I needed a warlock to defeat Keir. Freeing me from his mental bonds will help see such an end. Besides, it needed to go a verra specific way. 'Twas unlikely they'd allow you to travel through time to seek a warlock for such a simple thing."

"Nay," Coira said, wounded. "We would have encouraged it all that much more."

19

Yet in his one statement, Sheila realized how little Grant thought his kin cared about him.

All watched warily as he approached. Sheila couldn't help but feel bad for him. Taken from his clan at such a young age, he now returned to a family that didn't trust him. When Malcolm made a move forward, Sheila grabbed Grant's hand and they left the bars behind together. Leslie's eyes connected with hers briefly. Not convinced, worried, that look said it all. It didn't matter in the least what Grant had already done.

He was *still* the enemy.

"You'll come to our tent beside Torra," Arianna said as she and Iain led the way. "It has been requested that all fishing be done on the other side of the loch. Less eyes watching."

"Once we get there you will tell us how to free Torra from her dragon form," Coira said.

Sheila didn't miss the strain in his mother's voice. God knows this had to be hard on Grant's parents but they were staying strong. While they were no doubt glad to find out their son was alive and now with them, there remained years of uncertainty in between. And Malcolm? Though Cadence had certainly cheered him up tremendously lately, having Grant at the castle clearly re-soured his attitude. But Sheila didn't much blame him. After all, not long ago Grant had aided the enemy when they tried to kill their father, William.

Nobody said a word as they made their way out of the dungeon then veered left down spiraling stairs. When they stepped out of the backside of the castle she swore she heard Grant take a deep breath…as if it was his first.

Lord, did she empathize.

There was nothing like that first true moment of freedom. That moment when you knew that nobody owned you anymore. In her case, it'd been the first time she stepped outside of the townhouse she and Jack shared for seven years. Medieval Scotland, modern day New Hampshire, it didn't matter…freedom was freedom.

Night had fallen. The dragon slept in the loch, her great body submerged beneath the water and her head resting on the shore. Several torches lined the castle wall and flickered off her white, gold, silver and copper scales. As long as the side of the castle, Torra was an impressive sight.

When her cousins Cadence and McKayla joined them, Sheila pulled them in for a group hug as the others walked ahead.

"I'm so glad you're back," Cadence said. "I would have come down to the dungeons but Malcolm was being grouchy about the baby."

Sheila's eyes rounded. "Baby?"

Cadence's eyes glistened and she put a hand on her belly. "Yes, we discovered its vibration when Torra helped revive your life."

Sheila thought back to the battle that'd nearly ended her. The last she remembered of it, Colin MacLeod's evil sister, Nessa had just thrown dark magic at her. The next thing she knew she awoke in Grant's arms. Apparently through his magic, Torra's and the magic born of her cousin's rings and the MacLomain's marks, she'd died then been resurrected.

Determined to push all that oddity aside she said, "That's wonderful!" Sheila hugged Cadence tightly. "But I thought...well, I thought you couldn't get pregnant."

"Me too," Cadence whispered. "Adlin MacLomain believes it likely happened at the baby oak. Apparently it's a tree of life for lack of a better explanation. Being near it promotes fertility."

"Oh wow." Sheila met her eyes as understanding dawned. "When we went there to release the magic that barred the tree..."

She trailed off. Cadence and Malcolm had gone around the back side of the mountain to access the baby oak by going through the waterfall. That had to have been when it happened...which explained how they harnessed the powerful magic that freed the oak.

A nervous little tingle rolled through her as she glanced at Grant. She knew precisely how that particular brand of magic was ignited. If the Broun girl's ring burned and glowed for a specific man then he was the one she'd have to sleep with in order to ignite the immense power between the ring and the MacLomain's tattoo.

While it was one thing to admire Grant's good looks it was another thing entirely to imagine sleeping with him. She barely knew him! And there *was* that whole 'he's the enemy' thing. Yet Leslie hadn't known Bradon long and Malcolm and Cadence knew one another for even less time. Regardless. This was Grant...and her. Besides, did he even *have* a tattoo like the rest of the men?

Cadence seemed to follow her train of thought because she said, "Grant's here now. Once we get Torra settled back into her human form you'll be able to talk with him more, get to know him a little."

Leslie eyed Grant. "Gotta admit he's as hot as the rest of them. It shouldn't be too difficult spending time with him."

"His looks really aren't my main concern," Sheila muttered.

"No but they certainly help," Leslie said.

McKayla eyed Leslie. "Usually I try to head off arguments between you two but not this time around." She shook her head. "Shay's got a lot on her plate." She gave a pointed look at Leslie. "And you already found your knight in shining armor...or medieval highlander in a plaid. So no bickering until we have all this squared away, okay?"

Leslie huffed but gave no response other than a nod as she threw her arm around Sheila's shoulders in a show of support. Even though she and Leslie had come a long way since first traveling back in time they still could trip into an argument quicker than most. But that was just them.

"Don't worry about me," Sheila murmured to the others. "I've made it this far. I'll make it the remainder of this adventure."

Cadence eyed her. Sheila knew her cousin worried about her mental state since leaving Jack. But if all this traveling back in time had done nothing else for her, it'd slowly but surely helped her heal. How, she couldn't be sure, just that it had.

Her gaze flickered between McKayla and Cadence and she smiled. "So both of you are pregnant. That's truly awesome."

And she meant it. Both wanted children and deserved this.

When she looked at Leslie and raised her brows, her cousin put her hands up in the air and shook her head. "Don't look at me. Bradon and I are *just* fine being married for now."

McKayla's eyes widened in surprise. "That almost sounds like you're entertaining the thought of having kids eventually."

All stared at Leslie, amazed. She'd always made it clear she wanted nothing to do with children.

"Oh, don't look so shocked," Leslie said. "Bradon's amazing with kids. Besides, I wouldn't be opposed to a little version of him."

Cadence's brows arched. "Or a little version of you."

"Oh, God! A little Leslie?" But Sheila grinned and winked at her cousin. "Now wouldn't that be something."

Sheila only warmed further when she spied the small smile Leslie tried so hard to hide.

McKayla was about to speak but stopped short, eyes saucer round.

When Sheila turned, curious, her heart skidded to a stop.

Grant leaned back against the dragon's neck.

And Malcolm, set to kill, had a dagger pressed tightly against his neck.

Chapter Two

Grant remained calm and waited.

If his brother meant to kill him he would've done so already.

But Malcolm's eyes only narrowed dangerously, their golden depths alight with magic.

"Release him, Malcolm," Coira said, frustrated. "He wasnae hurting Torra, merely touching her."

"And how do we know his touch is not meant to hurt," Malcolm said through clenched teeth.

"You must push past this fury you have with your brother," William said, voice low.

"Please, Malcolm. We've all come so far," said the tall redhead called Cadence. As they had before, her words clearly had the most impact because the knife at his throat loosened some. Though he could easily be out from beneath the blade, Grant repressed his rage and only glared at his brother.

The more he lashed out against his kin the less likely they'd trust him.

And earning their trust was necessary.

Now that he was free of Keir's mental grasp, he knew he'd be able to set his plans in motion. Plans, of course, that would require help from his brethren.

"Malcolm, remove the knife from his neck," Sheila pleaded. "*Please.*"

Grant knew how much Malcolm cared for her as well and so with great reluctance he slowly pulled the blade away and stepped back.

"You're lucky you've such champions," Malcolm spat and turned away.

With a quick flick, Grant ran his thumb over the trickle of blood on his neck. At one time he'd worshiped his brother. But that was a lifetime ago and now he knew better than to worship anyone.

It was no easy thing knowing his kin had never searched more extensively for him. That they'd so easily given up when told he was dead. In fact, he'd had no contact with anyone at the MacLomain castle until Sheila.

His eyes flickered to her. The first time he'd seen her was at Keir's castle. While he'd never had much of a chance to study her he'd certainly seen the glow of the ring on her finger. Unsure what to make of it, he'd said nothing to the others. Laird Hamilton clearly didn't realize what he'd seen or something would have been said.

The next contact Sheila made was via telepathy. If he hadn't noticed her before he certainly noticed her then. Erotically charged, her mind had made an impact. But not just because of the sensuality behind it. Nay, though interesting, he set that aside. What really surprised him was that his master had no inkling of their mental connection.

That's when a nugget of hope surfaced.

Then at last when Grant had kidnapped Sheila and her cousin Cadence, he'd had the chance to not only teach her how to use the pentacle that connected them but to truly look upon her.

And he wasn't disappointed.

There was a fragile, mesmerizing beauty about her that stirred his blood. Long and curling, her thick auburn hair haloed a delicate face. Long thick lashes framed the softest blue eyes he'd ever seen. Plush and pink, her lips complimented sun-kissed, lightly freckled skin. He knew of her previous desire for his brother and thought Malcolm more the fool for turning her away.

Yet might he not end up doing the same?

Certainly not because he wanted to but because there might be no other choice.

"In order to free Torra from her dragon form we will need all the rings and all the marks ignited here," Grant said, eyes running the length of Torra's long body.

Coira frowned. "Impossible. Colin and Bradon are with the war party."

"We need them for but a moment," Grant said, not quite ready to look at his mother. "I know you've the ability to transfer them here then back in little time."

Still she hesitated and he knew why. It would be a reunion, however brief, that united all the younger MacLomain men. This, in effect, would throw together far too many emotionally charged wizards.

Finally, his eyes settled on her. "They willnae hurt me." His eyes grazed over Malcolm then returned to her. "The only MacLomain who wants me dead stands with us now."

His father's brows pulled down as he looked between his sons then spoke to his wife. "I'd say he has the right of it, lass."

Malcolm said nothing, only kept his blade drawn and his eyes narrowed.

Coira hesitated a few more moments before she finally nodded. "Then I will go get them."

After a few quick chants, the air warped around her and she was gone.

Meanwhile, Iain urged the women to sit under the large tent erected beside the castle. A storm was incoming and random snowflakes had started to spit. However, Sheila opted to stay with Grant.

Malcolm, arms crossed over his chest, hovered nearby.

Sheila tossed a glance at his brother. "Why don't you go hang out with Cadence?"

"Nay," Malcolm muttered, frowning.

She dished out a frown as well. "Hey, I didn't hover around you and Cadence when you wanted time alone did I?"

"Much different circumstances," Malcolm said.

"Malcolm," Cadence called. "It's Kynan."

Grant looked up at the black wolf on the battlement above and kept a grin to himself. The beastie was making a warrior up yonder very uncomfortable. Malcolm muttered under his breath and headed that way.

"You know that wolf, don't you," Sheila said softly.

Oh, he knew the wolf all right and appreciated the distraction it'd caused.

"'Tis of no importance." His eyes fell to hers. "'Tis cold, lass." He nodded at the tent. "You should seek shelter."

Sheila wrapped her arms over her chest and shook her head. "I'd rather keep you company. After all, you helped save my life."

"I wouldnae have you die if I knew of a way to save you," he said.

"And I appreciate that." She looked at him curiously. "But at what cost to you?"

"'Twas no cost but freedom you offered me," he murmured. "So 'tis safe to say we saved one another's life."

Sheila contemplated this as the wind twisted her hair around her slender shoulders. "I can't tell you how sorry I am that...all of this has happened to you...that Keir..."

When she trailed off he shook his head. "You need not be sorry. Though difficult 'twas God's will. Because of Him, I kept hope and faith in my heart."

Her brows perked as she nodded. "I'm glad He was there for you."

"As He was for you as well," Grant said softly. "Or so I'd like to think when He brought us together."

A rosy hue spread over the tops of her cheeks. "I suspect you know far more about me than I do of you though."

"Aye," he said, honestly. "And so I must say sorry for all that you have endured with your previous love."

Sheila shook her head, frowning. "I don't think the love between my ex and I was ever real...though I'd hoped."

"Nay, 'twas no doubt the wrong word to use," he said, tempted to take her hand, to offer comfort. "But now you face what it truly was and work through the pain in your heart, do you not?"

Her head moved a fraction as if she meant to nod, her words a mere whisper. "I think maybe I do."

"'Tis good." He met her eyes, tried to offer strength. "You will see through the hurt done to you and be better for it, lass. Of this I dinnae doubt."

Sheila pulled back her shoulders and notched her chin. "If I don't, he wins."

Grant more than understood that line of reasoning. He'd thought the same of Keir Hamilton far too many times over the years.

Malcolm had just exited the castle when the air warped nearby and Coira reappeared. Colin and Bradon were by her side. Grant crossed his arms over his chest and clenched his jaw. Now he would confront his brother and cousins all at once when not in the midst of battle. For fourteen winters he'd imagined this moment, wondering if it would ever come.

Malcolm fell in beside the other two and they all focused on him. Grant didn't miss how Sheila repositioned herself between him and them. Gallant lass to be sure. Yet little could she do if they decided to attack rather than trust.

All studied him, each with their own take based on their varying expression.

Colin, now chieftain of the MacLomains, appeared cautious.

Bradon, upset yet curious.

Malcolm, angry as ever.

If he'd make peace with any of them, Bradon was likely the one. A year apart in age, they'd been close as bairns. In fact, he'd been with Bradon moments before he was taken so long ago.

"We'll not have strife." Coira waved the other women over. "But get to helping Torra."

Colin's eyes met Grant's. "And how is it we're to do that then?"

"'Twill take a tremendous amount of magic," Grant said, not looking away from his cousin's intense regard. "I will touch the spot above her eyes while holding the hand of one of the lasses. She in turn will touch the mark of her MacLomain and he will have a hand on Torra. Then the next lass will touch the lass next to her and she will touch her MacLomain. With seven of us interconnected harnessing the power of the rings and marks, we can shift her from the dragon to the lass."

"Why must you touch her as well?" Colin asked, a heavy frown on his face.

"Because I am the strongest in magic," Grant said dryly. "Did you never wonder why *I* was the one taken by the MacLeods?"

Though his parents didn't seem surprised in the least, his brother and cousin's certainly did. While none responded to his revelation, he saw a miniscule softening in Bradon's eyes.

"If such is true it seems foolhardy to allow him to do this," Malcolm said. "There's no way of knowing what he might do."

"Do you want her saved?" Iain held his wife's hand. "My daughter is trapped in dragon form with only half a soul. 'Twould be unforgivable if we had the power to save her but didnae."

"He's absolutely right." Sheila frowned at Colin, Bradon and Malcolm. "I know my cousins will help so you're all that stands in the way of this."

McKayla, Leslie and Cadence nodded.

Leslie said, "Yep, I'm with Sheila on this."

"Adlin says it's the right thing to do," Cadence added.

Malcolm's narrowed eyes slid her way. "Aye?"

"Oh, *aye*," Cadence assured.

Grant knew through his telepathic connection with Sheila that Cadence was a necromancer who was in constant contact with Adlin MacLomain, he who all but birthed the MacLomain clan. How convenient that he supported this, perhaps a bit *too* convenient. But Grant could only be thankful even if Cadence wasn't being entirely truthful.

Malcolm ground his jaw and once more looked at Grant. "If this is but a ploy and you betray us so help me—"

"I'll help," Bradon interrupted and tossed Malcolm a shrug. "Even if this is a trick I'd never forgive myself for not trying to help my sister."

Colin's stern eyes went to Grant's and a long moment passed before he finally said, "Aye, I'll help as well." He looked at Malcolm. "I cannae force you to do this cousin but I'm with Bradon. I cannae help but try to save my sister."

Malcolm and Colin locked eyes and another long, uncomfortable moment stretched before Malcolm reluctantly nodded. "Fine then... I will help."

Grant understood that Malcolm especially worried over the babe in Cadence's belly. His brother hadn't liked unpredictable outcomes when they were bairns and that hadn't changed.

"Let us do this then," Grant said and turned to the dragon's face.

Snow fell harder, whipping across the shore as everyone got into position.

As it turned out, Leslie took his hand as he touched the space above and between the dragon's eyes. There were few places as powerful as the third eye of a dragon. Eyes closed, Grant first murmured a prayer to God then began to chant.

"*Pone te, Domine. Dilige bestiam, et invenietis requiem.* Place you be, come to me. Love thy beast, but find release."

Over and over he chanted, clenching his teeth as pressure built and a pentacle rose in his vision. Unlike the one he went through when he communicated with Sheila, this one reared up and swallowed his mind. Caught in blank space, Grant found his calm center and focused. If for a moment he paid attention to the otherworld in which he'd been thrust, his soul would instantly be ripped into shreds.

"Torra, take my hand," he whispered into his mind and held out his hand.

Then he waited and waited…and waited.

Through the darkness a small light started to twinkle.

"Aye, lass, this way now," he murmured.

As if one of the Fae flickered through the branches of a shadowed tree, the little light grew larger and larger. Bit by bit, it took shape. When it first appeared a small dragon flew toward him but then it blurred and took the shape of a woman.

"Grant," she whispered into his mind.

"Aye, I'm here."

Relief flooded him when Torra's human hand slipped into his.

Now came the hard part.

Betraying his clan once more.

Caught together in the dark underbelly of magic but at the same time in its very glory, Torra's eyes met his and she said, "You have no choice."

That didn't make this any easier.

Grant again prayed to God for forgiveness then started to chant. *"Tamen ego me quinque, erit devenire ad novam.* I take with me but five, to a new place we must arrive."

Everything warped around them then they fell.

And fell.

The smell of burning sugar filled his nostrils.

Torra released his hand and he grabbed another.

When he thumped softly to the ground, Grant immediately made sure Sheila was well beside him. Wide eyes blinking, she looked at him. Instead of asking where they were she said, "How are you still holding my hand? *Nobody* can do that when traveling like we just did!"

Startled, Grant almost grinned but didn't. Now was not the time for humor. But he'd *never* nearly wanted to grin so much.

"Ugh, sick of traveling like this," Leslie muttered.

Frown pulling at his lips, Bradon helped her up, his eyes shooting to Grant. "What the bloody hell did you do?"

But Grant offered no answer as he helped Sheila stand.

Leslie peered around as Bradon helped her to her feet. "Swept us away from the MacLomain castle no doubt. All I see is endless forest." She sniffed. "With an ocean nearby I'd say."

"You're getting good at this," Bradon murmured to his wife then said to Grant, "What did you *do*?"

But Grant's eyes were on Sheila whose eyes were on someone they'd be far more interested in talking with.

Torra.

No longer a dragon, she was once more a lass.

Braced against a tree, she eyed them and whispered, "So sorry you were pulled along with me."

All had been left behind but five of them.

Bradon blinked several times then took a few steps toward her. "Torra?"

Eyes tired but happy to see him, she said, "Aye brother."

"Oh, God, Torra." Bradon quickly pulled her into his arms. Gently putting her head against his chest he murmured into her hair, "I never thought I'd see you again…like this."

Too long had Grant hoped this for Torra. A greeting betwixt brother and sister when one truly understood what the other was. Colin would have his greeting in time, but for now at least Bradon had it.

When Sheila squeezed his hand, Grant looked down at the gesture then at her.

Grateful, she offered a small smile and nod.

Might she always offer that to him.

But he knew better.

"We must travel soon," Grant said. "Verra soon."

Torra and Bradon pulled apart yet she still looked at her brother fondly. "Aye, I suppose we do."

"Where to?" Leslie asked then paused when Torra's eyes met hers. "Good to see you again." Then she shook her head. "Sorry, all the time travel has me turned around. Good to meet you…for the first time."

Torra shook her head and smiled. "Nay, lass. I remember meeting you." Her eyes lowered then raised, her words soft. "Was it not the first time I met Colin MacLeod then?"

Leslie appeared caught off guard but she quickly regrouped. "Yes, it was. You were younger."

31

"I was indeed." Torra's eyes met Bradon's and Sheila's. "You were there too...when I met Colin."

Distressed, Bradon nodded. "Aye, but we dinnae need to speak of that, lass."

Trying to catch her breath, Torra shook her head. "I think mayhap we do."

Understanding her weakened state, Grant went to her.

When Bradon stood in his way, she said, "Worry naught, brother. He is here for me."

"We're *all* here for you," Bradon bit out not moving an inch.

"Aye." Torra put a hand on his shoulder. "Then I shall be more direct. Grant means no harm. He will protect me always."

Bradon shook his head, his tortured gaze flickering between Torra and Grant. "'Tis hard this."

"Not if you just hear her out," Leslie said, worried eyes on Bradon. "Hear her out, sweetie."

Grant locked eyes with Torra.

It was up to her how much she shared.

This was all for her.

Torra looked at her brother. "I am so verra sorry that I took you from the MacLomains but I wish you to see something here, something that will make a difference."

"'Twill be a bit of a walk south," Grant added. "But we will get you there."

"Why does it always work that way?" Leslie said. "If we're traveling around via time travel or portals, why not plunk us down in the heart of the matter?"

"Because the heart of the matter always has more to do with the journey," Sheila said softly.

Pleased with her observation, Grant's eyes swung her way.

But she wasn't looking at him. Nay, her eyes were on the forest and all that lay ahead.

"You see a bad outcome," he murmured.

Sheila kept her eyes to the trees. "I see a questionable outcome. Any time I do this 'travel across Scotland' or 'time travel' thing, there's a lot of unpredictability."

Leslie nodded. "I agree."

As if she sensed there was so much more to why they were here, Sheila's eyes met his. When they did he nodded toward Torra. "'Tis time for her."

"Nay," Torra said softly. "Now is the time for Colin MacLeod."

Chapter Three

Colin MacLeod? Now that couldn't be good.

Unsure, Sheila and Leslie glanced at one another then at Torra. It was so surreal seeing her once more as a woman. Just as beautiful as she'd been when they time-traveled to the original Highland Defiance, her long wavy black hair was streaked with a unique blend of colors and her blue eyes were nearly luminescent. Yet unlike when they'd met her before, her soft skin was drawn, her petite frame clearly weakened.

"I will carry you, lass," Grant said, eyes on Torra.

Torra shook her head. "You'll do no such thing. I need to use my muscles."

When Sheila peered closer she realized Torra's eyes seemed to shift colors, going from blue to opaque then back to blue. As if she understood Sheila's curiosity, she said. "Dinnae mind my eyes. 'Tis part of being down half a soul. The half I still possess struggles to find the other."

"That sounds awful," Leslie murmured.

"'Tis not as bad as all that," Torra said. "Just disconcerting at times…and draining."

Sheila could only imagine.

"What is this about Colin MacLeod?" Bradon said, his concerned eyes still on Torra. "I remember the way you two looked at one another when you met. What came of that lass? Why did you never speak of it all these years?"

She was about to respond when his eyes widened a bit. "And listen to you speak! Not just the sixteen words a year at the solstices and equinoxes."

Torra put a tender hand on his arm. "All will be explained in good time, brother."

"We must go soon," Grant said. "The day wears on."

Sheila eyed the forest. "I can't help but notice the season has changed. It feels like early autumn now."

34

"Aye," Torra said. "'Tis a fortnight before the Samhain and the year is no longer 1254 but 1250."

Leslie's brows shot up. "Wow, we didn't travel far this time."

They certainly hadn't. Usually it was forty to hundreds of years into the past. Not to mention the eight hundred years back in time they traveled to get here to begin with.

Grant held out his arm to Torra. "You will at least take my arm as we walk. 'Tis not up for debate."

Torra agreed and they all made their way through an ever thinning forest. This area had the feel of when they'd traveled back in time and met the younger version of Adlin MacLomain. As if her cousin read her mind she said, "Are we near the original Highland Defiance?"

"Aye, 'tis just north of here," Grant said.

"North?" Bradon said. "Then might we be near the MacLeod castle?"

"Aye," Grant said.

"Are you sure your magic will hold?" Torra said to Grant.

"Aye, 'twill indeed."

"What magic are you referring to?" Leslie said.

"That which I now possess having had Keir Hamilton in my mind for fourteen winters," Grant said gruffly. "'Twill mask us from not only him but Colin MacLeod if I so desire."

"Why would you *not* desire?" Sheila asked, confused.

But Grant gave no answer to that. Instead, he remained silent as they walked. While he was most certainly mentally strong, she was beginning to suspect that he repressed a great deal. Then again, he obviously kept many secrets.

For the most part everyone remained silent as they continued walking. What felt like hours later, they finally stopped at a small river. Though weary, Torra's eyes had a certain light in them as she scanned the wood line beyond. The sun was nestled low in the sky, illuminating the foliage from the inside out.

Grant crouched and clenched a handful of dirt, murmuring something before he washed off his hand and splashed water on his face. Then he nodded toward a thick grouping of bushes nearby. "We will hide over there."

"I thought your magic was going to disguise us," Bradon said.

"'Twill," Grant said. "But even then I wouldnae have us stand in plain sight. Not with these two."

Oh, she really didn't like the sound of that.

Where they crouched allowed them a clear view through the branches. Grant again murmured under his breath and she swore a tingling sensation covered her skin as though a light mist fell. Then the feeling passed. Sheila narrowed her eyes at who now walked toward the river and wished they had not a few bushes but a mountain between them.

Colin MacLeod.

Almost brutally handsome, he was taller and more muscled than most. With sun-streaked hair and quicksilver eyes, his strong features were fiercely masculine.

Sheila didn't miss it when Grant's hand slid into Torra's or the pain in her eyes as she watched Colin. She recalled with vivid clarity those first few moments when Torra and Colin met when they had time-traveled over two hundred years further into the past. She'd apparently been traveling through the Defiance to escape the heavy burden of what she'd become. It was still unclear why Colin had been there as well. Yet none of it mattered in those seconds when their eyes first met.

It had been powerful.

Romantic.

Profound.

Colin crouched and as Grant had, splashed water on his face. Then he seemed to pause, almost as if he sensed Grant had been there before him. Then, in a lightning fast move, he stood and spun, drawing his sword.

Sheila forgot to breathe when she saw who emerged out of the forest behind him. Tall, kilted, with a black cloak over his broad shoulders...

Keir Hamilton.

Holy hell.

It was impossible not to tremble. She'd met this man a few times and he was the epitome of evil. He walked it, spoke it, *oozed* it. Grant took her hand and squeezed gently. She found the gesture touching and selfless considering this man had held him captive for so long. Sheila couldn't tear her eyes away as Keir slowly approached Colin.

Sword up, the MacLeod said, "Who are ye?"

Keir's inky eyes narrowed. "Someone who has been watching ye for some time…someone who has been watching ye both."

Alarm flickered in Colin's eyes then vanished. "What do ye speak of?"

"I think ye know, lad." Keir continued to study him, his regard dark, cunning. "Torra MacLomain."

Sheila bit her lower lip. Oh no. Keir knew of them? Obviously.

"I know naught of what ye speak," Colin bit back and raised his sword higher. "Again, who are ye?"

"Too long then has it been since the MacLeods and Hamiltons came together for ye not to recognize an ally," Keir said.

"Ye are no ally of mine," Colin said through clenched teeth.

"Oh, but I am," Keir said, legs braced, arms by his side. The man teemed with both confidence and repressed black magic.

Colin clearly sensed the latter because he kept a firm grip on his blade.

Keir clasped his hands behind his back. "Ye willnae be marrying the MacLomain lass. Instead, yer sister will marry whoever will be their next chieftain."

"Who are ye to tell me who I will or will not marry, stranger?"

"*I* am yer new laird and master," Keir said.

Chills raced through Sheila. *What?*

Colin moved closer. "My laird is my Da and ye are soon to feel my blade run through yer chest."

Not concerned in the least, Keir quirked a black brow. "'Twould be unwise, lad. If ye want Torra to live that is."

Colin visibly bristled, his voice soft. "What say ye?"

"I've long known what she is. Born with the heart of a woman and the soul of a dragon, I know everything there is to know about my lass." Keir cocked his head. "And I know precisely how to kill her."

A strangled roar came from the MacLeod and he swung his blade, fire rolling off it toward Keir. The overlord laughed and thrust his hand. The fire sizzled out immediately and Colin's sword whipped out of his hand into Keir's. Colin growled, obviously both stunned and furious, when his own blade was suddenly brought tight against his neck. He froze, hand gripping a dagger he'd pulled free.

"While amusing, dinnae try such a thing again," Keir said. "For ye will always lose."

Hamilton stepped back. "Now would ye like to see how Torra shall die if ye dinnae obey my every order?" Before Colin could respond, Keir flicked his hand. Though they saw nothing, the MacLeod clearly did. His dagger clattered to the ground as he fell to his knees, tortured gaze witnessing something meant for his eyes only.

"Nay," he whispered, severe emotion in his voice as he trembled.

"Aye," Keir murmured, his dark gaze on Colin, relishing the MacLeod's response. "But it doesnae need to happen. If ye but come stand by my side and fight for my cause, ye will see Torra become one of the most powerful lasses in Scotland."

Apparently released from the horrible vision, Colin closed his eyes and a muscle leapt in his cheek. Keir, meanwhile, sauntered around him, watching the MacLeod's every response. "Do ye not want to see her alive and well? Do ye not love her as much as that?"

"Ye mean to make her yours," Colin whispered.

"Och, but of course." A terrible grin slithered onto Keir's face. "In every way possible."

"But first," Keir said, "I must continue with what I so long ago started."

When Colin's eyes met his, Keir's grin widened further. "Have ye not heard the tale of the mauled MacLomain lad, Grant?"

When Colin looked surprised, Keir nodded. "Aye, I took him all those years ago. Under the disguise of a MacLeod my men went right in and stole him." His voice grew nostalgic. "I still recall his cries, his tears, those first beautiful moments when I started to break him. There is nothing quite like ruining a bairn's mind, watching their verra sweetness seep away."

Colin frowned heavily. "Torra's cousin."

"Indeed, Torra's cousin." Keir shrugged. "Yet another reason why ye dinnae want to go against me. She would never forgive ye if she found out ye'd been given the opportunity to get closer to him and didnae take it, aye?"

Colin slowly came to his feet, hands clenched by his side. When he started to speak, Keir shook his head sharply.

"Now we are at the point where ye speak when spoken to." Keir's grin fell away. "Yer kin is allied to mine therefore I will give ye a much higher rank than you likely deserve." His eyes narrowed a fraction. "And mayhap, if ye train him to what I know he's capable of, Grant will be rewarded as well."

Keir continued. "As of today, ye will have no more contact with Torra or your kin. Ye will defect from your clan and over the years, urge more MacLeods to join you. Ye will lead my armies and together we will ensure Torra's safety."

Colin hung his head, defeat obvious.

Pleased, Keir made a flourish with his hand and colored leaves started to pour down. Caught in the dying rays of a brilliant sunset, they swirled and glowed. As they twisted around his hand they soon mixed with blackened fog. Raspy, evil, he said, "'Twas always…trying, watching her travel through time to go see ye. But I made the best of it and grabbed just a little slice of her essence. Yet it was enough," he whispered.

Suddenly, the twirling leaves whipped together and blended into a colorful mix of hues. With a hard swipe, he cupped them and slammed his hand against Colin's upper arm. The MacLeod flinched in pain, sweat beading on his brow.

"This," Keir said, his hand still on Colin's arm. "Will forever draw her and someday, when the time is right, 'twill be used to bring her to me."

Sheila couldn't help the tear that slipped free when Keir pulled his hand away.

Angry, red flesh revealed a massive tattoo of Torra. The one he still had to this day. A mark made not to worship her love but to imprison it.

"'Tis time for us to go," Keir said. "Word will be sent to yer clan."

Jaw clenched, Colin slowly picked up his dagger, eyes seething and magic simmering around him.

"Dinnae test me lad," Keir said. "Ye will *never* win."

It seemed Colin saw something in the Hamilton's dark look because he made no movement against him.

"Come." Keir walked into the forest.

Colin hesitated a few moments before he slowly trailed the overlord into the woods until they vanished.

Sheila turned and sat, still trying to process what she'd just witnessed. It seemed the others were as well because everyone remained silent for some time. When at last she pulled herself from heavy thoughts, Sheila's chest clenched. Poor Torra. Heart in her eyes, the woman continued to stare into the forest after them. Bradon had a hand on one of her shoulders, Grant the other. It was clear in the forlorn look how deeply her feelings ran for Colin MacLeod. To this day, the MacLomain woman still desired him, most likely even loved him.

But then look what he'd done for love.

He'd defected from his clan and joined with true evil so that he might keep her safe.

Sheila looked at Grant but he too stared after Colin. In those few words Keir had spoken of him, she had just a small glimpse into what he'd endured. Total mental annihilation at the beginning to be sure then only God knows what after that.

"I knew of this moment because Colin visited my chambers a few times," Torra murmured. "But never beyond the flames of my hearth, never as a whole man. Through those visits I learned of Grant's imprisonment." Her eyes glistened. "Colin told me I must stay away and not to give in to the dragon within lest Keir hurt me." She shook her head, chin jut out. "But 'twas long past time that secrets be revealed."

Bradon cupped her cheek, words tender. "If there is one thing you can be sure of sister, no MacLomain faults your actions. We will always support you no matter what."

Torra nodded slightly, eyes grateful. "For so verra long I thought to share the things I knew but 'twas a double edged sword. Keeping the dragon repressed allowed me but sixteen prophetic words a year that could be spoken to my kin. Only freeing the dragon freed my tongue."

"Such a hard thing," Bradon murmured and embraced his sister once more. "'Tis good then I suppose that Colin found a way to give you conversation beyond the few words you were able to say to us." His eyes turned to Torra. "How was he able to in light of Keir's threat?"

"I dinnae ken," she murmured, eyes flickering to Grant then back. "But I didnae question such a gift."

Bradon's brows drew together as if he wasn't entirely convinced of her words but he said nothing more about it.

"They're gone now," Grant said at last and helped Sheila stand. "We're safe enough to sleep for the eve."

Concerned, Bradon looked at Torra. "Do you really want to stay here?"

She nodded and whispered, "More than anything."

There was heartache in her words. She wanted to stay close to where she'd last seen Colin, no matter how terrible the encounter.

"There is a wide conclave in the mountainside nearby," Grant said. "We'll find shelter there."

Bradon eyed Grant, a tentative look on his face. "Thank you for bringing us here, cousin…for showing us this."

Torra and Grant exchanged a quick glance before Grant said, "'Twas not just me that wanted you to see this. While I ken the anger my brother has toward me, everything that has happened and will happen is so that you might better ken what you are up against."

"I'm getting a better idea by the moment," Bradon said and nodded at them both.

"Torra will show you where we'll rest," Grant said. "I've been too long in the dungeons and will join you once I've bathed."

Sheila followed the others, glancing over her shoulder as he turned away. Say you want to bathe too. Just do it. She nearly shook her head. What was she thinking? But the further she walked away, the more convinced she was that a dip in a cold river might just do her some good. Or being near him. She couldn't be sure which. So as soon as she knew where they'd be sleeping she made up her mind. She was going with Grant.

"I think I'll go for a swim too," Sheila said.

Yet as she walked, she slowed. Did she really want to do this? The man deserved his privacy, some time alone to finally be free of all that bound him. But for the life of her she couldn't stop walking. By the time she was a few hundred feet away she halted and watched Grant through the trees.

Already in the river, he lay back in the water. Not so much that she could see the whole of his body but enough that she could see his broad glistening shoulders. Licking her lips, she stared as he dipped beneath the water then surfaced. When he turned his head slightly and froze she knew he sensed she was there.

Okay, enough of this. Don't be such a coward, Sheila. Shoulders back, she walked the remainder of the way and then stopped at the river's edge. Grant said nothing, only watched her. Set to ignore her thumping heart, she started to undress. Not sultry and slow, but quickly. The truth was she'd never been naked in front of any other man but her ex and there hadn't been much sexuality involved in that relationship.

So when she whipped off the last of the twenty-first century, her bra and panties, Sheila made fast work of getting into the water. She couldn't really blame Grant for *not* averting his eyes. After all, he'd been imprisoned. Still, she knew her cheeks were flaming red and that was *never* a good look with her hair color.

Brrrr, cold. But she'd deal.

After she dipped beneath the water for a good long while, truly to the point her lungs nearly burst, she finally surfaced. Grant continued to eye her, not bemused as she thought for sure would be the case but fairly serious. Ignited by the river in twilight, his pale smoky blue eyes were contemplative.

At last, he held out his hand. "Let me show you something, lass."

Her eyes widened. Seriously? She could just imagine what he wanted to show her.

A smile reached his eyes but not his lips and he curled his fingers. "Come. 'Tis not what you think."

Determined to trust him, she kept shoulder deep in the water and took his hand. So close that she could all but feel his heat beneath the water, she was once again wowed by his good looks. A light layer of stubble had formed on his jawline but instead of taking from his appearance it somehow enhanced it.

When he spoke his voice was huskier than before and his eyes to the forest. "There is something that happens within the trees at this hour, something truly divine."

"Divine?" she murmured, looking up.

"Aye," he said softly. Pointing up at the pines and oaks, he continued. "Verra soon what you think is a darkened forest left behind by the sun will come alive with new light. A light that ignites both our God and those of the old religion."

Sheila looked at him. "But there is only the one true God."

42

"Aye, He exists but He didnae shun the others, lass," he whispered. "Watch."

Eyes to the trees, Sheila did just that, eyes widening as twilight descended. His hand wrapped around hers and she knew that she witnessed something born of magic. Something nobody else saw. A truth of sorts. Streaming, glorious, a light shone through the trees. A purple light made not of the sun or the moon but something else. Beneath it, or maybe within it, sparkles and flecks ignited. Warmth and energy filled her, sorrow and beauty, perfectness and flaws, everything.

What she viewed was truly in all sense of the word…divine.

It encompassed the life of the trees and everything alive around them then it took of the air and the water and all the in-betweens. In it she found forgiveness and happiness. Two things that she pretended to have yet realized she knew nothing about. Even so, one thing rose above all of it…love.

Thorough.

Penetrating.

Just out of reach.

"*This* is what Adlin MacLomain always wanted his Scotsmen to see, to ken, that all can co-exist and all are there to worship. One doesnae shun ye if ye dinnae have faith in it. And neither shuns the other or who might worship them."

Sheila murmured, "So you're pagan as well?"

"I believe that all exists and 'tis not my right to judge another for their beliefs. 'Tis all there for you to see." His voice grew softer. "The difference is my heart grows warmer with the light from above, that given from the one God, but it doesnae mean I dinnae respect the others. I love God above all but will always value the others. To not do so would be a disservice to my God."

She couldn't help but say, "That almost sounds blasphemous."

"Mayhap 'tis," he admitted. "But I have prayed and look where I am now. If what is in my heart is so wrong would my God have brought me to this moment now," his voice turned to a whisper, "with you."

Her eyes went to his.

While desire was there so was something else, something searching, curious, eager.

Though aware of the profound moment he'd allowed her to see within the trees, she couldn't pull her gaze away. In his eyes she saw not only his convictions but also his want for her to understand.

"I've read every word of the bible...several times," she murmured.

"So you have," he said. "'Tis good that." He paused, reflective. "But might you free yourself from memorized words and *see* what is around you. Feel what is here."

Sheila swallowed hard. He asked a lot.

Eyes once more to the forest she could admit to seeing and feeling more than just one God here. And that scared her beyond reason. For too long she'd prayed to her deity and in the end He'd come through for her.

"Enough with heavy thoughts for one day." Grant squeezed her hand. "Enjoy the river then we'll go eat."

Though he pulled away, she still felt the warmth of his touch. When she once more looked at the forest it was dark, all light faded. But something of it remained in her mind, in her thoughts as she swam further out. At the water's deepest point, she could still stand but didn't want to. No, she preferred sinking beneath its depths, reveling in the way it made everything else vanish.

When she finally surfaced and turned back to the shore, Grant was wrapping his plaid. But not before she caught a glimpse of his tight backside and...the tattoo on his upper back. He had one too! But of course he did. It must've been covered by his hair before. Sheila twirled her ring, thoughts consumed with what that meant. She'd yet to ask him if her ring's stone glowed for him and wondered if the time would ever be right.

When he leaned against a tree, his eyes on her, Sheila knew she shouldn't wait too long. If the power of three couples could shift a dragon into a woman, what might the power of four couples do? Yet still. There was a lot of ground to cover with Grant before she saw them ever being more than...whatever they were.

Unlike when she'd entered the water, Sheila exited with less shyness, less mortification. Why, she'd never know, just that something about this man was lending her comfort. He'd not take what she wasn't willing to give. In fact, she wasn't entirely sure he meant to take anything at all, or so said his now averted eyes when she left the water and dressed.

When finished his gaze turned to hers and he held out his hand. "Let us go eat, then rest."

Though she took his hand she still wondered why he'd averted his eyes. Had she done something wrong? Did he find her undesirable?

As they walked, he said softly, "Have you not learned of the MacLomain's ability to hear thoughts?"

Darn. That's right. Sheila bit the corner of her lip. "I have. What of it?"

"Would you like me to teach you how to bar others from reading your thoughts?"

Embarrassed but not about to avoid what he'd implied, she pulled her hand away.

"Yeah, that'd be great." She hesitated but would rather get everything out in the open. "But why don't you just cut to the chase and say what's really on your mind."

He considered a moment then nodded. "Aye 'tis true I heard your thoughts and so will give you honesty." His eyes flickered to hers then the forest as they walked. "Why would you think I find you undesirable or think you'd done something wrong?"

Ugh, this was uncomfortable. But she might as well share some of what was troubling her. "You have the magical tattoo created by Torra, Colin MacLomain and Seth. That means you fit into a puzzle, one made of magic and rings and…maybe even me."

Oh shoot. Had she just said he might *fit* into her?

Don't overthink it. Just say what you need to say.

Before he could talk she spit out the rest, afraid if she didn't she might not. "With Colin and McKayla, Leslie and Bradon, even Malcolm and Cadence, the romance was ba-bang fast." She took a deep breath. "Now here I stand with this ring and you're the only MacLomain left with a tattoo," she trailed off, mouth dry.

Silence descended.

She couldn't say it was necessarily an uncomfortable silence but it was silence and that was hard right now. About to speak because she couldn't stand it anymore, he cut her off.

"Few lads can say they know a lass's mind so thoroughly before they even meet her." This time his voice wasn't soft but firm. "I know you verra well, Sheila. More so than anyone I have ever met."

He took her hand as he continued. "And if there is nothing more true about you 'tis that you are still weakened by the hand life dealt you. I willnae harm you more by taking you where you are not ready to go. Nay, 'tis best that you recognize yourself first. Whilst you might be a bonnie wee lass and bright as well, 'tis not in my eyes that you need to find yourself but within your own."

A burn spread through her that had nothing to do with the man standing so close. No, it was more the reaction of someone who felt themselves judged. "You think you have me all figured out, eh?"

Grant gave no reply.

Sheila pulled her hand away. She didn't need this crap. Sure, he might mean well but who was he to tell her what she needed to figure out about herself? His words were just one more layer on her growing frustration. As it was, her cousins were convinced that any happiness she showed was forced and their opinions were getting pretty old. As far as she was concerned, she'd come far since she'd left Jack and intended to keep on healing.

When they rejoined the others, a rabbit already roasted on the fire. Torra was sleeping, curled against a rock. Leslie and Bradon spoke softly. With a murmured chant, a fur appeared in Grant's hand and he put it over Torra. Bradon and Leslie looked at him, grateful for the gesture.

After Bradon tore off a few pieces of meat, he handed some to them both.

Sheila nodded. "Thanks."

Grant said thank you as well and sat across from her. Determined not to look at him, she made a point of studying the flames. Low, crackling, they offered no relief from her turbulent thoughts.

"How are you doing, Shay?" Leslie asked.

Startled by her cousin's soft inquisition, her eyes met Leslie's. "I'm good. You?"

"As good as possible considering the day's events," Leslie admitted. "Want to go for a walk?"

"Not really."

"Good." Leslie said. "Let's go then."

"Like I said," she started but Bradon cut her off.

"I could use a moment alone with my cousin."

Of course he could. And she understood that.

46

Not sparing Grant a glance, she followed Leslie. They didn't go far, just a five minute walk or so along the river. When at last they sat, it was on a flattened rock just beyond a small waterfall, or so said the bubbling and crashing of water. With nothing but a half moon to oversee, the river ebbed away in darkness.

Leslie, surprisingly enough, didn't say anything right away. When she did it was the last thing Sheila expected. "I think the first chance you get you should return to the twenty-first century."

Sheila ground her teeth. Of course her cousin would think that. "Right, because all of this is getting a little too intense and now that you know what I went through with Jack, well, I don't need one more thing."

While she expected Leslie to agree one hundred percent, she said something totally off the wall. "Actually, I was thinking you didn't need one more screwed up man messing with you but yeah, escaping back home doesn't sound like such a bad idea."

"Why, because you now realize all the hell Grant's been put through?" Sheila frowned. "And what a massively warped game he's part of."

"Partly." Leslie's eyes met hers. "But mostly because you're now starting to recover from all your ex put you through and healing would be a whole lot less jarring in the twenty-first century."

"You don't know that."

"Of course I do."

"So it's okay that you faced your demons here with Bradon but I'm not allowed to."

"What demons?"

Sheila clenched her teeth. Though McKayla had sworn her to secrecy, Leslie deserved the truth. "I know about Patrick's death."

Patrick had been Leslie's long-time boyfriend who died of cancer.

Leslie swallowed hard but never lost eye contact. "That has nothing to do with this."

"No more than what I went through with Jack," Sheila said evenly, sad as she looked at her cousin. "That said, I'm so sorry, hon."

Instead of biting out a sharp remark like the old Leslie would of, her cousin nodded then cast her eyes to the river. "Thanks."

That was Leslie. One word answers. But it was far more than she expected so she said the last thing she intended. "Every morning Jack would wake me up with the same words, "Look how beautiful you are.""

Leslie's eyes met hers. "That doesn't sound so bad."

"No, it doesn't," she murmured, eyes to the shore, lost in thought, and memories. "Only he ended every day saying how stupid I was, how I could've done this differently or that differently. One way or another, I was never quite as beautiful by the end of each day." Leslie said nothing but Sheila felt the weight of her eyes. "I'm sorry." Sheila said. "You don't need to hear this."

But, why was she sorry? Mostly because she'd shared such heavy thoughts when Leslie was just breaking free from her own. And because they were words she'd become too accustomed to saying. She always apologized. Even though most of the time she had nothing to apologize for.

A small sound suddenly came from her cousin and Leslie's hand slid into hers. "You have no need to be sorry."

"Yes I do," Sheila said. "You don't need to hear this stuff. I guess I'm still a little screwed up. Who knows. I'm not half as strong as you. That probably explains why I'm always so quick to bicker with you. Gotta stop that...I just don't have any fight left in me."

While she expected her cousin to soften and be sympathetic, she did something altogether unexpected. She shook her head then stood, hand on hips as she glared down. "Enough." Her nostrils flared. "You're the only one who ever stood up to me now you're gonna just give up the good fight? Now when you need to be stronger than ever?"

Give up? That was about the last thing she intended to do. Wasn't it?

Irritated, Sheila was about to respond but Leslie put her face in hers, noses inches apart. "Pull yourself together. I'm sorry for all you've gone through but we haven't got time for this. Be stronger. Be better." Her eyes narrowed. "Be a *Broun*."

Broun. Yeah right.

Tense, Sheila frowned. "I'll be a Broun but not one that needs this MacLomain connection to make everything all sweet again." She shook her head, not sure why it was suddenly part of her frustration. "I won't go running back to the twenty-first century either so I guess I'll remain unhealed and see this through…without the romance part."

"Whatever in regards to the romance. Totally not what I'm getting at here." Leslie flung her hands up and turned away. "Life's screwed you. I totally get that. But what of it?" She spun, eyes narrowed. "What are you going to do about it, Sheila? You always hide behind one project or another." Leslie flung her eyes to the trees. "You'll save the forest, everything around you." Her eyes landed hard on Sheila. "When all along *you* were the one who needed saving."

Sheila pulled up straighter and released an exasperated breath. "God has saved me. Everything else is falling into place."

"Awe hell, *really?*" Hands on her hips, Leslie frowned. "So we're back to that."

"Back to what?"

Leslie leaned close, eyes super narrowed. "*Religion.* What you've clearly hidden behind all these years."

Sheila couldn't help it. She saw red.

Thwap.

She slapped Leslie hard.

And there was a whole lot more where that came from.

If solid arms didn't hold her back, she would've totally unleashed. Remarkably enraged, Sheila tried to pull away from Bradon but he'd have none of it. His low, aggravated yet somehow soothing words fell by her ear. "No more, lass. *Enough.*"

Blinking, she watched as Grant took Leslie's elbow, his eyes on Sheila. "He's the right o' it, lass, enough."

Sheila wanted to scream, flail, rant, but what she'd become over the past seven years resurfaced, another beast entirely, one that was subservient…silent.

Leslie brushed off Grant and stared at her as she put her hand to her cheek. Silent, she eyed Sheila for a long moment before she left.

As the last of her anger drained away, Sheila stumbled back and once more sat.

Bradon crouched in front of her, worried. "I'm going to my wife but first…" His concerned eyes roamed her face. "Are you well, lass?"

Blank, lost, she nodded.

Bradon looked long and hard before he nodded and pursued Leslie.

Head in hands, she closed her eyes. What was the matter with her? Leslie hadn't deserved that. But Sheila knew what her cousin had done. She'd tried to help the only way she knew how...via anger. Leslie had been right. Sheila was wrong.

There was no way of telling how much time went by, maybe minutes, maybe hours, before she stopped beating on herself. At last calm and as centered as she was likely to get for now, she looked at the river. When she did she was startled to realize Grant sat nearby. All this time he'd remained quiet and allowed her space. Slightly embarrassed she said, "Sorry about all that. Just venting I guess."

"There is naught to be sorry for, lass," he said softly, eyes on the river.

The guy *had* to think she was ten types of crazy. Way to make an impression, Sheila. Since she'd traveled back in time and started this little adventure, she'd been pretty much in control of her emotions. But it seemed that her cousins might have been on to something after all. Maybe she wasn't at a hundred percent yet. Rather than get upset about that revelation a certain peace settled over her.

Grant's eyes turned to her almost as if he sensed the small change in her outlook. When both warmth and compassion entered his eyes, Sheila realized that her previous speculations that she didn't need a MacLomain on this journey might just be wrong.

Then something else entered his eyes. Something she couldn't quite put her finger on.

Sadness? Or maybe regret mixed with determination?

One thing was clear however. Whether or not she needed him, he certainly needed her.

Chapter Four

Grant stood and held out his hand to Sheila. "Come. 'Tis time to rest."

Composed, Sheila nodded and walked silently beside him. It was impossible not to sense her emotions. Acute, painful, they were at last starting to bubble to the surface. Yet they needed to if she was to find peace. Though it was a difficult thing to watch he well understood her turmoil, the broken, dark place she slowly but surely left behind.

Leslie had taken a different approach with her but then her cousin seemed to respond with anger when sad. The physical violence Sheila had dealt was not meant for her cousin but her former lover. Yet this passion was needed.

Release was needed.

He pondered this…her. The more Grant and she were together, the more he knew she'd soon need another type of release altogether. Truth told, it would be no difficulty lying with this lass…when she was ready.

And they *would* have to lie together sooner rather than later.

The image of her slender, nude body as she walked into the river was at the forefront of his mind. He'd never seen a lovelier creature. Fine-boned, with slightly flared hips and breasts made to fit his hands, it had taken tremendous strength not to pull her into his arms.

But the time wasn't quite right yet.

When they returned to the others, Leslie sat against a rock, Bradon's head in her lap as he slept. Grant wondered at the intimacy and love his cousin had found with his wife. Though he could admit to desiring Sheila and feeling close to her, he knew nothing of love. Mayhap a faint memory of how his parents and kin had once loved him, but not what was shared between a lad and a lass.

Sheila sat across from her cousin and eyed her red cheek sadly. "God, Les, I'm so incredibly sorry…especially after the whole Patrick thing."

Leslie looked at her for a long moment. "I purposely tried to rile you up so you'd vent a little, Shay. So I'm sorry about the cruel words."

"I figured maybe you had, sort of."

"Sort of?"

"You were sad for me too," Sheila said. "So you got angry."

Leslie stared at the fire. "I suppose you're right." She didn't seem bothered that Grant sat nearby. Though he'd leaned back against a rock and closed his eyes, he was still there.

"I'm just worried about you," Leslie murmured.

"I know but I *am* getting better." He heard a small smile in Sheila's voice. "Especially now that I got out some aggravation."

Leslie snorted but said nothing more.

When Grant opened his eyes a while later, Leslie's eyes were closed and Sheila lay curled on her side. Bringing forth a few more furs, he covered all three, then sat down, eyes on Sheila's face. He'd never been able to simply sit and admire a lass's beauty. Slightly darker in color than her hair, her eyelashes curved against her cheeks, a graceful fan over soft, luminescent skin. The tip of her nose upturned ever-so-slightly and her kissable lips opened just a bit as she slept.

As if somehow pulled from slumber by his gaze, her eyes slowly opened. For a long time, they simply stared at one another. Then, as if she'd been sleeping all along, her eyes slid shut. Though tempted to lie beside her he wouldn't. Not this eve. She'd had an emotional day and didn't need to wake up with him pressed against her. Not to mention, he doubted he could hold her in his arms and not want more. So though he slept some, he was up before the others, game hunted and already roasted when they awoke.

Sheila's eyes immediately went to him. "Thanks for the fur…and for breakfast."

He nodded and handed her and the others some food. Torra, her breathing somewhat heavy, stared into the fog draped forest, her words murmur soft. "The solstice comes soon. I must get back to my brethren. 'Tis best to be surrounded with as many of the next generation of MacLomains as possible." Her eyes went to Grant. "Meanwhile, you must go to him."

"Who?" Bradon asked, eyes narrowed.

Grant hadn't been looking forward to this. "Colin MacLeod."

"What?" Sheila asked, wide-eyed.

"I cannae abandon my friends, lass," he said. "They have been like kin to me."

"But they're not your kin, Grant," Bradon said vehemently. "We are."

"He has been with them longer than us," Torra said softly.

"Colin will kill you for sure!" Sheila said.

Before he could respond, Leslie spoke, eyes narrowed. "Not if they're friends."

Sheila's shocked eyes met Grant's. "Is Colin MacLeod...your friend?"

"The verra best," Grant whispered.

Bradon cursed. "Bloody hell."

"'Twas Colin who told me Keir had Grant," Torra reminded. Her voice grew stronger as she met Bradon's eyes. "You might not believe it now, but you've more to be thankful for to Colin MacLeod than you know."

"He tried to burn Cadence and Sheila alive not that long ago," Leslie said. "So don't mind me if I'm not convinced he's one of the good guys." Her eyes went to Grant. "Nor you for that matter."

Grant said nothing to that but looked at Sheila. "I willnae leave him alone beneath Keir's rule. Though his mind is not under Hamilton's control, he is as much his victim as I am...was."

Sheila shook her head. "But won't Keir be furious that you slipped free from his mental hold? Won't he likely kill you or at the very least cast you beneath his spell again?"

"He will likely try and will think he succeeded but he willnae," Grant said. "And for all Keir knows 'twas not me who ripped free from his mental grasp but 'twas forced by the enemy. I will convince him that I remain devoted to his cause."

Bradon shook his head. "You have a lot of confidence in yourself, cousin."

"Aye," Grant said. Confidence had nothing to do with it.

"If 'tis the enemy's army you go back to 'twould be best if you didnae go back empty handed," Torra said.

Leslie's eyes narrowed. "That doesn't sound very promising."

Grant frowned. "I dinnae need a prisoner with me."

"Aye, but you do," Torra said. "If the MacLeod's and Hamilton's are to believe you escaped with vengeance in your heart then you should claim a MacLomain prize."

"*What?*" Leslie's voice trailed off.

Sheila's eyes remained on his face as comprehension settled over her. She knew what she had to do so said, "There's no way I'm letting my cousin go and none of the MacLomain men will be joining you to be sure."

Leslie's eyes swung to Sheila, incredulous. "You're seriously not considering this."

"No, I'm not considering," she said. "I'm going."

"Absolutely not." Leslie shook her head. "For all you know Keir will show up and kill you in an instant. And just look at what Colin MacLeod did the last time he saw you. He nearly charbroiled your ass!"

"I assured him Sheila and Cadence would be saved from that fire," Grant said. "Or he wouldnae have done it."

"Pft, yeah right," Leslie muttered.

"If this will help Grant stay safe, I'm going," Sheila said. "Simple as that."

Torra looked at her, a pleased flicker in her tired eyes. "'Twill without doubt, lass. Many thanks."

"Ugh!" Leslie stood and shook her head. "Haven't you already been through enough, Shay?"

"This is *my* choice," Sheila said. "And having the choice to think on my own isn't something I've experienced a whole lot of in the past seven years."

"Oh damn," Leslie whispered. "This is just so crazy dangerous."

"All of this is dangerous," Sheila countered. "But we're strong and we'll make it."

Though he spoke to Leslie, Bradon's proud eyes went to Sheila. "She's the right o' it."

Leslie frowned as she continued to look at Sheila. Finally she said, "Well I can't stop you if you're determined." Then her eyes went to Grant. "If she gets hurt I'll hold you personally responsible."

"As will we all," Bradon assured.

Grant would never let anything happen to her but understood that trying to convince them of such would be pointless. His eyes went to Sheila. "Are you sure you want to do this, lass?"

She nodded, determined.

But he meant to give her honesty. "You need to ken that if you do…" He paused, not entirely sure how he wanted to phrase this. Best to say it simply he supposed. "When with the MacLeod's you will belong to me."

"And there's the convenient little catch," Leslie muttered.

Sheila's eyes narrowed just a wee bit. "What *exactly* does that mean?"

"Nothing as bad as it sounds," Torra said. "Grant is first-in-command of Keir's armies which gives him much authority. If he claims you as his 'twill keep unwanted hands off of you."

"Bonus," Sheila murmured, receiving a skin of whiskey from Bradon. After a deep swill she nodded. "When do we leave?"

Grant, as always, was impressed by her courage.

"Now," Torra said. When she tried to stand, Grant took her arm and helped her up.

"I have another question." Leslie frowned at Grant. "What does Keir know of the tattoo marks Torra put on you guys and these Claddagh rings that we Broun's wear?"

"Verra little unless he possesses Torra in her entirety," Grant said. "The power of the marks is well protected by Torra and he doesnae know of the rings. Created by both a warlock and a MacLomain wizard, their powers are masked as well."

"Almost too convenient that, wouldn't you say?" Bradon asked. "Assuming you have a mark, how has it gone unnoticed by Keir?"

"Aye, I've a mark," Grant said. "He thinks I had it inked during celebrations with the men."

"Wow, really?" Sheila said. "The man doesn't strike me as that naïve."

This treaded alarmingly close to the precarious dynamics that had existed between himself and his former master. "'Tis safe to say Keir has come to trust me most thoroughly."

"And how does one earn that kind of trust with a monster I wonder," Bradon said.

"With a cunning mind and knack for both warfare and magic," Torra said. "And of course, the most unlikely of allies."

Sheila looked at him curiously. "I don't understand. Does she refer to Colin MacLeod?"

Grant held out his hand and opened his fist. "Nay, Adlin MacLomain."

As he knew they would, her eyes rounded and her mouth fell open. "You have a pentacle just like mine!"

"Aye," he murmured. "Given to me by Adlin MacLomain, it has allowed me to travel to the Defiance over the years without Keir's knowledge. Because of this I learned much and was able to give Keir invaluable advice."

"Advice that he thought you'd come up with on your own," Bradon said, a small grin on his face. "Good old Adlin, meddlesome wizard."

As they made their way through the forest, Sheila fell back and walked with Bradon and Leslie. This gave him a moment alone with Torra before they once more went their separate ways.

"You know Sheila had to go with you no matter what. Why did you give her a choice?" Torra said softly.

"She has been through too much to have been taken against her will," he said. "This needed to be her decision."

"'Tis good then that she cares for you. This could have gone another way entirely."

"But it didnae," he said.

"Nay, it didnae," Torra murmured. "'Twill get more difficult for you now, my friend. I know you dinnae go back only for Colin."

Grant frowned. Nay, there were others. "I willnae leave Kenzie and Bryce behind."

"Might they not escape if the MacLomain's win this war?"

"Assuming the MacLomain's win," he said.

Her big blue eyes met his. "They will win. *We* will win."

Grant wished he could be so optimistic but there were still so many things that could go wrong. They remained silent the remainder of the walk, both deep in thought. Eventually they arrived at the point in which they'd travel back through time. None knew it but the inconspicuous small boulder nearby was in fact a Defiance. And though most thought the Defiance's now inactive, he'd found a way to harness their power.

Torra embraced him, her words close to his ear. "I will see you again soon enough, my cousin. Meanwhile, keep a close eye on your Broun lass, aye?"

It could be no other way. "Aye."

Sheila hugged Bradon then Leslie, her cousin muttering, "I better damn well see you again, sweetie."

Sheila worked at a grin. "Look on the bright side. At least we'll be in the same era and only a few days ride apart from one another."

"Yeah, on opposing sides of the same war." Leslie shook her head. "Be careful, okay?"

"No other way to be," Sheila said.

With a solid nod, she came to Grant's side. "I guess it's time to go."

"Aye," he murmured and began to chant. Hand on her elbow; he braced himself against the swirl and fall of time travel. The scent of sugar filled his nostrils and colors swirled by before they thumped softly to the ground.

Now it was time for her to meet his clan…

And the lass who'd been his for so long.

Chapter Five

There was nothing quite like coming out of the haze of time travel surrounded by the enemy.

Frigid wind whipped and heavy snow fell, the perfect seething backdrop for the man who stood over them, legs spread and arms crossed over his wide chest.

Colin MacLeod.

Sheila swallowed as his hard silver eyes flickered between her and Grant.

Holy heck, what had she been *thinking* when she agreed to this?

But look at that...she now wore a dress! Grant must've had something to do with the change of clothing. No doubt her jeans and t-shirt might've looked a tad bit strange.

Men sheathed their weapons, grins on their faces as Colin held out a hand to Grant. "Good to see you, my friend."

All Sheila could think of as the men embraced, clapping one another on the back, was how vicious they'd been when they kidnapped her and Cadence before. Not so much to her and her cousin but to the oncoming MacLomains's. That little battle had ended with Grant and Colin taking Iosbail MacLomain.

Now here she was, once more in the position of prisoner.

Because she'd volunteered!

Grant grabbed her elbow and pulled her up. "I dinnae return without a prize."

Colin's eyes narrowed a fraction as they met hers. Not once had this man looked her dead in the eyes and that was okay. His regard had a way of stripping a person down to their bare soul. The last time she'd seen him, Malcolm's wolf had made a meal out of Colin's sister, Nessa who moments before had been battling with Sheila and Cadence.

So this couldn't be good.

Yet instead of lashing out at her, his gaze returned to Grant and he disregarded her as if she wasn't standing there to begin with.

"'Tis good you brought a MacLomain wench, 'twill please our men."

"She's my prize," Grant ground out. "Well-earned after what I suffered at the hands of the MacLomains."

Lord, was he convincing. Gone was the even-tempered Scotsman who showed her God in the trees. In his place, the man she'd first witnessed at the Hamilton castle. A stern, near emotionless warrior.

Colin eyed him for a few seconds before he clapped him on the back, grinning. "Aye then, take your pleasure with her if 'twould please you." The MacLeod slid him a sly look. "Much to the displeasure of your whore I'm sure."

His *what*?

"How fares Kenzie?" Grant asked.

"Set aside for you as always," Colin assured, his gaze flickering over Sheila briefly before returning to Grant. "Will ye be wanting both this eve then?"

"Aye," Grant said. "But whiskey first."

Please let her be hearing wrong because it certainly sounded like Grant intended to bed her and some woman named Kenzie...at the same time.

When Grant pulled her after him it was a really easy thing to plant her feet firmly and not allow it. The truth was she was becoming more and more frightened. What if everything Grant had said was a complete lie? Though she'd been determined to trust him it was becoming more and more difficult as she truly started to take in her surroundings.

MacLeod and Hamilton warriors as far as the eye could see.

Sheila yelped when Grant threw her over his shoulder. "Have I a tent then?"

"Aye." Colin nodded to one of the larger ones. "There."

Grant wasted no time but flipped her down and shoved her in. Before she could say a word he put a finger to his lips, winked then growled, "Ye will stay here until I return. If ye attempt to leave even once, ye will be given to my men. Do ye ken, lass?"

Relief washed over her.

He'd winked.

So she nodded and said not yes but, "Aye."

Then he was gone, his stern voice just beyond the tent skins. "Have a fire lit. I'll not have her cold skin against me."

As she gazed around, Sheila realized how well-liked Grant must be that the MacLeod's had set up a tent like this not knowing if he'd return. Soft furs lined the ground as well as several plaid blankets. Soon after Grant left, a Hamilton warrior entered. Tall, rugged, he had blondish hair and dark hazel eyes. Crouching, he cleared a spot in the center and dumped some wood.

Wary, she inched back and watched him.

His eyes went to hers. Sheila was surprised to see warmth in them and even more surprised by his deep albeit soft words. "Fear naught, lass. Our Grant willnae hurt ye."

Not interested in engaging a complete stranger, she said nothing.

"Bryce is the name," he said as he lit the fire and then nodded toward a satchel in the corner. "There's some food and a skin o' whiskey in there if ye be needing it."

Unable to help herself she at last murmured, "Thank you."

Bryce nodded but said nothing more. Once he seemed convinced the fire would stay lit, he left. Sheila wasted no time but crawled over to the satchel and pulled out the skin. After she took a few deep gulps of the burning liquid, she eyed the dried meat. Not hungry in the least, she crawled back over and peered out the thin strip of opening to the fire beyond.

Grant, Colin and many other warriors sat around it, laughing and toasting to Grant's safe return. When several 'women of the night' wandered over, Grant pulled one onto his lap. Rather striking, she had pale blond hair and deep brown eyes. Sheila took a long swig of whiskey as she watched the woman wrap her arm around his neck and plant her lips softly against his cheek.

A burning started in Sheila's chest that had nothing to do with the alcohol. This had to be *his* whore. Knees pulled against her chest, Sheila knew she should look away but couldn't. Instead, she kept with the whiskey as the Scotswoman tossed back her head and laughed.

Why would Grant do this to her?

But then what had he really done? Just last night she'd decided she wasn't meant for a MacLomain. So why get jealous now? But Sheila knew precisely why. She *wanted* to be part of this Broun/MacLomain connection.

More than that…she wanted Grant.

It'd been no small thing having this man in her mind, the sensual sensations connected with it. Then there was something entirely too romantic about having a man save your life the way he had. Could it be she'd just been caught up in the thrill of the ride? Sure, she wore a ring and Grant had a tattoo but what if this was just another twist in the story. Could it be they weren't meant to be together after all?

Time seemed to pass far too slowly as she watched Grant with his warriors and his woman...because that's certainly who the blond girl appeared to be. Sheila could see it in the fondness in their eyes when they looked at one another. She could see it in the way they held hands, genuinely affectionate beyond simple lust.

When at last Grant stood and pulled the blond up with him, Sheila shimmied back.

Though she'd fully intended to pretend she was asleep when he returned, she just couldn't do it. Instead, she stared wide-eyed as he pulled the pretty woman in after him. Wind and snow blew hard, but the sound couldn't drown out the pounding of her heart.

Tying off the entrance behind him, he gestured for the woman to sit.

Graceful, she did just that…right next to Sheila.

Oh God, he really *did* intend to have them both.

That'd be the day!

So when the woman made to speak, Sheila shook her head and looked at Grant. "You are out of your ever loving mind if you think—"

"Nay," he whispered sharply, his eyes going to the woman by her side.

"Nay is right," the woman said softly. "Sorry I couldnae say hello sooner, lass. 'Twas not my place." She held out her hand in greeting. "I am Grant's friend, Kenzie."

"Yeah, caught that," she muttered but didn't take the proffered hand.

Kenzie put her hand in her lap and eyed Grant. "She has the wrong idea about us."

"Aye." Grant plunked down on the opposite side of the fire, his eyes on Sheila. "Like me, Kenzie was taken against her will and has been with the Hamilton's nearly as long as I. Where I was trained to help lead his armies she," he cleared his throat, "was trained for other things."

Oh Lord. *Really?*

Her eyes flickered to Kenzie, uncomfortable. She had no idea what to say. Was Grant serious? Though there was most certainly a sadness in the girl's eyes there was also a great strength as she looked at Sheila. "'Tis true, lass. I am a whore." Kenzie made a loose gesture with her hand in Grant's direction. "Well, mostly his whore but a whore nonetheless."

Sheila seriously had no clue what to make of this. What to say to a woman enslaved into such a life? Still a little unsure as to how to approach this she kept things simple. "I'm so sorry." Then she held out her hand. "My name's Sheila."

Perked up some, Kenzie took her hand and smiled. It was hard not to be aware of how beautiful the woman actually was. Yet there was more than that. Sheila realized that Kenzie wasn't aware in the least of her own beauty.

Kenzie soon leaned back on her hands, a devious grin on her face as she looked at Grant. "So here we three be having our way with each other." Her brows shot up. "Aren't ye something, Grant MacLomain."

Grant took a swig from his skin and offered a charming grin. "So it seems." He winked at Kenzie. "Now work your magic, lass."

Sheila clamped her hand over her mouth in shock when Kenzie flung back her head and started to moan. Long, breathy and startlingly sensual, she panted a few times then released a long groan. After a few more of these sounds she slowed down some before unleashing another round.

Then suddenly she cried out, "Oh, Grant! Aye, that's it, right there, lad. Ohhhhh, aye, ohhhhh!"

Sheila couldn't help but chuckle…muffled in her hand of course.

What was *up* with these people?

But she knew it was being done for the benefit of those beyond the tent. Nothing but 'genuine authenticity' would do for curious ears.

When finished, Kenzie shot her a wicked grin and cocked her brow. "Are ye up for it, lassie?"

"Making those sounds? Heck no." Sheila shook her head. "Besides, I'm being taken against my will. No pleasure in it for me, right?"

Kenzie considered this, eyes narrowed on Grant. "Well with this one ye never know." But then she patted Sheila on the shoulder. "But ye've the right o' it."

Grant tossed Kenzie his skin. "For all your hard work."

"'Tis always about pleasing ye, my friend." She took a long swig. "How long do ye want me to stay?"

"As long as you like." Grant pulled the dried meat from his satchel and handed it to her. "Here. Eat."

Then he handed some to Sheila. "You too."

"Thanks but I'm not hungry."

Grant continued to hold the meat out. "Please. You need to keep up your strength."

Though it was a simple request she saw the concerned look in his eyes so she took the meat.

Kenzie looked between Grant and Sheila before she said, "'Tis good that you came, Sheila."

Came? Like willingly? She looked at Grant then Kenzie and said what she thought she should. "I didn't have much choice in the matter."

"Right," Kenzie said slowly. "Of course you didnae."

"Kenzie knows of all of this," Grant said softly to Sheila. "She is a dear friend."

Sheila was certainly sensing that. But wow, she knew about everything? She looked at Grant. "Isn't that a little risky?"

Kenzie stood and stretched. "I think 'tis time I go."

Grant frowned. "Why?"

Skin and meat in hand, she made her way to the tent entrance and started to undo it. "Because where I have truths," she tossed a look over her shoulder, "Sheila still doesnae."

Grant sighed but nodded. "Go to the tent beside this one. You need not service others this eve."

"Aye, m'laird," she murmured.

"I'm not your laird," he muttered.

"Nay, but ye should be," she said before vanishing into the night.

Grant retied the entrance but instead of sitting on the opposite side of the fire, he sat next to Sheila and removed another skin from the satchel. She pulled her knees against her chest, stared at the crackling flames and tried to process what she'd learned in such a short time.

"I'm sorry I didnae tell you of this before you came," Grant began. "But I'd rather you didnae judge the lass before you met her."

"What makes you think I'd judge her?" Sheila said, a little offended. "Honestly, I would've rather understood your relationship with her before watching what I did between you two out at that fire."

She felt Grant's eyes on her face.

"Then forgive me if I handled it wrong. I didnae realize it would hurt you to see such."

Nothing like making it clear she'd been jealous. Sheila took a swig from her skin but didn't look at him. "You just caught me off guard is all."

"Is that all?" he murmured and shifted closer to her. "Then let me give you honesty."

When he paused she looked at him.

His eyes locked on hers. "She is one of many lasses enslaved by Keir Hamilton. While Keir has given me many whores…lasses, over the years, she was one I favored above the rest and so he allowed me to claim her as mine."

Sheila couldn't believe what she was hearing. He claimed her? How unbelievably barbarian. "That's terrible."

"Not so terrible," he said honestly. "We were each other's first but there was never love betwixt us only deep friendship."

Christ, he lost his virginity to her? Wasn't that just the icing on the cake. But what type of cake exactly? If nothing else, theirs had been a friendship born of dreadful circumstances.

Before she could respond, he said, "Though I've not lain with many of them, through Kenzie I've learned the name of every lass taken by Keir." His voice grew impassioned. "When the time comes, I will see them all set free."

Officially speechless, she could only stare at him. He'd been enslaved for fourteen years and it seemed he was less concerned with that than he was with freeing other prisoners. The pure gallantry, the humaneness of such a thing was phenomenal, yet so very sad.

When at last she found her words there were but four that she knew all would agree with. "That's amazing. Thank you."

"Och, me wee geal, I need no thanks."

Oh, but he did whether he knew it or not. Caught in his entrancing eyes, she murmured, "Why do you call me geal? What does it mean?"

His hand slid into hers and the gray in his eyes sidled past the pale blue. "When in this darkness that has been my life I saw a spark of light, 'twas when the pentacle first brought you to me." He put the back of her hand to his lips and gently kissed. "Geal means bright, clear…pure… 'twas you, lass."

After years of mental abuse about the last thing she felt was clear and pure but that didn't matter in the least as his eyes searched hers.

"Might I kiss you?" he whispered.

Before she could respond, which would have been a definite *yes*, he tilted her chin and brought her lips to his. Her eyes fluttered shut and the world became entirely made up of him, his talented caress involving nothing but his mouth against hers. And it was just that, an artful brushstroke of his lips over hers. Tender, testing, his lips fit over hers as though melding and memorizing…exploring.

Slow warmth scorched and flared to fast heat. It fanned from her lips over her cheeks until it crashed like a tumbleweed caught in harsh wind down through her body. Sheila grasped his arm, frightened almost by the free-fall she was taking.

In no rush to take advantage of the instant passion he pulled from her, his kiss remained rather chaste, as if he relished the innocent contact. Wind gusted against the tent, the fire flickered, but he kept his administrations tempered.

At last impatient, she flicked her tongue out and skimmed his lower lip. As if he'd been waiting all along for an invitation, his tongue flicked against hers. Wanting more, she licked into his mouth. It seemed, perhaps, that was more than he could handle because he suddenly half growled, half groaned.

In a flash, and she'd never know how he did it so quickly, he knelt between her bent, spread legs. He cupped her cheeks and slanted his mouth over hers. Now more aggressive but not overpowering, she could feel the desire he held back in the swirl of his tongue around hers.

She hadn't been with a man in a very long time. Though she'd only left Jack a few months ago, they hadn't been intimate for a good year before that. Now this...Grant. His tongue continued its sensual, curious adventure in her mouth. Grasping his arms, she sunk further and further into the wickedly deep abyss of eroticism that he offered.

When his arm snaked around her lower back and his hot lips trailed over her chin and down her neck, her head fell back. Lips open, eyes closed, she released a low groan when he pushed her back and his large hands rode up her legs. Working from both sides, he started at her ankles, feeling her calves with reverence, as though he'd never touched anything so precious. Then he ran his palms over her knees before he flattened them against her upper thighs and pushed up her dress.

A heavy, needing throb had already started between her legs. Drawing in deep breaths, she released a strangled moan when his lips met her inner thigh. It seemed the enemy was pleasuring the prisoner after all.

I'm so ready for this. Please, yes, pleaaaseeeee.

"Is he here then," a deep voice boomed.

Oh, yes, I'm nearly here...or there, just let him keep on going.

But it seemed that wasn't just a bizarrely masculine voice in her head based on Grant's reaction. Jerking back, his eyes met her. Worried, he shook his head sharply and left the tent.

What was happening?

Adjusting her dress, Sheila crawled to the tent flap and stared out. Oh, but how she wished she hadn't. Standing before the remnants of the fire, black cloak whipping in the wind, was Keir Hamilton. She pulled back and closed her eyes.

Dear God, no.

Why was *he* here?

Despite the late hour, men snapped to life, quick to rebuild the fire and bring forth food and skins of whiskey. Even Colin MacLeod reappeared. Grant fell to one knee in front of Keir and lowered his head. "My laird."

Why had she ever believed for a minute Keir wouldn't come when he knew his number one slave had returned? Sheila bit her lower lip harshly and worked at not trembling.

"Nay, stand my lad, you have done *well*," Keir's raspy voice applauded.

He had? Petrified by what that might mean she reigned in her courage and peered out.

As if he knew she was there, Keir's dark eyes swung her way and he barked an order. "Bring her out!"

A strong pair of arms reached in and grabbed her, dragging her out until she was set in front of Keir. Sheila shook so hard she nearly threw up. Petrified, she looked at his black-booted feet and started to inwardly pray. If this was it, if this was the end, she'd go with God.

Claw-like, his hand grabbed her chin and whipped her head up. In that moment, staring into the face of pure evil, Sheila shuddered.

Then she went deadly calm.

Funny, when you knew you were drawing your last breaths you didn't think about all the harmful things in your life but of all those who mattered, who you loved. She thought of McKayla, Cadence and Leslie, she even thought of Bradon and Malcolm. What she refused to think of because she didn't want this evil bastard anywhere mentally near him was Grant.

"Oh, aye," he hissed softly, his dark gaze on hers. "She will do."

Hand in the air, he curled his fingers. "Bring forth the holy man."

The holy man?

Did Keir actually have it in him to have a holy man say a prayer over her grave?

When she was yanked forward and her wrist bound by a scrap of plaid with Grant's, she was more than confused. So they'd die together then?

"She'll not be your prize but your wife," Keir said, pleased as he stepped back and allowed the clergyman to finish wrapping their wrists. When she looked at Grant it was only to find his eyes on Keir.

"'Twill infuriate the MacLomains," Keir declared through a toothy, rotten smile. "Mayhap not as much as it would have had it been Colin but 'twill do."

Way beyond understanding what was going on, her eyes went to the clergyman when he started to mumble words quickly. Her eyes widened. Was this guy marrying her to Grant? And why again did this make Keir so happy?

Grant, voice low, offered the clergyman a few words in what had to be Gaelic before his eyes went to hers. Hard, distant, she barely recognized them. The clergyman's words were now aimed at her. Mouth agape, she could only stare at them all.

Keir's hand suddenly came around her throat and his hot breath by her ear. "All ye need to do is say aye."

Pinned by the dark overlord's gaze, she knew if she didn't it would mean Grant's death. How she knew that she'd never be sure. But to make such a vow in the eyes of God? As if he read her thoughts, Keir's eyes narrowed further.

Okay, no offense to God but she'd be darned if this monster sunk his teeth into Grant. She gave a sharp nod, the best she could manage with his hand around her throat.

After another long, dank look into her eyes, he released her and nodded.

Though she didn't understand a word coming out of the clergyman's mouth, she swallowed hard and nodded, unable to look at Grant as she said aye. Did she want to? With all her heart. But at this point she didn't dare allow Keir to see something other than hatred. Truly, Sheila had to wonder if she was marrying in the eyes of God or the Devil himself.

When their vows were apparently complete, an evil ripple of laugher buried itself in Keir's chest. "Verra good indeed."

The next thing she knew she was being dragged away by some nameless Hamilton warrior. All she heard behind her were Keir's words to Grant. "I will keep your wife safe at my castle. Fight the bloody MacLomains and win. This marriage will be yet another thing to weaken them. Then," she heard the dark promise in Keir's voice, "you can do with her what you will."

When the man next to her started to murmur, she knew magic was once again whipping her away. This time, however, it had nothing to do with time travel. No, this was but a shift north. Sheila clenched her teeth when her vision cleared and the Hamilton castle once more stood before her.

This wasn't supposed to be happening.

Or was it?

She just didn't know anymore. Trying to bank her fear the best she could, she didn't struggle as she was led over the drawbridge. The last time she'd been here she and Leslie had been running alongside hundreds, all determined to either fight or flee from the dragon flying overhead. Smoky, battle-ridden, this place had been far different than it was now. Quiet, with a few torches burning, there were barely any people about.

If anything, the castle was all but abandoned with little to no commerce. Perhaps that was what came of war in these times but the MacLomain castle wasn't like this. There, people still sold wares and life flowed. Was it subdued? Of course, their clan was off to war. But they kept on with duties so that their clan wouldn't fail. So what of this? How could a castle this massive maintain itself without activity of some sort?

Sheila kept emotions at bay as she was led in the front door of the castle. She couldn't bear to look around because if she did she'd recall too vividly what happened when last here. Too much destruction, not only because of Keir but also because of Colin MacLeod and even Grant.

This was their lair.

While she tried to convince herself Grant had nothing to do with it, she still remembered the deadly look on his face when he'd stood in this place, when he'd tried to kill his parents. Yes, he'd had no choice…still.

Memories were memories.

Sheila again swallowed hard when she was led through a door off to the side, down a long, spiraling set of stairs. Having recently been in the MacLomain's dungeon, she recognized the putrid, damp smell of the place she was being led to.

The wife of Keir's slave would not be offered comfortable chambers but a prison cell.

And it was a good long walk down into the belly of this castle.

By the time they reached the bottom, Sheila knew any hope of escape was non-existent. She'd just walked into her tomb. They didn't go much further before the man unlocked a cell and shoved her in. When the bars slammed shut, she flinched.

Welcome to helping out a MacLomain.

She didn't mean to think that way but seriously, this sucked. A filthy pot sat in the corner on a dirt floor. There was nothing else. One torch burned in her cell. It smelled horrid against the murky scent of brine that somehow seeped in from the sea. Not even a slit of a window existed.

Sheila sunk to the floor against the wall and braced her head in her hands. For seven years she'd lived in a prison but it looked nothing like this. No, if anything this might've been Grant's prison. She flinched. Had this been where he was kept or was he given a chamber in the castle or even the warrior's quarters befitting his station?

She didn't know because she hadn't asked.

Why hadn't she?

Sheila leaned her head back against the wall. She knew damn well why…it would have hurt too much to hear that it might've been. Nobody deserved to live like this. It was hell in the purest sense.

"And yet another Broun arrives," came a flippant, echoing voice through the dark shadows of the dungeon.

Startled by the feminine octave, she raised her head. Was she somehow thinking aloud?

"Stop feeling sorry for yourself and stand. Go to the bars."

Now she knew she would not have thought that. Not to mention, she had no accent. Eager, Sheila jumped to her feet and looked through the bars.

A slender hand gave a small wave from the opposite cell. "Greetings, lassie."

Sheila blinked. Beyond beautiful despite imprisonment, a woman with black curling hair wrapped a slender arm around one of the bars and said, "Ye be a Broun to be sure. Where be your MacLomain then?"

Sheila never had the chance to meet her when Colin MacLeod kidnapped her but she knew without doubt who spoke.

Iosbail MacLomain.

Adlin MacLomain's sister.

Sheila wasn't quite sure how to answer but decided it best to be honest. "My MacLomain's been shotgun married to me then ordered by his master to fight his own clan."

"Och," Iosbail said, eyes gleaming almost merrily through the bars. "Now that be exciting, aye?"

Exciting? Not. But this was Iosbail MacLomain. She'd heard stories about the woman. Crazy, bold, live-on-the-edge, that was her...or so they said.

Sheila decided to stick with honesty. "I would have preferred marrying the old fashioned way, in a church and perhaps asked first. Oh, and knowing the guy more than a few days would've been nice."

A very unfeminine snort echoed off the walls. "Aye, but 'twould not have been so memorable."

Sheila frowned. Thank God it hadn't been Colin MacLeod. "I still don't get Keir's reasoning for such a thing outside of thinking it'll infuriate the MacLomains."

Which might've been true if he *was* in fact the enemy as Keir so clearly thought.

"Is that not enough?" Iosbail said. "There is much the Hamilton can accomplish with a Broun lass married to his MacLomain. Such an alliance alone gives him extra sway over what would remain of his enemies if he wins this war."

She could hardly see herself as being important enough to the MacLomains and their allied clans that their marriage would make much impact.

As if Iosbail heard her thoughts she said, "You underestimate the value of we Brouns and the power of a Scottish marriage pact."

Maybe. Maybe not.

Sheila tried to get a better glimpse of Iosbail but the one torch flickered low and there was little to see. "They'll get you out of here before you're hurt."

"Who?" Iosbail said. "Me MacLomains?" She chuckled. "Mayhap."

"Definitely," Sheila assured.

"Where be the Sinclair?"

Iosbail referred to her love, King Alexander Sinclair, of course. "He's with the MacLomain army ready to battle the MacLeod and Hamilton armies."

Silence.

Too much silence.

Sheila was about to speak when Iosbail said, "How fares Torra?"

So she knew of Torra MacLomain? How? Sheila wasn't about to divulge too much information in case Keir Hamilton somehow listened.

Tentative, she said, "As far as I know trapped in this castle. So I'm guessing she's not so good."

Iosbail seemed to contemplate this. "Even Keir knows he's only got half her soul, hence the need for me, lassie."

Sheila was about to speak but suddenly saw the gleam of one of Iosbail's eyes. It almost felt like the distance between them was ripped away when the MacLomain wizard murmured, *"Intelligit autem anima ad percipiendum cum Viking magica. In otherworld, spatium inter se et immolato serpentes ad me des Torra animae dimidium."*

The air grew alarmingly thin and Sheila struggled for breath. Grasping at the bars, she tried not to panic. Her arms, legs, heck everything was growing weak. Even her vision blurred. Unable to stand, she started to sink to the ground.

Then, out of nowhere, she was lifted into a strong set of arms.

Grant?

How was he here?

But she had little time to wonder as the unmistakable pull of time travel twisted around them. Fast, furious, it ripped everything away until they thumped to the ground. Sheila barely had time to process where they were before a sword was at her throat…

This time held by Adlin MacLomain himself.

Chapter Six

The MacLomain Castle
876

Though the sword was to her throat, Adlin MacLomain spoke to Grant. "Who are you? Speak fast or she suffers my blade."

Sheila had never seen Adlin look so vicious but then based on the remarkably different appearance of the MacLomain castle beyond she suspected she was meeting a much younger version of him. She swallowed hard and tried to ignore the sword, never mind the several others surrounding them.

"I am Grant, your kin from the future," Grant said calmly. "We have traveled here through one of your Defiances." He paused, as if to let the information sink in. "If you kill her you threaten the verra existence of the MacLomain clan."

Adlin's eyes narrowed on Grant. "Toss aside your weapons."

Grant complied. Meanwhile, Adlin's eyes began to glow as he stared at Grant. She knew that look. His magic ignited. That meant he was likely crawling into his descendant's mind.

Surprise lit Adlin's face and his eyes returned to normal. Sheathing his blade and motioning for his men to do the same, he held a hand out to Sheila. "My apologies lass. I've never had kin visit from the future. 'Tis an honor indeed!"

Oh, thank *God*. As Adlin pulled her up she realized they hadn't traveled alone. Kenzie and Bryce were with them.

Grant made brief introductions and Adlin nodded. "Come into the castle so that we might talk." He began walking. "No doubt you've quite the story to tell."

As they followed him over the drawbridges, Sheila's eyes widened. Though still an impressive sight the castle was no longer stone but wood. Curious, she asked what year it was. When Adlin said 876 she nearly tripped. She'd come to think of the year 1254 as her home away from home so that meant they'd traveled 378 years further back in time. Nuts!

Though the innards of the castle were fairly similar many of the tapestries had yet to be hung including the monster Viking tapestry that was certainly the great hall's overseer. Adlin urged them to sit in front of a low fire. Here was another feature that hadn't changed. Definitely the heart of the castle, the hearth was monstrous with ancient faces carved into the mantle.

Adlin gave them a few moments to settle after they received mugs of ale. As handsome as he'd been when she'd last seen him, the MacLomain's patriarch surely broke hearts with his black hair and pale blue eyes. She'd also met him in his later years and the two of them got along fabulously. But he hadn't lived those moments yet so he wouldn't remember.

Gaze settled on Grant, Adlin was blunt. "So what brings you this way with a futuristic girl, a Hamilton warrior and your lover? Because it surely wasnae one of my Defiances."

Sheila bit her lip, overly aware that she was *not* the lover Adlin referred to.

"Nay," Grant conceded about their method of time travel. "It was a different sort of magic altogether."

Sheila frowned then her eyes widened when she glimpsed her ring.

The stone glowed!

Not how it normally did but much brighter. Her eyes flew to Grant. His gaze, however, was still on Adlin. "You saw inside my mind so ken the magic used to get us here. In fact, our simple contact gave you a thorough look into your clan's future, did it not?"

"Aye," Adlin murmured. "As it also showed me the reason why you chose to come here now."

Sheila's mind was spinning as she looked at Grant then Adlin. "Now you know of the great MacLomain/Broun connection and about many of the romances ahead. Sure, Fionn Mac Cumhail and the goddess Brigit were the weight behind it all but you played a pretty big part yourself. I'll bet this visit will help you make sure all that happens, won't it?"

A little gleam lit Adlin's eyes. "So it would seem."

Yet did he know about his one true love, Mildred when he looked into Grant's mind? There was no way. Grant didn't know her. But Sheila did...or at least *of* her. Sheila was about to ask more when there was a commotion at the door. Adlin stood as a very pregnant woman strolled into the hall, a sword strapped to her back. With braided golden hair and amber eyes, she was stunning.

"My lass, come meet our visitors." Adlin held out his hand. "They've quite the tale to share."

His lass?

Good thing she hadn't mentioned Mildred!

Adlin kissed the woman's cheek then helped her sit as he glanced at the others. "Allow me to introduce Meyla Naðr, daughter of Naðr Véurr, king of the Vikings in his own right."

Sheila's jaw dropped. *What?*

Meyla's sharp eyes took them in as she nodded in greeting. "You've a different look about you to be sure."

Adlin filled her in on where or better yet *when* they were from.

Meyla's eyes shot to Grant.

Grant's eyes narrowed slightly.

"Aye, lass," Adlin murmured. "You have the right o' it."

The right of *what*? Sheila was thoroughly confused. After a few sips of ale she waited, hoping for more information. It didn't take long.

Adlin sat beside Meyla and rested his hand on her stomach as he looked at Grant. "I know you sense him, lad."

Grant's eyes widened slightly and he whispered, "'Tis Iain's Da."

Sheila blinked several times. Iain? As in Iain MacLomain? Torra, Colin and Bradon's father?

Adlin's eyes softened as he looked at Meyla's stomach. "So that is to be my grandson's name is it."

"But how is that possible?" Sheila said. "The time frame isn't right."

"Unless," Grant murmured. "The baby isnae raised in this time period but in the future."

Meyla's eyes connected with Adlin and she nodded. "So it is as you said it would be."

Adlin pulled her hand onto his lap, gaze tender. "Aye."

Though there was sadness in the Viking's eyes there was also strength.

Sheila couldn't help but think of what Adlin had told her and her cousins so recently when they traveled to the original Highland Defiance. About how the last woman he'd had children with birthed the direct lineage to Iain, William and Ferchar which of course led to the younger MacLomain men, the next generation.

Meyla, so it seemed, was that woman.

Sheila couldn't help but stare at Meyla as everything sunk in. Kenzie and Bryce, however, remained quiet, their eyes averted. Her heart clenched a little. They didn't feel like they belonged here…that they were beneath such a conversation. But they weren't. They were equals. And if they were here for this then they'd likely play an important part. Yet hadn't they already simply by being friends with Grant through such a difficult time in his life?

Grant didn't seem overly fazed by what Adlin had shared but then he most likely considered himself more MacLeod or even Hamilton than MacLomain at this point. As such it didn't surprise her when he said nothing to Meyla but directed his next question at Adlin. "What know you of Torra's dragon bloodline and why Keir Hamilton might want your sister Iosbail in order to harness the entirety of my cousin's soul?"

Again, Adlin and Meyla locked eyes for several moments. When the woman nodded, Adlin turned his attention to Grant. "Meyla's Viking bloodline seems to have shown truest in Torra." He squeezed Meyla's hand. "The blood of the dragon comes from Meyla's Da, Naðr Véurr. In English his name means serpent protector. But his story is a tale better told another time."

Sheila knew her eyes were round with shock. Dragon blood? So this particular strand of DNA could have ignited in any of Adlin's descendants? Pretty mind-blowing. Which made her wonder if that wasn't why Grant was more powerful than the others. Did he use some untapped dragon voodoo to whip them back to this time frame without the use of a Defiance?

Adlin's eyes drifted to Sheila as though he heard something that she never said. "'Twas not only the glow of your ring and Grant's mark that brought you to me but my sister, Iosbail's magic."

All right, scratch the dragon voodoo theory. At least for now.

"The glow of my ring and Grant's mark?" Sheila said, confused. Unless she was going batty, they'd yet to ignite the two!

Adlin ignored her question, his eyes once more swamped with magic as he looked at her. Oh no! But if he'd been inside her mind he made it quick and painless. Then, to confirm that he'd actually done such a thing, he said the words Iosbail had spoken moments before Grant had whisked her out of the Hamilton dungeon. *"Intelligit autem anima ad percipiendum cum Viking magica. In otherworld, spatium inter se et immolato serpentes ad me des Torra animae dimidium."*

Grant grew disturbed as he repeated the words in English. "He means to draw her soul with Viking magic. In the otherworld, the space in between, he'll sacrifice her to the serpents and they'll give him the other half of Torra's soul."

"Hell," Adlin muttered. He looked at Grant. "I know what Iosbail did and I dinnae doubt she did such on purpose." The arch wizard shook his head, words wry. "For all I thought I was one step ahead of my sister, all along she's been one step ahead of me." He looked skyward. "Bloody Brouns!"

But Sheila didn't miss the small smile on Adlin's lips.

And she knew there was one on her face too. After all, she was a Broun and it wasn't the first time she'd heard the curse muttered from a MacLomain mouth.

"The version of Iosbail that is now imprisoned by Keir Hamilton is a reincarnate. Where hails Iosbail from this era?" Grant asked.

"As far as I know, ruling her clan in East Lothian," Adlin said. "Or so I assume."

Assume. Tricky word. If Iosbail knew enough to enter Leslie's horse and save William from death with old Viking magic, then she clearly knew she'd be needed long before that. But how?

Sheila went to take a sip of ale only to realize she'd already finished it. As if they'd been waiting, a servant delivered another. She thanked them and took a sip. While she should certainly be focused on Iosbail and her role in all this, her mind was still locked on someone else entirely.

Grant.

Before anyone could speak she looked at him. "I'm confused. I thought my ring and your mark couldn't ignite unless..." She cleared her throat, overly aware of the others but determined to get an answer, "Unless we ignited them first."

Adlin cocked his head, a grin in his eyes. "And how is it you do that?"

Sheila narrowed her eyes at the wizard. "You've been in our minds. I think you know darn well how."

When her eyes skimmed over Kenzie and Bryce it was to see them looking anywhere but at her and Kenzie burying a smile in her drink. *Hmph!* It seemed these two were really close to Grant if even they knew how the magic was sparked.

But she didn't care. She wanted an answer. So her eyes remained fixed on Grant.

All he offered her was a shrug. "I dinnae know, lass. My mark started glowing after you were brought to the dungeons. When it did I knew I had the magic I needed to get Bryce, Kenzie and you out of there."

"What about Colin MacLeod? I thought he was one of the main reasons we needed to rejoin your armies to begin with."

"Colin is safe enough. Keir doesnae suspect him as traitorous," Grant said.

"Then why scurry the rest of us out of there so fast?"

His eyes met hers, the crackling flames of the fire reflecting in their depths as he softly said, "If I had a means to free the three of you of Keir Hamilton, 'twould be done."

"At risk to you no less," Kenzie murmured.

Sheila frowned. Of course this put Grant at great risk. In truth, it probably put him in more danger than all of them. Suddenly angry, she said, "What did you do?"

"Saved you, I'd say," Adlin cut in. "And for such you should be grateful. Are you not his wife then? It seems he had no other choice."

Oh right. The 'wife' thing. But she'd not focus on that right now.

"And I *am* grateful," she replied readily but didn't back down as she looked at Grant. "But at what risk exactly to yourself." Determined not to let go of her other line of inquisition she held up her ring finger. "Is there another way I don't know about to get this shining so brightly?"

"Nay," Grant said. "Not that I know of."

Sheila twirled the ring. Darn. She didn't know why she was so frustrated. Wasn't it a good thing his mark and her ring were ignited without sleeping together? Sure, she supposed. But despite herself, she felt denied of a right her cousins had enjoyed which mortified her even more. Had she really wanted to sleep with Grant that much?

Thoughts of their kiss in the tent surfaced and she blushed. *God*, maybe she had.

"We have learned much already because of this visit," Adlin declared, standing. "You are my guests and as such, I urge you to partake of my hospitality. Chambers are already being prepared. This eve marks the harvest so 'twill be a celebration. Until then, enjoy my castle and clan."

"M'laird, we will house with the servants," Bryce said, head down.

Adlin frowned and shook his head. "Look me in the eye lad."

So Bryce did.

"Any friend of a MacLomain is kin. You will sleep in a chamber and celebrate with us all, aye?"

This is why she loved Adlin so much. None were kinder…once they got past the whole 'sword held to your throat' part that is. There could be no blame though. He didn't know any of them until today. Lord, was that going to change over the years. She shook her head. Now she knew everything would happen partly *because* of them arriving here. Wasn't that something!

"I will show you to your chambers," a young woman said as she approached.

"No, let me," Meyla said, standing.

Adlin frowned. "'Tis not necessary, lass. Too many stairs."

Meyla cocked a brow. "Stairs?" A throaty chuckle broke from her. "I could sail the high stormy seas like this and walk away stronger than any man." She urged them to follow. "I've a good mind as to where Adlin's put you."

Grant nodded to Adlin before taking Sheila's hand and pulling her after him. Not entirely comfortable with the display of togetherness, she pulled her hand free as they climbed the stairs. As it was when the castle was stone, torches lined the hallways and soon enough they'd arrived at a chamber.

Meyla looked at Kenzie. "This one's yours." Then her eyes went to Bryce. "The one next door is yours."

Both nodded and looked at Grant.

"I'll be back soon enough. Wait for me after you bathe," he said.

It seemed Grant and Sheila's chambers were up another set of stairs. When Meyla stopped at a room and nodded to Sheila, her eyes nearly popped. It was huge.

"Yours is the next one," Meyla said, her eyes sliding to Grant then back to Sheila.

Grant nodded. "Many thanks."

Meyla said nothing but vanished back down the hall. It seemed Grant wanted to say something to Sheila but decided against it as he held out his arm as if to usher her into her room. "Go, relax. I'll look for you later, aye?"

Sheila nodded. Though she had a lot to ask him now didn't seem the right time. When he turned and entered his own room she did the same. A fire crackled on the hearth and a dress lay across the large bed. Best of all, a tub of steaming water lay waiting.

Eager to wash away even a brief stay in the Hamilton dungeons, she tore off her clothes and sank into the hot, welcoming water. She leaned her head back, closed her eyes and released a long, slow breath she had no idea she'd been holding.

One second she was volunteering to be taken by the enemy, the next she was literally taken by the enemy…then this. Bliss. Yet uncertainty. So many things had been answered yet so many things had not. Still, she didn't feel as discontented as she probably should.

Instinctually, her hand went to the pentacle around her neck. Funny how important it had become to her. Why? Because of Grant. She'd liked the connection they had through it, no matter how brief. She'd liked that it was something all hers…all theirs. His thoughts had melded with hers and through them she'd gained strength. *His* strength. Or so she assumed. There was that word again.

Assumed.

What if through him she'd found strength that'd been inside her all along? Sheila nearly snorted. Yeah right. Had it been inside her all along Jack would've never been able to warp her thoughts so easily. No, she could only have a weak mind. Right? Hands trembling, she opened her eyes and gripped the sides of the tub.

With a deep inhale then release of breath, she practiced at blowing out all the negative thoughts. They had no room in her mind. They didn't belong to her. Eyes drowsy, she gazed at the chamber. Three torches burned. Wind billowed skins inward and a cool breeze swept over her skin.

"Sheila."

The whisper was so soft she thought it was the wind.

"Where are you?"

Her eyes slid shut as the feminine words slipped upon the wind. Iosbail?

"Just run already! What are you afraid of?"

I won't. I can't.

"Now. Go! I'll not say it again."

Sheila looked between the dark clouds and the cool welcoming water. No, she thought, I can't do this. If it meant saving herself or saving the tree...

"Sheila, you're living, breathing. The tree? There are naught but embers in the branches."

But the tree was more than that.

More than her.

Fire started to roll along the rock, the grass, until it snaked her way. Petrified, she watched, aware but unmoving. I won't leave the tree! Determined, she ran into the flames, felt the pain and screamed.

And screamed.

Over and over.

"Sheila!"

Why was the tree shaking her?

"Sheila," the voice said again.

Then the tree was warm, soothing. Not sure what else to do she wrapped her arms around its trunk only to feel warm flesh. Petrified, she pulled back.

Grant?

"Shhh," he said, burying his face into her neck. "Shhh."

Startled, shaking, her arms fell to her side and she whimpered, "I don't understand."

"'Twas but a vision," he murmured.

A vision?

As reality returned in increments, chills raked over her and she shivered. When at last the room resurfaced, she was swathed in a blanket on his lap. When had this happened?

She pulled back and met Grant's eyes. "Why are you here?"

Though he said nothing, his fingers brushed her cheek. Only then did she realize tears streaked down her face and neck. Panicked, she tried to squirm away but he held tight, his blue eyes ignited in magic. "Nay lass, this is nothing to run from."

Weakened, vulnerable, she cried, "You, this, everything should be run from. I hate that you're seeing me this way. I'm not weak. I'm strong."

"Aye," he whispered.

When she tried to push away again it was not against his hard body but against the jarring sensation of waking up from a harsh dream. Flailing, water splashing, she grabbed onto the sides of the tub. Fingers clenched, jaw tight, she stared...

At nobody.

Her room was empty.

Nothing but the fire and torches flickered.

What the *hell*? Biting back a sob, she sunk her mouth beneath the water and blinked several times. Was she going insane? Sweet Jesus, it felt that way. While she wanted to immerse entirely beneath the water she was too frightened. Releasing air, bubbles burst on the surface of the water much like her emotions.

Tired of the all the things in her mind she didn't understand, Sheila stood and dried off. Crawling into the chemise and light blue dress provided, she grabbed a comb and raked it through her hair. When another tear rolled down her cheek, she wiped it away, frustrated. Why the hell was she so emotional?

"Sheila?"

His words seemed so close she thought she still sat on his lap. But when she turned, Grant was leaning against the door jamb, eyes soft. Her breath caught. It was the first time she'd ever seen him in the blues and greens of the MacLomain plaid. It suited him. Potently handsome with a few small braids hanging by his strong jaw, he wore new boots and a fresh tunic.

When she said nothing he came, took the comb from her and urged her to sit down next to him on the bed. Still shaken, she folded her hands in her lap to hide the trembling.

As if he understood, one hand closed over hers, words gentle. "You should rest. We've been given a reprieve here. Lie down, get some sleep."

"No," she mumbled.

"You've learned so much. You're tired. No one would fault you for resting this eve, lass."

Sheila stared at her ring. He was right. They wouldn't. Neither would he for that matter. But she couldn't. Not right now. Being here was too important. Their arrival was one more notch in this journey's gondola ride, straight up not the real thing but a rhetorical mountain of truths.

"I need to be part of this," she whispered.

Grant's gaze remained concerned. "Aye."

More and more aware of his touch, of his proximity, she struggled to remember all the things she wanted to ask him. Thankfully, he asked a question instead.

"Something happened when you were in here alone. What?"

"How do you know?"

He threaded their fingers together, the gesture soothing yet intimate. "Our minds have been joined. It's made me more aware of your emotions even when you're not with me. I knew you needed me in here so I came."

Somehow that didn't surprise her. Should she tell him what happened? Mostly likely. Maybe he could make sense of it. So she shared the dream, including his part in it, leaving out that she hadn't wanted to appear weak in front of him. She guessed that had more to do with her insecurities than anything else. Insecurities she was determined to push past.

Yet as he contemplated what she'd told him, their eyes still locked, she'd swear he saw the parts she hadn't shared. Why, she had no clue. His expression hadn't changed any. Then again, he could read minds if he was so inclined.

"It sounds as though you saw the baby oak. You mentioned fire, that the tree burned." He frowned. "'Twould be bad indeed if that tree burned for 'tis more special than most know."

"I've never actually seen it, only its mother oak, but have heard about it. Pretty amazing tree by the sounds of it," she said. "And connected to Torra somehow, right? Outside of the obvious reasons why a tree burning is bad, you're referring to more than that I take it."

His eyes turned to the fire. "Aye, I dinnae ken your vision outside of my part in it but that you had such can only help us."

"I wasn't actually sure I was a visionary until now." Her eyes remained on his face. "Do you understand your part in my vision?"

"Aye." His eyes returned to hers. "I will always be there to soothe you if I'm able, Sheila. 'Tis the verra least I can do."

The very least he could do? That sounded awfully...obligatory.

When she stood, he grabbed her wrist. Their eyes again locked.

"I didnae get the chance to tell you how bonnie you look, my wee geal," he said softly.

Something about the way he said it, the way he looked at her, sent trembles everywhere.

"Thanks," she murmured.

When he stood, she went to step back but he'd have none of it. One arm came around her lower back and pulled her close. Her heart started to hammer. Instead of kissing her, he simply held her like that. Admiration in his eyes, he touched her hair then ran the tips of his fingers along her jawline. "It has never been my place to simply enjoy a lass's beauty, to feel the softness of her hair and skin for more than a few moments."

Her chest tightened at the sadness in his voice, the gratefulness. Sheila leaned her cheek into his touch, more than willing to give him ample opportunity.

"You are a selfless lass." Grant cupped her cheek. "More than I deserve."

"Why would you say that?" she said. "If anything, I'd say you deserve this more than most."

"'Tis a hard thing to think myself deserving of anything," he said. "'Twas not the way I was raised."

Her heart broke for him. To hell with Keir Hamilton for this.

"No, I suppose it wasn't." She stood on her tip-toes and kissed his cheek. "So I guess we both need to change our way of thinking."

"Aye," he whispered. It seemed he wanted to kiss her by the way he stared at her lips but instead pulled away. "Kenzie and Bryce need to eat, feast. They have been denied so much in their lives."

"Of course," Sheila said. "Let me finish combing my hair then I'll join you downstairs."

Grant's gaze lingered on her hair for a long moment before he nodded and left. While she might've liked him to wait, she understood his urgency. It was hard to imagine what his friends had been through. Now they'd been offered freedom and he wanted them to enjoy it.

As she ran the comb through her long locks, it occurred to her she'd forgotten to ask him any of the questions weighing on her mind. What did he *really* think about why his mark and her ring glowed? And were they actually married or was that some sort of farce?

Ready at last, she headed downstairs to the hall.

But she wished she hadn't…

Grant and Kenzie embraced on the second landing.

And the woman sobbed her heart out.

Chapter Seven

"Ah, there ye are, lass!" Bryce said. "Keep me company then?"

Grant looked over Kenzie's shoulder at Sheila. Frozen on the stairs, her wide eyes met his. It was clear she misunderstood what she saw but now was not the time to explain.

Bryce held out his hand to Sheila. "I dinnae want to go down alone, aye?"

Sheila dragged her eyes from Grant and offered Bryce a small nod as she took his hand. Grant continued to hold Kenzie after they left. The poor lass was dealing with all the overwhelming emotions that went along with finally being free of Keir Hamilton. Bryce, it seemed, was handling things much better. But then he'd been a warrior, not forced to be a whore.

After some time, Kenzie's sobs finally abated. She pulled back and said, "I cannae tell you how thankful I am."

He tilted up her chin and met her eyes. "'Tis said lass and I dinnae want to hear it again. This is a freedom that should have always been yours. Not something you feel you owe me, aye?"

She pressed her lips together. "I'll try my best but can make no promises."

Grant sighed and wiped away her tears. "Now 'tis time to celebrate. Dance, feast, but remember you belong to no man. Not that 'twill likely happen here but if any lad makes untoward advances, let me know."

"Aye," she said. "But I can handle myself, Grant."

He nodded and took her hand. "Let us go down then."

Kenzie pulled her hand from his as they walked, shooting him a wink. "I don't want your new lass getting the wrong idea."

"Sheila's not mine," he replied.

"Oh, sure she is." Kenzie smirked. "You two just need to figure that out is all."

"I dinnae think either of us are ready or capable of such a thing right now."

"And I dinnae think 'twill much matter when it comes to love." She shook her head. "Either 'tis there or not."

"I know nothing of love. No more than any of us who have been imprisoned by Keir," he assured.

"So you say but might be surprised," Kenzie informed. "I see the way you look at her. 'Tis different than how you look at me."

Grant frowned. "She isnae as strong as you. I worry for her."

Kenzie's eyes widened. "The lass is far stronger than you think. Just watch."

While he appreciated her optimism he wasn't so sure. But then he'd been inside Sheila's mind and saw clearly her struggles.

Kenzie nodded at the crowd dancing in the MacLomain great hall. "Well, if ye've love for the lass ye'd best let my brother know."

"I dinnae have love," he grumbled, his eyes on Bryce and Sheila dancing. She looked genuinely happy as they spun. Bryce, naturally, pulled her close soon after.

"Well, look at you all done up in the MacLomain plaid!" Adlin declared, handing over skins of whiskey as he joined them. Kenzie smiled her thanks and wandered off.

Grant nodded. "'Tis strange to once more wear my clan's colors."

"No doubt, my lad." Adlin patted him on the shoulder. "But 'tis good this." He eyed him proudly. "Verra good indeed."

Uncomfortable, Grant wasn't sure how to respond. He'd not been treated this kindly since he'd been a bairn and still at home. But those memories were nearly lost to him because of Keir. His master...former master, had forbid them.

Now, of all people, he was reconnecting first not with his immediate kin but with his clan's patriarch, Adlin. Though his mark and Sheila's ring had certainly helped them flee the Hamilton castle, they had nothing to do with why they were brought here.

That had been all Iosbail MacLomain's doing.

Adlin's eyes twinkled as he looked at Grant. "I was going to give you and your wife one chamber but 'tis a new matrimony, is it not? One not quite ready for a single bed?"

Grant scowled. Not for a moment had he forgotten what Keir Hamilton had forced on Sheila...on him. "'Twas not a marriage of our choosing," he ground out.

"Aye." Adlin shook his head and watched Sheila and Bryce dancing, voice amused. "And to such a bonnie lass at that. 'Tis a poor thing that you were forced into such."

Grant arched a brow at Adlin. "'Tis not a good marriage if the lad and lass are not willing."

Adlin's wise eyes met his. "Were you truly unwilling then? Or mayhap this was the kindest thing Keir Hamilton ever did to you, however unknowingly."

Grant ground his teeth. He'd give Keir no credit for anything. Not even this. But he was curious about something and mayhap Adlin had an answer. "You know of the glow of my mark and her ring. What make you of that shaman?"

Adlin shrugged. "My guess is that you two found a way to ignite them." His lips curled up. "Mayhap you do so when here hence them igniting somehow in the future. One of those strange time travel loops. You cannae have one without the other. You couldnae travel here without the glow but without igniting the glow here you couldnae travel back to begin with."

"That sounds like a riddle," Grant muttered.

Adlin beamed. "I always did like a good riddle."

The MacLomain chieftain eyed Meyla across the way and said, "I'm off now. Though 'tis windy there's a bonfire out on the field. Mayhap you'll want to take your lass that way once you've tired of her dancing with other lads."

Other *lads*?

Sure as a thistle blooms she was no longer in Bryce's arms, but another clansman's.

Grant swigged from his skin and grabbed a piece of bannock as he watched Sheila. There was something exceptionally captivating about her. The way she smiled and laughed. The way she seemed to genuinely care for everyone and everything she came in contact with.

His thoughts drifted back to the kiss they'd shared in his tent. He hadn't expected the sweet taste of her nor the way she'd responded. The need to devour her was instantaneous. Though the intimacy hadn't lasted nearly long enough, he knew without doubt he wanted to sample every part of her. From the arches of her small feet to the soft skin at the nape of her neck, he envisioned flicking his tongue and learning what she liked.

Though his time with whores was always brief, he'd been well-trained in the skills of pleasing a lass. In truth, he'd made a point of it. Not for his benefit but for those enslaved. Fulfillment was not something they received from Keir's warriors so he urged them to show him what they liked, what truly pleasured them.

After he finished his bannock, he grabbed another and headed Sheila's way. Though tempted, he didn't force her to abandon her current partner but merely hovered nearby. While he could admit to feeling less than pleased she danced with another he wouldn't take this happiness from her. Like him, she'd been denied it for far too long.

In little time her eyes grazed over him. When she continued to dance, he ground his jaw, determined not to get frustrated. He'd always been trained to take what he wanted when he wanted it. Men listened to him or faced Keir Hamilton. It was as simple as that. Some might say that in time his men no longer felt forced to obey Grant but wanted to. Yet during moments like this is was hard to separate what he'd been molded into from what he aimed to be...a decent, honorable Scotsman.

Ballocks, what was he thinking looming over her like this? She didn't owe him anything.

Disgusted with himself, he headed out to the fire.

The moon was full and bright, illuminating the field and woodland in a soft glow. Cool wind gusted and soothed his heated skin. It was still so odd to have no sense of direction, to be free to go where he wished. With the Hamilton's, every day was one of training and routine. Now...he was aimless.

Though lasses made eyes at him, he kept focused on his destination. As he walked over the second drawbridge onto the field memories started to bombard him. One in particular that Keir never managed to take away...his last day with the MacLomain's. Or better yet, the last time he'd walked onto this field. As if it was yesterday, he remembered the eve's festivities. Hundreds of people were celebrating, the crowd merry.

"I'll grab it then we'll run," Bradon said. "She'll have no choice but to follow, aye?"

Grant glanced over his shoulder, once more seeing his cousin as a young lad. They were both tall for their age but far too gangly to turn a lass's head. At least the one they wanted.

"Och, you dinnae have it in you!" Grant cried, his heart thundering as he urged Bradon to prove him wrong.

"Nay?" Bradon winked and started into the crowd with Grant right behind. "Just you watch."

Grant smelled sweets roasting all the way from the kitchen as the bonnie lass turned away from her Ma, basket in hand. Bradon slowed. A smile crawled onto his face as they approached. Eyes narrowed, the lass watched them.

"What be ye up to, Bradon MacLomain?" Grant didn't miss the flirtatiousness in her voice. Even at such a young age, Bradon had a way with the lasses.

Bradon grinned. "I thought mayhap you'd like to take a turn or two with me and my cousin."

Not bashful in the least, her eyes slid to Grant then back to Bradon. "Both of ye then?"

"Aye, lass." Bradon shot her a crooked grin. "'Tis always better with two of us."

While Bradon was more than at ease beneath her regard, Grant wanted nothing more than to have the ground swallow him whole. The last thing he truly wanted to do was dance with a lass. He'd rather throw a rock at one. But not Bradon. Nay, it seemed since he'd toddled he wanted them around.

The lass's eyes flickered once more to Grant, suddenly shy. "I dinnae know. He's awful young." Her gaze roamed over him. "But strapping, aye?"

Her Ma frowned at the three but soon turned back to her conversation.

"He's but a winter younger than me," Bradon assured. "And taller than ye besides."

The lass considered this long and hard before she finally looked at his cousin and shook her head. "Nay, I know ye too well, Bradon MacLomain. Ye've always the lasses comin' round, you do."

Bradon shook his head. "That's a shame." He tossed a look at Grant. "Are ye ready then?"

Bloody hell, he meant to see it through.

So when Bradon snatched her basket and started to run, Grant followed. Exhilarated, he chased after his cousin, positive that the lass followed. About to look over his shoulder to confirm, he was surprised when a strong set of arms grabbed him. Before he could yell at whichever uncle was jesting with him something came over his mouth.

Then all went dark.

When next he awoke, he was in the Hamilton castle's dungeon. He'd never forget those first awful moments chained against the wall, staring into Keir Hamilton's dark eyes.

"If you'd just waited a few more minutes I would've joined you."

Ripped from dark thoughts, Grant realized he now stood in front of the great bonfire with Sheila at his side. He blinked away old memories and handed her the bannock. "You should eat."

Sheila eyed him curiously but took the food. "Thanks."

Grant unclenched his fists and tried to unlock his tense muscles. "'Tis good that you have fun, lass. I didnae want to take you from that."

Munching, she shook her head. "Something tells me I'd have more fun with you."

As if she realized what she just said, she swallowed hard and took a swig from her mug. "I mean..." She stopped talking and shook her head. "Never mind."

Pipes trilled and soon enough, music caught on the wind and surrounded the crowd.

"I havenae ever danced," he mentioned softly, not sure in the least why he'd said such.

Her eyes widened at him then soon softened. "That totally sucks. I'm so sorry."

"Sucks?"

Sheila polished off her bannock. "Sorry, I mean that's terrible. And I'm sorry too...that you've never danced that is."

"You've naught to be sorry for, lass. While lower ranking warriors like Bryce were allowed to dance during rare celebrations, 'twas not something Keir promoted with warriors such as me and Colin." He shrugged. "'Twould have taken from our men's regard of us."

The fire glittered in her bonnie blue eyes as she looked at him and held out her hand. "Then why don't we give it a shot. No nasty Keir Hamilton here, is there?"

Shot? Nasty? Though he didn't know these words he understood her meaning. "I dinnae think 'twould be such a good—"

Sheila set aside their drinks. "Oh, it'll totally be good." She pulled him into the dancing crowd. "Bear with me. I'm just learning these Highland jigs but," she wrapped her elbow with his, "if we just skip around and have fun that seems to be good enough."

Skip around? Grant frowned. "Nay, lass."

"Then we'll just walk in circles with our elbows locked like this," she started to walk, forcing him around. With a wide smile she said, "See, this isn't too bad, is it?"

Grant looked down into her eyes as they slowly circled. Nay, this wasn't too bad at all. The red in her dark brown hair seemed to catch fire, ignited by the nearby flames. The dress hugged her slender curves nearly as well as he'd like to.

If they moved a little faster, he didn't notice. But he did notice the little extra spring to her step and the way her cleavage plumped up in response. When she laughed, he smiled, eyes once more on her bonnie face. Sheila spun and caught his opposite elbow, spinning them in the other direction. This time he chuckled, enchanted by the unabashed joy in her face.

"See, you can do this dancing thing." She grinned. "Just feel the music."

If there was one thing he'd absolutely *never* done in his life, it was *feel* music. Yet as they danced he could admit to getting caught up in the rhythm…or mayhap he was just getting caught up in watching her. The way her long hair spun around her shoulders and her slim waist twisted. Either way, there was a new freedom in the movement, in swaying to the pipes, or in his case, circling with her a wee bit faster than before. Twirling, happy, they did this for several songs.

Laughing the whole time, she bumped her hip off his. Entrenched in the moment, happy, he wrapped his arm around her waist when she did it again. Thankfully, the pipes trilled down to a song better suited to slower movement because he wanted her against him. While he might be free from Keir Hamilton he didn't feel it…unless with her. Something about Sheila took his mind elsewhere, somewhere he didn't recognize but very much liked.

Her hand flitted over his chest when he pulled her close.

Where the rapid movement of dancing was foreign to him, this slow sway felt more familiar. Not all that different than lying with a lass, there was a much appreciated sensuality about it. Hand wrapped around the back of her neck, he stared into her eyes. It didn't shock him in the least to see fear and uncertainty. While he sensed she certainly liked intimacy, Sheila was frightened by her own intense emotions.

Determined to give her the same pleasure dancing slowly that she had offered them when they moved faster, he repeated her own words. "See, you can do this dancing thing." But his tone was deep, purposeful, meant to make her feel secure and desirable.

And it seemed to be working.

As they moved, she slowly relaxed, the sway of her hips as fluid as they'd been before. When she leaned her cheek against his chest, Grant closed his eyes to the unfamiliar feelings washing over him. Aye, he was aroused but it was more than that. His muscles warmed and clenched as though he braced for attack. His heartbeat kicked up as though he battled.

It made no sense.

He was but dancing with a lass.

Yet he'd never been more aware of another in his life. The press of her breasts against him, the scent of flowers in her hair, the way her slender body filled his arms. Long after the piper trilled a faster beat, they stayed that way. Slow, swaying, lost in time, lost in one another. If Kenzie and Bryce hadn't happened over, they might have spent the entire eve that way.

When Bryce cleared his throat, Grant looked his way. "Aye?"

"Adlin's requested you over yonder." He nodded toward the courtyard. "It seems there's to be some battling."

Never once had he turned from battling but right now he had no desire. "Nay, not right now."

Sheila pulled away, her eyes dewy, lost, but quickly focusing. "If Adlin wants you then you should go."

Grant took her hand. "Are you sure, lass? I much prefer dancing with you."

A warm smile curved her lips. "Nothing says we can't get back to it later."

Kenzie grinned. "Sounds like she has the right o' it lad."

"Come on then." Bryce led the way.

They didn't go too far. Men were already sparring in the courtyard. A small fire had been lit and a few trestle tables dragged out. Adlin, arms crossed over his chest, watched the men fighting.

By his side, the lovely Viking Meyla watched as well. When they joined the outskirts of the crowd, she nodded at them then whispered something in Adlin's ear. The MacLomain chieftain's eyes met Grant's and he waved them over. When they joined them, Meyla part strode, part wobbled into the armory.

"There's nothing like swordplay during a celebration, aye?" Adlin asked, his regard tossed between Grant and Bryce.

"Nay," Bryce agreed, eyes eager as he watched the warriors.

Grant could admit to enjoying it just as much. After all, this had been his entire life, everything he knew outside of sleeping, eating and…he glanced at Sheila…lying with a lass. She was watching the men battle as avidly as everyone else. It seemed that outside of dancing this was a part of Scotland that had captured her attention just as much.

"What make you of what you see?" Adlin asked softly.

Grant didn't need to look at the chieftain to know he spoke of his warrior's talents. He also knew that they were young men without much experience, certainly not Adlin's more seasoned warriors. Never one to be less than honest, he said, "I think they'd lose if put against my men."

"Would they," Adlin murmured. "Might you fight a few of them?"

His eyes swung to the shaman. He was serious. "Nay, 'twould be unfair."

Adlin's brows arched but he saw pride in his gaze. "Are you so sure of yourself then?"

"Aye, I am."

"Then might you fight now," Meyla said when she returned. "With this."

Grant eyed the blade she gave him. Impressed, he studied it. Heavy, crafted perfectly to his height and size, it was fit for a king. The intricate hilt was inlaid with gold, its head crawling up the blade in a pattern much like a crown. Without a central fuller, this blade worried less about blood and more about conquering. Intrigued, he stepped away from them and swung the sword, felt the cut of it through the air. So well made, it seemed an extension of his arms.

"'Twas given to me by my Da, Naðr Véurr," Meyla said. "It carries the heart of my kin in it."

Grant looked from Meyla to the blade, still twisting and turning it before his eyes went back to her. He held its hilt out. "I shouldnae fight with this, lass. 'Tis too important."

Meyla stood tall, hands on her hips, eyes locked on his. "Fight with it." She nodded at the blade. "Then I'll know how important it is."

Truth told, he had no desire to release the sword. It already felt part of him. Honored, he asked, "Who will you have me fight then?"

Meyla nodded at the warriors already sparring. "Start with them." Her eyes turned to Bryce. "Then him."

He and Bryce locked eyes and nodded. Grant pulled off his tunic then brought the hilt of the sword to his lips. He murmured a prayer to the Lord then strode into the battling. Neither lad saw him coming, he but slashed the sword down and cut their parry in half.

Clang. The harsh interception echoed.

Sensing a good show, the crowd quieted.

Grant pulled back and held his blade eye level between them. Eyes skirting between the two he said nothing…just waited.

He already knew they wouldn't go about this correctly. When both swung at once he used not his blade but body, kicking one in the stomach while ducking and punching the other in the face. Eyes on both he said, "If you mean to fight with your blade then fight with your blade."

One wiped the blood from his mouth but soon held up his blade. The other recovered slower. Or so it seemed. Grant didn't hesitate but kicked the crouched over man in the side of the face. This time he staggered and fell to his knees. As he suspected the other man came at him with a good clean swipe of his blade.

Relishing the first thrust of his sword, Grant met him and the blades rung.

As always, bloodlust rushed through him and he started a dance he was far more familiar with. One made of angles, weakness and strength. One made of quick slashes and precise movements. The sword Meyla gave him was perfection. While a normal blade might have taken him three moves against this warrior, this one took but two and he fell.

The other came at him.

Without nearly a rush to his blood, he swung four times hard and the enemy was on the ground. When the other man regrouped he ducked and parried, driving the man back so quickly he fell to his arse and cowered.

Only one harsh breath left Grant's lungs as he looked around. "Who's next?"

"Och, me, every time." Bryce started to circle him.

Grant grinned, welcoming someone he'd trained himself. He nodded at Bryce's sword. "Hold it high and aim to kill, lad."

Bryce came at him as fast. While an excellent fighter his mistake was always in his excitement. But Grant would not show him up in front of the crowd... not yet.

Bang. Bang. Bang. Their blades clashed together as they parried fast and ferocious.

Both were happy but determined to put on a good show, one they'd done many times before as Keir Hamilton watched for flaws. But now they could do it for fun...for the joy of fighting. On and on they went, clashing swords, parrying, aiming high then low but never quite getting the other.

Suddenly, a loud voice boomed. "Enough of this. 'Tis no fun watching friends fight, aye?"

Both stopped, breathing harshly as Adlin approached, sword in hand. Grant grinned at Bryce. "Off with you. Time for me to truly battle."

Grant pulled his sword close and centered himself. Adlin MacLomain desired to fight him? What good would come of it? He had no desire to show up his patriarch in front of his clan. As if he heard his thoughts and no doubt did, Adlin offered a small smile, muttering under his breath, "You're an arrogant MacLomain to be sure."

The tallest of his lot, Grant looked down but a small fraction on Adlin. "I dinnae wish to fight you."

"Of course you do," Adlin said easily, swinging his blade. "You wish to fight everyone, Grant."

He watched the way Adlin handled his blade, the angle of his body. It was unlike what he was used to. His brethren treated the sword much like he did himself, as though it was an extension of who he was.

"This is who you are," Adlin's words whispered into his mind. *"Or at least everything you think you should be."*

Wasting no time, sensing an equal, he narrowed his eyes and raised his blade high.

Adlin did the same then nodded.

Grant came at him fast, eager to seek out Adlin's weaknesses.

Clang. Clang. Clang.

Three touches of their blades. That's all it took for Grant to know Adlin had no weaknesses. He was a master swordsman. With a quick spin away, he paused but a moment before coming in fast once more. Over and over their blades met. Of equal strength and drive, neither was pushed back far before moving forward again. As he fought his patriarch, Grant continued to look for weaknesses; a bend of a knee that shouldn't be there, an elbow held too high or too low, but found nothing.

But every man had a weakness.

Even Adlin.

Slashing, parrying, they fought, sweat drenching their bodies. And as they did, Grant shifted and moved ever-so-slightly. With a harsh thrash here, a deep drive there, they met strike for strike.

The crowd was silent, breathless, waiting.

Determined, eager, Grant baited his kin, slamming his blade fast and furious...until...the moment was nearly there. Focused, driven, he made only one mistake. He looked into Meyla's eyes. Lined up, ready for the final drive to victory he paused...all but froze.

What the bloody hell was he doing?

Is this what victory meant? Such destruction? Such annihilation?

Though loath to practice the dark arts, he now had no choice. Harnessing what he could manage of the power taught to him by his master Keir Hamilton, he slowed time and swung his blade fast. In effect, he blocked Adlin's sword before it slid where Grant had manipulated him into aiming it...

Straight into Meyla's belly.

With a weird *thwarp* and gush of air, Grant sped up time and Adlin's blade fell from his hands. Everything went silent save the sound of the wind and crackle of the fire. All anyone saw was Grant's blade pushing away Adlin's. Nothing else.

Meyla grasped the edge of Grant's blade now resting on her stomach. She studied the sword for a long moment before her gaze finally rose to Grant's eyes. "You fought well. Naðr Véurr's blade now belongs to you. May you honor him in victory."

Adlin's soft voice followed hers, as if to bless the blade. "And may you forever remember that you are more than just a warrior."

Grant barely heard their words. The blade his? Nay. Nothing had been more undeserved. Turning away, he lowered his head and again murmured a prayer to his God. What had he done? Had he nearly killed a bairn before it was born? Disgusted, he tossed aside the sword and walked away. The taste of metal filled his mouth and it felt as though spiders crawled over his skin.

Evil.

Right here.

Right now.

Inside of him.

How had he thought for a moment he'd escaped his master's clutches?

Though Keir Hamilton wasn't present he was still somehow part of Grant's mind if for no other reason than he now *thought* like the dark overlord. He'd never be free of Keir. Not for a moment. He'd been trained to be a ruthless warrior and would always be one.

Not interested in the forest, he strode into the heart of the enemy, determined to allow the people to flay him if they so desired. But none seemed all that interested. So he climbed. As many stairs as he could find before he searched for more. At last, he arrived at the top of a tower he'd not been in for a very long time. The highest in the MacLomain castle, it oversaw everything. Sad, lonely, petrified, angry, he looked down over what should have been his home.

"Torra," he whispered and sat on the window's eave overlooking the courtyard. "I'm so sorry."

"Well you shouldn't be," came a soft voice.

When he turned it was to the last person he wanted to see…

Chapter Eight

There was only one way to handle this.

Gently.

Sheila leaned against the wall beside him. "Are you all right?"

Grant said nothing as he looked out the window.

What to do? She had no desire to force him into a conversation he obviously wasn't ready to have. As had everyone else, she'd watched the fight between him and Adlin. It'd been impressive. Grant was a hell of a fighter.

Sheila eyed his muscled torso illuminated in moonlight. Lord, was he hot. And how he fought? She swallowed and licked her lips. She'd never seen anything like it. And since traveling back in time to medieval Scotland she'd seen a whole lot of fighting.

But nothing that equaled Grant's talent.

What he did with that sword was mesmerizing, graceful, lethal...brutal. In some ways it reminded her of how his brother, Malcolm fought with an axe but so much better. How could she find his destructiveness attractive?

Yet Sheila knew why. Grant manifested in his sword what he felt in his soul.

After eyeing him for a long while she went to the hearth. Firewood was already stacked. All she needed to do was light it. But how? Suddenly a fire sprang to life. She glanced at Grant. He hadn't moved.

Clearly, talking to him more about the fighting in the courtyard wasn't an option. Obviously he was hurting. Whatever he worked through was his to tackle. She got that. But it was hard not to reach out and help.

The last she'd seen Grant had knocked Adlin's blade from his hand. He didn't gloat or grin. Nothing. And though it appeared as if it ended amiably enough, he'd left upset. So why had Grant fled?

Why was he so closed off now? Perhaps he felt bad he bested the chieftain in front of his clan but even that seemed unlikely.

She'd debated whether or not to come up here to begin with but once she saw him, the raw pain in his eyes, she knew she had to come. But what now? He continued to stare silently out the window.

Okay, she had one of two options.

Stay or go.

Sheila rubbed her lips together. What would she want him to do if their positions were reversed? The answer was simple. Stay. She'd want someone there even if she wasn't ready to talk to them. So she lay on the cot and continued to watch him. Not once did he move or say a word. But at least she was there.

Eyes on him as long as she could manage, she must've drifted off because the next time she cracked open an eye the fire had sizzled out. Drowsy, she drifted in and out of slumber. At some point a warm body cuddled up against her and she opened her eyes one more time. Grant no longer sat in the window. No, he was at her back now. He'd wrapped his arm around her waist and buried his face in her hair. With a deep sigh of relief that he was as okay as he could be, she closed her hand over his and shut her eyes.

Still, as they rested, she felt his distress, his unease. Often times she'd squeeze his hand. Not once did he respond until he did…just a whisper. "Thank ye, lass."

"You've no need to thank me," she responded only to realize she was alone and bright sunlight shone through the window. Confused, discombobulated, she sat up. "Grant?"

But there was nothing left in the room but smoked out embers and a chilled wind.

Not true.

A fresh chemise, dress and comb lay by her side.

Wishing he was still here, she dressed, staring out the window as she combed her hair. The day was as blustery as the one before but the air was slightly warmer. With a heavy sigh Sheila realized she missed her cousins. This was the first time she'd traveled through time without at least one of them along.

"Greetings, lass."

Sheila turned to see Kenzie standing in the door with a small tray and a warm smile. "Good morning."

She vividly recalled her and Grant embracing last night. Though Kenzie had assured her otherwise, Sheila still couldn't help but wonder if more existed between them.

Kenzie set aside the tray, joined her at the window and handed her a cup of mead. "'Tis a bonnie day. Ye should join us soon. Mayhap cheer Grant up some."

Sheila flinched. "So he's still upset then? Not sure I'm the one to cheer him up."

"Our master...I mean Keir, did horrible things to him." Kenzie's lips pulled down. "And even though 'tis behind him now 'twill take some time for him to truly realize it."

"I'd imagine it will." Sheila wasn't surprised by this information. No, she completely understood. "Did you see him and Adlin fight last night?"

Kenzie shook her head. "Nay, but Bryce told me of it."

"Did he have any thoughts about Grant's reaction afterward?"

"Nay, just that he suspected Grant didnae like his own ruthlessness."

"I watched the whole thing." Sheila shook her head. "He seemed as ruthless as any other man fighting."

"Bryce would have seen something in his expression to say such." Kenzie's eyes met hers. "'Twould be good mayhap if ye tried to seek these answers from Grant."

"I tried last night." Sheila sighed. "But I didn't want to push. I think Keir Hamilton did enough of that to him."

"But ye are not Keir Hamilton." Kenzie cocked her head. "I sense ye have a strong bond with Grant. Dinnae let that go to waste, lass."

That was the last thing she intended to do. But if she couldn't get through to him then she couldn't get through. No sooner did she think it, Sheila frowned. It almost felt like she was quick to give up on him which wasn't fair in the least. What had he said to her just last night? *I will always be there to soothe you if I'm able, Sheila. 'Tis the verra least I can do.*

Yes, she'd come up here to soothe him but had she given up too easily? Should she have urged him to share? It was impossible to know if she handled things correctly.

"Come," Kenzie said gently, obviously seeing the distress on Sheila's face. "Eat then we will go join the others."

Sheila nodded, grabbed some berries and nibbled. The food seemed tasteless. "Thanks so much for bringing this up but I'm not all that hungry."

Kenzie nodded and picked up the tray.

"No." Sheila took it from her and headed for the door. "I can bring this down."

"I dinnae mind taking it," Kenzie started.

"Absolutely not. I've got two hands and two feet just like you." Sheila worked at a grin. "You're free now, sweetie. Enjoy!"

"Aye," Kenzie murmured as they walked down. "'Twill take some getting used to."

They'd just reached the great hall when a servant took the tray. Sheila nodded her thanks and she and Kenzie exited the castle. Heavy wind gusted and she held her hair out of her face. "Wow, super windy today."

"Laird Adlin says the rains come," Kenzie said. "'Twill be a bloody good storm upon us soon."

Sheila eyed the clear blue sky. "Really?"

Kenzie shrugged. "'Twas what he said."

They'd just reached the bottom of the stairs when Adlin appeared. "Good morn to you, lassies!"

It was impossible not to smile. "Good morning."

"Good morn, my Laird," Kenzie murmured, lowering her head. It seemed it would take a while for her to learn not to be subservient.

Adlin focused on her first, kissing the back of her hand. "Ye need not lower yer head to me, lass."

Sheila always thought it interesting how his words, even his brogue differed based on who he spoke to. Kenzie blushed and met Adlin's eyes. "Thank ye, my Laird."

Adlin continued to smile. "Might I steal away yer new friend for a bit?"

Kenzie's eyes rounded as she glanced at Sheila. "Aye, my Laird!"

After they'd put some distance between themselves and Kenzie, Adlin muttered, "'Tis a poor thing indeed what Keir Hamilton did to his prisoners."

"I couldn't agree more."

"Might we take a stroll down to the loch?" Adlin asked.

"Sure." She'd gotten along amazingly well with Adlin's older version and suspected she'd enjoy his company at any age.

Sheila eyed the courtyard then field, hoping to glimpse Grant but he was nowhere to be found. They didn't go far before they reached the shore of the loch running alongside the castle. Interestingly enough, it was the very shore on which Torra in her dragon form had laid.

"She must have been verra beautiful," Adlin said.

Naturally, Adlin had been in her mind and knew of what would come to pass. "She was…is, in both forms."

"As I'm sure you know, I've seen your thoughts lass and I know of Mildred."

It took everything she had to show no reaction. "I'd say sorry but the truth is I didn't give you the information willingly."

He urged her to sit next to him on a log. "Nay, you didnae and whilst I'm sorry to take such from you I must put my clan first."

"Which means invading a stranger's thoughts."

"Aye," he conceded.

Sheila wasn't upset. "No worries. I get it." She eyed him. "I just hope Meyla doesn't possess the same gift."

"Nay but it wouldnae matter if she did. Meyla is stronger than most lasses." Adlin gazed at the loch. "And our love isnae all that deep. There is another from where she hails. 'Tis he she will return to."

Ouch. "And how are you okay with that?"

Adlin didn't seem upset in the least. "She is not the love of my life so I can only ever be happy that there's another for her."

Sheila had to wonder why they were having a child together but certainly wouldn't ask. It was none of her business. And it seemed Adlin wouldn't be offering any more information about it either because he switched the line of conversation altogether. "What know you of Grant's distress last eve?"

"Nothing but I wish I did," Sheila said, hopeful that he'd enlighten her.

"Grant has a certain sense about who he is," Adlin said softly. "And cannae see far beyond it."

"Because of Keir's influence," Sheila said. "Makes sense. But what does that have to do with last night?"

Adlin's eyes met hers. "He meant me to slay my bairn before 'twas born."

Sheila gasped. "No way." She shook her head. "I don't believe you."

"Aye," Adlin said. "But not because he wished ill will to the bairn. After all, had he killed him he himself would never be born. Nay, 'twas done simply because he was trained to never accept defeat no matter what it takes."

Still shaking her head, she said, "But I watched the entire fight. Neither of you stabbed at Meyla's belly!"

"But where did Grant's blade rest when last you saw it?"

Sheila swallowed and tore her eyes from his. Though she'd thought it odd she figured...well she wasn't sure now. "It was resting on Meyla's stomach."

"Grant has been well-trained in the dark arts. The magic he used was taught to him by Keir."

Her eyes met his, confused.

"He slowed time, lass." Adlin shook his head. "'Tis not even something I'm capable of as my magic doesnae work that way."

"Then how do you know he did?"

"Because I saw it." Adlin's eyes narrowed. "In the air around him, in the air around everyone. 'Twas black, 'twas evil."

Her stomach soured. "You must be wrong."

Adlin quirked a brow at her.

"Okay, so you're never wrong." Sheila again shook her head. "Then why did you and Meyla all but bless him afterwards?"

"Because he overrode it." Adlin nodded, pleased, whispering again, "He overrode it."

Before she could respond, Adlin continued. "Grant is like me. He is a white wizard, a believer in God. Other MacLomain's are dark wizards, they are the pagans. But their magic is not evil, just shadowed, different. However, they are more likely to ken the black magic. So 'twas a shock to me that Grant, a white wizard, was able to not only use black magic but fight it if need be."

Adlin hesitated for a moment, fresh pride in his eyes. "In all honesty, he's done a remarkable job at overcoming a great deal of the anger he deserves to harbor. He has a strong spirit and will about him." His eyes locked with hers. "'Tis safe to say outside of myself and mayhap Torra, he is the most powerful wizard to be born of my lineage."

A little shiver rippled through her. "He knows."

"Aye." Adlin took her hand. "Such power is a heavy burden to carry most especially when combined with the long, dark life he's lived."

Before she could speak, Adlin said, "But beneath the magic is just a man...one who could stand to be loved."

Sheila wasn't sure what to say.

"Do you love him, lass?"

"I barely know him," she murmured. Sad, she looked to the water. "Like him I'm not really familiar with what love's supposed to be."

"I dinnae think there's a set way to love." Adlin squeezed her hand. "But 'twill not be hard to recognize when it comes, neither for you nor for him."

She closed her eyes and sighed. "You say it as though it's already happened."

Adlin's voice grew very soft. "I say it as though I would like nothing more."

Sheila swung her eyes to his. "You've a good heart, Adlin MacLomain."

"As do you," he said easily.

Suddenly, it seemed as though she sat next to not a young highlander but an old man, his wise eyes and warm soul comforting. "Though we haven't known one another long, less so in your case, I'll always consider you a good friend."

Adlin grinned, eyes fond. "As will I you, Sheila." He pulled her to her feet. "Let us get back. The weather will soon change."

Sheila frowned at the sky. "But it's gorgeous out."

"For now but not much longer."

Not about to argue with an arch wizard, she left it alone and enjoyed idle chatter as they walked back arm in arm. They'd just stepped foot on the field when she spied Grant practicing at arrows across the way. "Lord, he reminds me of his brother Malcolm with that look on his face. I didn't realize how much they resemble one another."

Adlin chuckled. "So I've some brooding descendants, aye?"

"You sure do." She offered a wry grin. "But Malcolm's become a little less grumpy now."

"'Tis good this." Adlin smiled. "I look forward to meeting them all someday."

"When you do, in every time period, you act as though you've never met us."

"'Twould make sense," Adlin said. "If you were to know I met you here or at any other time, would it not influence these moments that we share now?"

Sheila had given this plenty of thought so nodded. "I'd say it most certainly might."

Thump. Thump. Thump. Grant released three arrows in rapid succession, all flush together on the bull's eye. Then he quickly released three more, all crowding around the others.

"And to think," Adlin said. "The bow and arrow is of his weaker skills."

Scary thought. But Sheila couldn't help but feel pride. If nothing else came of Grant's years in captivity, he deserved to have harnessed such talent.

No doubt sensing they were coming, he turned, eyes cutting not to Adlin but to her. He wore no tunic, just the MacLomain plaid and the boots with those braids interwoven into his hair. Corded muscles rippled over every last inch of him. Suddenly hot, Sheila pulled her arm free of Adlin's.

The MacLomain chieftain chuckled but said nothing.

Grant handed his bow to Bryce, eyes flickering between her and Adlin as he greeted them. "Good morn to you both."

Sheila nearly wiped the sweat from her forehead she was so darn hot. It felt like a fire had ignited beneath her skin. "Hey. Good morning."

Adlin nodded then turned his attention to Bryce. "Might we compete, lad?"

Bryce grinned. "Aye!"

Grant looked at her then nodded toward the forest. "Up for a walk, lass?"

The day might be sunny but the woods looked far too dark, welcoming and strangely intimate. Much like Adlin, he didn't give her a chance before taking her hand and pulling her after him. Sheila wasn't sure she wanted to follow him in his current mood because she knew darned well his spirits weren't up. She'd learned that by watching Malcolm. Quite honestly, she didn't want to deal with it right now.

They'd just reached the tree line when she dug in her heels and pulled her hand from his.

His heavy frown turned her way. "What is it?"

What *was* it exactly? But deep down inside she knew. For years she'd walked on eggshells around her ex. Would he say something kind or something mean? What mood was he in now? She shook her head and backed away. Sure, Grant wasn't Jack but he was sifting through a lot of emotions. Just like *she* was.

"If you don't mind I'd rather watch Adlin and Bryce shoot."

Grant's frown deepened and he grabbed her hand. "Just a few moments. Please. I want to show you something."

"Leslie was right," she murmured, a headache blossoming behind her temple. "I need to focus less on fixing others but more on fixing myself."

Grant's expression softened but he didn't let go of her hand. "Aye, lass." He reeled her closer. "'Tis the same for me."

Through all of this she'd been determined to be strong, to stand by him, but when she'd seen his growling face so much like his brother's, she realized how tired she was. Trying to understand the way a man thought had become too much a part of her life. At the moment, she had no desire to sift through anyone's emotions save her own.

The scowl had all but vanished from Grant's face as he studied her. "Please, give me a few moments alone with ye."

Realizing that he slipped into the deep brogue he was used to speaking with the Hamilton's, she paused, almost sighed. A few moments wouldn't kill her...would they? "Where do you want to go?"

"Anywhere you are."

Sheila blinked a few times. A heavy slew of sensations raced through her. "Grant?"

"Aye," he murmured, eyes all but eating her alive. "If you dinnae want me to communicate within the mind, say such and I willnae."

Not sure of anything at all, she reveled in the pure eroticism behind having his voice in her head. It was so entirely different than when they communicated via the pentacle. "No," she whispered then cleared her throat. "It's fine. Just...different."

Instead of letting him lead her, she walked into the forest. *She* led the way. "Come. Please show me whatever you'd like."

Grant walked alongside, a small smile on his face as he tied back his hair with a swath of plaid.

"Why are you smiling?" she asked.

The smile fell from his lips but not his eyes. "No reason, lass."

When she started to head in one direction, he gently grabbed her elbow and led her in another. They didn't go far before he urged her to sit beside him on a rock alongside a small river. Somewhere nearby she heard the bubbling of a small waterfall. Sheila pulled her hand from his. "No offense, this is beautiful but not all that different than many spots I've seen in Scotland."

"Actually 'tis." Grant looked at the sky. "Because of the storm that brews and who comes, I am able to show you something you couldnae see at any other time."

Sheila eyed the sky and shook her head. It was still clear blue. "Who comes?"

"That doesnae matter." Grant took her hand and his eyes swung to hers. "I wanted to thank you for being there for me last eve." Though there was pain in his gaze there was something else as well. Affection? "I'm sorry I couldnae speak with you about why I grew so upset. 'Twill take time for me to share such things. For too long I have kept dark thoughts to myself and dinnae know how to let another help me struggle through them."

Sheila was surprised by his easy admission...grateful for it. "No worries. I understood." She paused, debating if she should say more but decided she needed to know. "Adlin told me that you slowed time." When Keir had done such a thing at the Hamilton castle it'd scared the heck out of her. "I didn't know you could do that."

"And I willnae ever again," he pledged, darkness settling in his eyes. "'Tis harmful magic that I cannae be part of. To do so is to embrace evil." His tone grew cautious. "What else did he tell you?"

"Enough that I know you're going to be okay, that you're overcoming a lot of bad stuff in a really good way," she said, voice both soft and proud. "And enough to know that going to comfort you last night was definitely the right thing to do."

"'Twas more than I deserved," he continued. "So I wanted to give you something in return."

"You don't need to—" she began but he put a finger to her lips.

"But I do," he said. "I want to give you a glimpse of things that have happened here that brought you to this moment. I want to show you that you are an intricate and verra important piece of all of this."

Sheila said nothing when Grant's thumb made small circles on her palm and he began to chant. "*Discutiat et pro nobis, ut video, spiritus, nunc autem et mortale sit.* Unfold time for us to see, but spirits now then mortal be."

As the forest had done before, everything turned a light purple. Once more, a bright light shone amongst many other lights through the pine branches. Though transparent, a young couple appeared on the opposite side of the river. Two horses stood nearby as they gazed into one another's eyes.

"That is Iain and Arianna when they first traveled back to Scotland together. 'Twas her strength and courage that made such possible," Grant murmured.

No sooner had she glimpsed them when another couple entered the clearing on horseback. Ferchar and Caitlin! Yet they were just as transparent.

"This is the first time the Broun lasses from different centuries met," Grant informed. "'Twould prove to be the start of a bond between many because both are such admirable lasses."

No sooner had they all vanished then another couple appeared, sitting on a nearby rock. They could only be William and Coira, both far younger. If she wasn't mistaken there was the faintest hint of nostalgia in Grant's voice when he said, "'Twas the moment Coira admitted to herself that she loved William but was courageous enough to abide by the ring's magic and allow another to court her. Not of this clan or century, in a land not her own, she showed such strength of spirit, such perseverance."

When they faded so too did the purple light. "These lasses are your kin. The strength and courage they possess are within you as well. You will overcome your challenges in life with as much dignity as they have and lend strength to all of those around you. Dinnae ever doubt it, lass."

Touched, Sheila's eyes met his. Allowing her to see these women during such pivotal moments in their lives was indeed a gift. That he thought her of their caliber was flattering to say the least.

"Thank you," she whispered.

He shook his head. "You need not thank me. 'Tis important that you understand what lies within you...how far you've truly come."

Though she appreciated him saying as much, it would likely take time to be convinced.

Grant eyed her for several more moments before he stood. "I've been battling all morn so am afraid I must bathe before the storm comes." A small grin curved his lips. "Might you stay or should I walk you back first?"

"Well it wouldn't be the first time you bathed in front of me," she reminded with a smile to match. She rather liked how despite his unfortunate life, Grant didn't linger on heavy thoughts for too long. "And I'd hate to delay you before this supposed storm."

"'Twould be no delay." Yet he was already pulling off his boots.

So it seemed she'd be given one more memory of this river.

A wicked gleam blossomed in his pale gray-blue eyes. "Will you join me, lass?"

Sheila's mouth went dry when his plaid dropped and allowed her a full frontal view. Something she hadn't seen the last time he bathed. *Keep your eyes on his face. You can do it.* But nope, her gaze fell and eyes rounded. She tried to blink away her expression but no doubt looked more the fool for it.

"'Tis sweet how your cheeks turn so pink." A smirk curled up one corner of his lips. "I've never seen the like."

Oh, God save her. Sheila's skin was sizzling. Though she'd bathed the night before she figured she'd better join him. Anything to refocus her eyes which were still glued to where they shouldn't be. To make matters worse, or better depending on how you looked at it, her obvious appreciation was bringing him...*it* to life.

"Yeah, I'll swim." She nodded toward the river. "Go on. I'll catch up."

Of course the moment he turned, her eyes locked onto his incredibly tight, well-rounded backside. Nearly stumbling out of her dress, she never took her eyes off him the whole way in. In fact, she was halfway in when she realized that though she'd got her dress off she still had on her shoes and chemise.

Hell.

Though she whipped her sodden shoes onto the grassy shore, she figured she might as well keep on the undergarment. So she sunk down and wet her hair. Thankfully this water wasn't nearly as chilly as the last time they'd done this. Standing waist deep, she rung out her hair.

When Grant resurfaced from the water his eyes were on her.

Well, part of her.

A clingy, white wet chemise left little to the imagination.

Sheila had never felt a man's eyes like she did his. Desire made them darken and his lips parted just a fraction. "Bathing was not something Keir allowed verra often so 'tis good this," Grant said, gaze devouring her then moving to her face, "Especially with you."

Why she picked that moment to ask him about their marriage she'd never know. Maybe because she knew whatever this was between them was bound to get a whole lot more physical. "About what Keir made us do…getting married that is…" Then she trailed off, not sure in the least how she wanted this conversation to go.

As if the Heaven's answered for him, distant thunder rumbled. Sheila glanced at the darkening skies. They'd been right!

In that brief moment she looked to the sky, he took her hand, pulled her close and tilted up her chin. His voice was whisper soft. "What think you of what Keir did? What think you of this marriage?"

Interested in his gentle questions, she replied, "I think I'd rather hear your thoughts first."

"Nay, 'tis your thoughts that matter most."

Despite the intensity in his gaze, she was overly aware of his proximity. The way water trickled in little rivulets down his tanned chest and his arousal pressed against her belly. Doing her best to gather her thoughts, she murmured, "I think Keir made a big mistake…" He tensed. But she wasn't finished. "When he thought it would enrage the MacLomain's."

Though he relaxed slightly, Grant wasn't done. "But what think you of the bond we now share."

Sheila considered it. "I think it was done so in the eyes of our God which makes it pretty serious for me." Not sure what he wanted to hear she said, "Though absolving a marriage here is difficult, divorces are pretty common in my time. If that's what you want, we can do it."

"I dinnae want the marriage absolved," he said softly. "But I willnae have you forced into something you dinnae want. Too long have you suffered such at the hands of your last love…or as you call him, *ex*."

Grant *wanted* to stay married to her? But why? They barely knew one another. Still, the thought sent pleasant warmth through her. "I don't understand why you'd want this. Haven't you had so little choice in your life as well?"

"This is the first real choice I've had and I wish to keep you, lass," he said. "If you'll have me."

Not sure in the least that he was seeing things clearly, she offered no response.

Something in his eyes told her he was in no rush to have one either. It seemed he wanted her to decide if this was right at her leisure. Oddly enough, she was comforted by his lack of pressure. So she gave him a soft kiss on the cheek.

When she hesitated, her lips lingering on his cool skin, he turned his mouth to hers. Slow and easy, he cupped her cheeks, his kiss at first chaste.

But that didn't last long.

In a split second, they were back in that tent on enemy territory. An unforgettable kiss was reignited as his lips worked hers with a masterful skill she was unaccustomed to. Yet as before, she soon became just as hungry, tongues swirling and exploring.

Sheila was so completely lost that she didn't realize he'd walked her backward until sun-warmed grass was beneath her. Thunder might have rumbled closer, lighting might've flashed, wind might have bent the trees, but all went unnoticed. Nothing but the feel of his long, hard body pressing against hers got through.

"Sheila," he said against her ear, the sound hoarse, desperate…sexy. Then a whisper. "Let me have you."

Have me? Heck yes. *Please.* She gasped and arched when he tore her chemise down the front and his hot mouth latched onto her nipple. Painful yet delicious throbs started between her thighs and a deep groan buried itself in her throat. Unfamiliar with her body's response, she dug her hands into his hair and thrust her breasts up more.

Somehow he managed to continue to wring sensation after sensation from her breasts while simultaneously pushing up the lower half of her chemise. His hands were everywhere, stroking muscles she didn't know she had. He left no inch unattended. All the way from her ankles to her lower thighs.

As he ventured up her body, strange sounds came from her throat. It seemed if she made a particular sound he liked more than another, he'd linger wherever he touched.

When his mouth finally left her breasts and traveled below, she bit her lower lip. Ever so slowly, he inched up her chemise, his lips and teeth skimming first the lower thigh of one leg then the other. The combination of his hot tongue and the cool air had her chest rising and falling harshly. More than that, his slow, thorough stroll had the pressure between her legs building and building. She was already burning to such a blazing degree that she was ready to blow.

Sheila nearly came undone when his tongue flicked against her inner thigh. Clenching the grass, she closed her eyes, trembling. The sweet ache spread into her lower body and gooseflesh broke out all over. Almost as if he knew what was about to happen, he held her thighs and blew his steaming breath against her center.

Her eyes shot open and she cried out when a fast frenzy of harsh clenches rolled straight up through her body. By instinct, her thighs tried to come together but Grant held tight. Sheila swore she heard him moan, his heavy breaths wafting over the epicenter of her untimely release. Even her jaw quivered as the orgasm blasted through her.

"'Twill be quite the thing for ye both when ye get around to doing more than that," came a matter-of-fact voice.

Startled, struggling to cover herself, Sheila sat up abruptly.

Only to see Kenzie crouched by the river.

Chapter Nine

Grant frowned at Kenzie while helping Sheila adjust herself as best she could with a ripped chemise. He was about to help her on with her dress when she shook her head and nodded at his clothes. "Please get dressed. Even if we weren't married I'd be uncomfortable with you naked in front of another woman." Her eyes widened at his heavy erection and she buried her face in her hands, mumbling, "Especially after that and with you…ugh forget it."

"Och, nay," Kenzie said, splashing water on her face. "There is naught to be bothered by. I've seen him—"

"Enough, lass," Grant cut in, wrapping his plaid. Painfully aroused, he crouched and splashed water on his face as well. Kenzie truly didn't know better. She'd lived far too many years forced by Keir to prance around in the nude pleasing his soldiers. When his eyes went to her, he tried to keep his tone gentle. "'Tis no longer appropriate for you to be around such things unless with your own lad."

"My own lad," Kenzie quipped, standing. "'Tis hard to imagine such a thing."

Sheila had tied together the top of her chemise and was quickly pulling on her dress and squishy shoes, eyes skirting between him and Kenzie. "Listen, I'm gonna get back to the castle."

Grant had no choice but to use magic to cease his determined arousal so that he could follow her. Then, much to Sheila's surprise, he flicked out his hand and her shoes dried in an instant.

"That is why I am here," Kenzie said, following them. "Adlin requested that you return to the castle what with the storm."

As he knew they would, pitch black clouds were smothering the sky. Heavy wind gusted and thunder echoed. Grant didn't let Sheila go too far before he took her hand. When she went to pull it away, he held tight. Of course he didn't blame her for being uncomfortable with Kenzie appearing as she had but such things were bound to happen. His friends had endured a lot and it would take time for them to adjust.

Though she didn't try to pull away again, he knew she wanted to. Regardless, he wouldn't let go. Grant breathed deeply as he tried to force away images of her receptive body. He'd not expected her to respond so thoroughly to his touch. Her sensuality astounded him. He hadn't even taken that first anticipated taste and she'd exploded.

What would it be when he did all the things that typically brought lasses to their pleasure? What would *those* cries sound like when they broke from her lips? He cleared his throat, the sound nearly a groan, as he once more used magic to quell his fast returning erection.

Sheila glanced at him then blushed. Grant imagined his current expression was unmistakable. His need to be inside her was too great. It was bloody hard to focus on anything else.

"It seems the MacLomain's are hanging a tapestry soon," Kenzie said. "'Tis cause for celebration I'm told."

When Grant glanced at his friend, he realized she was feeling bad about interrupting them. "'Tis good then for us to be around a merry crowd, aye?"

"Aye," Kenzie agreed, her eyes on Sheila. "'Tis a grand tapestry. I remember seeing it when a bairn. Never did I look at it long though." She shook her head. "I was sure if I did 'twould suck me right in."

"You were at the MacLomain castle when you were young?" Sheila said.

"Aye," Kenzie replied, clearly unsure if she should say as much.

Sheila's eyes rounded at him. "You knew each other as children?"

"Aye," Grant said. "Kenzie is of the MacLaughlin clan. Longtime allies of the MacLomains."

Though he thought perhaps Sheila might grow upset she instead put her hand on Kenzie's arm and frowned. "I'm so sorry that Keir got you as well. And I'm sorry if I overreacted at the river. Just trying to get used to all this. Please know that it's got nothing to do with you personally, okay?"

"Nay, 'tis fine, m'lady." Kenzie smiled. "Worry naught."

Sheila shook her head. "No need to call me that. Remember, we're equals. Just two women making our way in the world, right?"

Kenzie shrugged. "Mayhap." She glanced at Grant. "But I always thought he should be laird of the Hamilton clan." Then she winked at Sheila. "Which makes *you* his lady to be sure."

"Laird of the Hamilton clan?" Sheila asked, astonished. "Why not the MacLomain clan?"

"Because my guess is the MacLomain clan already has a good chieftain and the Hamilton's are in need o' one." She grinned at Grant. "Besides, outside of the evil swine now ruling the Hamilton's, all love Grant, even the old folk and wee bairns."

Sheila's eyes met his then returned to the field they'd just arrived at. "I can understand that."

"Though 'tis sweet of you to think such, I wouldnae want such a castle. Too many memories," Grant muttered.

"Aye, true," Kenzie allowed. "For the people as well." Her eyes cut to him. "'Twould take a great and much beloved chieftain to help them heal."

Sheila frowned. "I hate to think of what the Hamilton clan has endured beneath Keir's rule. The first time I was there," she paused for a moment then regrouped as her eyes went to his, "You and Colin MacLeod were rallying the clans to go to war against us."

Sheila again paused and he knew she thought of him battling against his own family. Something he had no choice but to do. "Then the last time I was there Keir put me in the dungeons with Iosbail." Her eyes narrowed. "I didn't see anyone then. No commerce, nothing."

"You wouldnae have if 'twas the eve," Kenzie provided. "Unless there was a celebration, Keir ordered that all return to their dwellings. He preferred no distractions once the sun went down."

"Why?" Sheila asked as though she didn't want the answer.

Kenzie and Grant looked at one another and frowned.

"'Twas his time to connect with his dark magic," Grant finally said. "During those hours he cultivated it…learned from it."

Sheila visibly shivered. "That's awful but no big surprise I suppose."

This time when her eyes slid his way, Grant knew she wondered just how often he witnessed those practices, was mayhap even part of them. That was an answer he hoped he'd never have to give. But if she ever asked, he'd give it truthfully. Why? Because he wanted her trust, hell he wanted *her,* more than anyone on this God forsaken Scottish soil.

When Sheila was around, an undefinable weight lifted off him. She cast a light over his dark thoughts. Would he release her from their marital bond if that's what she ultimately wished? Aye. But it would be with a heavy heart.

The solace she'd offered the eve before remained with him. Somehow, through just her presence, he'd sifted through his morbid emotions until there was nothing left but her...and him. He'd watched her sleep on the cot in Torra's old chambers for hours. The dying flames on the hearth basked her complexion in what felt like peace, a deep solitude. Or mayhap that was merely his tarnished soul.

No matter, he'd felt unfamiliar stirrings, ones that went far beyond simple lust. As he lay by her side and pulled her into his arms, he knew Sheila was *his* lass. Somehow she always had been and always would be.

His deep thoughts rushed to the present as they crossed the first drawbridge. Wind started to gust so strongly that he had to hold both lass's hands lest they stumble into the moat. Swollen raindrops started to spit as they made their way into a courtyard nearly devoid of clansfolk.

Adlin held open the castle door as they all but staggered up the steps in what had fast turned into a driving rain. Thunder crashed and lightening flashed so quickly the castle stairs flickered rapidly in their vision. The moment they entered, the door slammed shut behind them. Blankets were put around their shoulders as the MacLomain chieftain waved them toward the fire. "Come, warm yourself. 'Tis a grand day indeed!"

Though a storm might bluster beyond, one would never know it based on the goodwill and happiness in the MacLomain great hall. They'd indeed had a good harvest for such a spread with too many types of bread to count. Grant eyed the mussels, scallops and moist shrimp. Wooden platters overflowed with capons, pheasant, goose meat, partridge and wood pigeon. Not in all his long years at the Hamilton castle had he seen so much food.

Grant hesitated when he went to grab a shrimp, convinced if he looked up he'd see his master glaring down and shaking his head sharply. But it didn't much matter when the darkness receded and Sheila held a shrimp to his mouth, her soft blue eyes warmer than ever. "Allow me."

If she wasn't careful, she'd be up in her chambers...or his, sooner than she thought. With a slow flick of his tongue, he brought the morsel into his mouth, all the while imagining it was something else altogether. Sheila didn't misunderstand the look in his eyes in the least and her gaze soon lingered on his lips.

The pipes trilled, their sound only slightly louder than the wind howling outside. They accepted mugs of whiskey as a long rolled up scroll of fabric was left at the foot of a huge, barren wall overlooking the hall. It'd taken twenty men to carry it.

"I can't believe I'm here to watch this being hung," Sheila said under her breath.

Grant wrapped his arm around her waist and pulled her back against him. Not likely his best move based on the feel of her wee arse tucked up against his front. But he enjoyed the simple affection that they might share.

And she *was* his wife.

Adlin grinned and took Meyla's hand as the ladders were brought out. Grant was surprised the shaman didn't use his magic but then mayhap he wanted this done the old fashioned way. That meant men would be going dangerously high because this tapestry was nearly as tall as the castle's great hall. By far, the largest ever hung in the MacLomain castle. They'd already rung up the rings to hold the great metal post. Grant sighed inwardly and felt his magic stir.

"What is it," Sheila said softly. "You're upset."

"Nay," he tried to reassure but his eyes remained on Meyla, pregnant and standing below the dangerous exhibition.

"Adlin knows what he's doing," Sheila whispered over her shoulder.

Grant narrowed his eyes. Oh, he did not doubt for a moment that the chieftain knew what he was doing. The hall quieted, even the pipes, as more ladders were brought and more men climbed. The sound of creaking wood and grunts accompanied the wind as well as the snap and pop of the fire on the hearth.

Why didn't metal strengthen these ladders? They were far too flimsy for how high these men climbed. Like the rest of the crowd, Sheila was in awe as the tapestry was slowly unraveled.

Grant was not impressed in the least.

To his eyes, it seemed a dangerous and much unneeded sport. Lives were at risk without good reason. So when the tapestry was only half unraveled and one of the men stumbled, he didn't hesitate to release his magic to stay the man before he fell. Adlin, naturally, sensed it and locked eyes on Grant.

Strangely enough, Meyla did the same.

A low growl rumbled in his chest and Sheila tensed, her eyes turning to his. "What is it?"

He had no time to answer before a few more men stumbled and the crowd gasped. Pushing forth his magic, infuriated, Grant pillowed the tapestry out and unraveled the rest before more men were put at risk. The crowd roared with approval, not realizing in the least that magic ushered in the masterpiece without more potential damage.

Caught in the light of hundreds of torches, the Viking tapestry found its home.

With nothing but storminess and a raging sea beyond, a heavily armored, horn helmeted Viking ran his sword though a man on bent knees begging for mercy. The tapestry was so well woven that the viewer clearly saw the look of triumph through the thin slices of metal that adorned the victors' head.

Grant knew exactly what that Viking was feeling.

He'd conquered.

He'd won.

And he would again and again.

"What?" Sheila turned in his arms. "What just happened? What do you see?"

It mattered little what he saw as Adlin and Meyla's eyes remained on his. They'd seen all of this before it happened. Frustrated that he was once more a puppet to a master, he shook his head and pulled away. "I see nothing."

Sheila glanced at the tapestry then once more at him, words gentle. "I think you see everything."

Grant let the last of his magic and anger seep away as he looked into her sweet, caring eyes. There was something in them that appealed to him. Was she weak? Nay. Was she as lost as him? Without doubt. But that wasn't what appealed to him the most. He cupped her cheek and stroked her chin. Sheila had something entirely different about her that he'd yet to witness in another human being and couldn't put words to it. While miffed at the MacLomain chieftain, he'd let it go for now so that he and his lass might enjoy their time together.

He brought his lips so close that they dusted hers as he whispered, "'Tis time for us to be merry, eat and drink."

Before she could question or worry further, he lifted his mug to her lips.

Her eyes remained on his as she drank, the fluid fluctuating her throat muscles in a way that made his groin tighten. When she was finished, he brought the cup to his mouth so that she might see that their lips touched once more…if only on the edge of a cup.

"Grant, Sheila," Bryce boomed upon greeting. "My glorious friends!"

Grant grinned at his friend. Bryce was well in his cups and happy. Never had he seen such a glorious sight. Clapping him on the shoulder, he raised his cup and urged Sheila to do the same. As she did, Kenzie came alongside and raised hers as well.

When the four clanked their drinks together, Grant felt something in it.

Something born of the future.

Eyes closed, he swigged from his drink before once more turning his eyes to Sheila. She watched him and his friends fondly and her stance was stronger than he'd ever seen it. Something had changed in his lass, something indefinable. Where before Sheila's gaze might have shied from everyone else's, now she made a point of meeting every eye turned her way. Her regard was less afraid, more self-assured.

"I'm not interested in hanging out down here too long."

When her words entered his mind, Grant breathed through his nose, eager for the smell of her arousal. What he'd really like to do right now is swipe the table clear and toss her down. He'd much rather devour her than the well-laid platters of food.

He slipped his hand into hers and squeezed.

Sheila squeezed back and urged him to sit. "Let's eat."

So they did. Everything they could put their hands on. Him more than her but it didn't matter. Grant actually sat at a table and ate. Nobody looked down on him watching his every move. Out of habit, he'd glance up every once in a while but there was never anyone there. This wasn't the Hamilton castle. Nay, this was the MacLomain castle.

Kenzie and Bryce sat across from him, smiling, eating and drinking as they all chatted. This moment felt more freeing than any he'd had before and as his eyes met theirs, he knew they felt the same.

All toasted their drinks over the table once more and laughed. His friends were genuinely happy. Aye, they might still be tentative but he saw the way they no longer ducked their heads but met people's eyes, their shoulders straightening more and more every time they did.

Grant felt such joy in this. When Sheila's hand curled over his on the table the feeling was all that much more so. She didn't need to look at him. They shared this moment without eye contact. Though the bagpipes rallied on and the clan danced around them, for a split second in time it was just him, his friends and Sheila. Slow, easy, under no watchful eyes, they simply enjoyed one another's company.

"I'd like to dance again."

When her gentle voice entered his relaxed mind, Grant smiled. She'd quickly got the hang of speaking telepathically. Wasting no time, he pulled her against him and blended into the dancing crowd. Aye, the pipes were lively and the clan boisterous but all he wanted was the feel of her body against his. As people closed around them, he pulled her closer still. When at last the two stopped, his arms around her, they stood in front of the great hall's monstrous fireplace.

"The faces in the mantle are alive," she whispered into his ear. "Do you see?"

Of course he did but how did she? "'Tis just good workmanship," he assured.

"No," she murmured into his neck. "They all tell me stories. One even speaks of how it will see Iosbail MacLomain and her husband, Alexander Sinclair fight in this very hall. No, they all have a different tale to tell and some far more intense than others. They didn't do that when I was in this castle before."

Grant cupped the back of her head and sighed. "'Tis not a mantle a true visionary should be near when her powers are just igniting."

Before she could question him, he grabbed a few skins from a servant and pulled her up the stairs. Nothing she'd overly enjoy would come of her staying in the great hall this eve. Between the Viking tapestry and the mantle over the hearth, her magic was slowly blossoming. While it was certainly doing so in a good way, it would also be overwhelming and he didn't want that for her.

Not right now.

They hadn't gone far beyond the first floor when he pulled her down a hallway he hadn't been down in far too long. When they arrived at the doorway to a chamber, he froze…remembering.

"Grant?" Sheila said. "Why are we here? Our rooms are upstairs."

Releasing her hand, he crossed to one of two windows in the chamber. With a flick of his wrist, a fire sparked to life on the hearth and a few torches lit. Grant put aside the skins, peered out the window then closed his eyes. It might be in a different time but he was right back where he began. When her light touch met his arm, he opened his eyes to see Sheila staring up, concerned.

He'd not shut her out as he had the eve before.

"Worry naught, lass," he murmured, "I but return to what was my chamber when a bairn."

Chapter Ten

There were no words that could ever suit this moment…but there were actions.

So Sheila wrapped her arms over his shoulders and rested her cheek against his chest. His arms slowly came around her and he rested his chin on the top of her head. She could only imagine how hard it was for him to stand in this room with all the memories that must be haunting him. But she gave him credit for seeking it out rather than avoiding it and felt privileged that he wanted her with him.

They stood that way for a long time before he finally spoke. "'Tis less the memories of my time in this room that affect me now but all that might have come to pass had I not been taken."

Sheila blinked away the moisture in her eyes and looked at him, not surprised in the least to see a single trail of wetness on his cheek. Standing on her toes, she peppered light kisses along the evidence of unchecked emotions, then brought her lips alongside his ear, whispering, "Let us, here, now, make a new memory, one that cannot be taken from you."

When his lips sought hers, she pulled back and shook her head. "Memories I want to give you."

Grant said nothing but leaned over slightly when she pulled his tunic over his head. When with her ex, she'd been told what to do in the bedroom…during those first few years. After that, there'd barely been any intimacy. Now she had the chance to think for herself and do what she wanted. And she wanted him to not worry about pleasing her and enjoy the moment. Yes, he'd all but been raised by women who serviced him but she had the feeling he'd focused more on pleasing them.

Did that make her jealous? Naturally. She was human. But it also made her respect him. Sheila wanted him to *see* her appreciate him, so she made a point of trailing her hungry gaze slowly over his wide shoulders, muscled chest and chiseled torso. It was no hardship to take her time enjoying his body. No hardship at all.

Starting with his wrists, she ran her hands up over his strong forearms then biceps, trailing her palms and fingers over every single sinewy muscle. Her tongue snaked out and wetted her lips in response to the way he tensed beneath her touch and gooseflesh broke out over his skin. She was only to the point of running her hands over his shoulders yet already an impressive erection billowed his plaid.

His arousal and the desire in his eyes empowered her.

Slow, thorough, she trailed her hands down his chest, followed by her lips. He tasted warm and masculine…delicious. His low groan rumbled against her lips when she hit certain spots. When that happened, she did as he had at the river and spent more time in those locations. When she fell to her knees, he all but growled.

As he went to move, she shook her head and stayed him. "Remove your plaid."

Jaw clenched, a vein pulsed in his neck as his lust darkened eyes looked down at her. Sheila kept her womanly smile hidden. It was taking everything he had to give her this control. Slower than she would have liked, he removed the plaid. When the material hit the floor, she inhaled deeply. Hell, what had she gotten herself into?

This was a position she'd been put in often when she and her ex were first together. But then it'd been under his less-than-gracious instruction. Now she'd chosen it…wanted it. And Grant certainly wasn't Jack. No, Jack didn't have anything this impressive.

Fearless, determined, she wasted no time.

When Grant's hands wrapped into her hair and clenched, Sheila closed her eyes. Pleasuring him like this, tasting him, ignited a whole new brand of fire between her legs. As a low groan broke from her mouth, vibrating around him, he gasped. Her eyes rose, pleased to see his head flung back.

Yet when she took him deeper it seemed one stroke of the tongue too far because he again growled and the next thing she knew, Sheila was in his arms, back against the wall.

"I dinnae want ye to…" he breathed heavily against her ear, hand encompassing half her neck, "I need to be in ye another way altogether, lass."

Her heart pounded nearly as loud as the thunder roaring across the sky.

Grant tore the skin from the window and rain sliced into the room. Fast, faster than she could've imagined, he untied and pulled her dress away. The chemise? Forget it...ripped entirely from her body this time. Sheila was shocked and excruciatingly aroused by how quickly he had her naked and propped on the edge of the window.

Cold rain pelted her back, a shockingly tantalizing counterpart to his hot arm around her back and his sizzling erection between her legs. One hand braced against the wall, his lips closed over hers. Starved, eager, they ravaged one another. There was no sense of time, only of sensation, the push and pull of lips and tongues.

He tasted of whiskey and male, of a passion she'd never imagined existed. Alive in his embrace, she rocked, teasing his arousal, teasing her desire. Together, through nothing but the glide of their bodies against each other's and their ravenous mouths, they climbed higher and higher.

Suddenly, with one strong arm still around her back keeping her safe from a long fall, his free arm snaked beneath one of her legs and pulled it high. He didn't give her long to be startled by the feel of the cool wind at her core before his fiery heat replaced it. Sheila quivered at the feel of his girth pressing into her.

"Easy, lass," he whispered against her ear when she tensed. "I willnae hurt ye."

A thousand icy hailstones could've pounded her delicate flesh and done nothing to quench the hellish heat spreading through her. When his gentle finger found her clit and made small circles, she lost sight of his slow invasion but languished in the sweet, bone-deep pleasure he pulled from her.

Inch by precious inch, he pushed forward.

By the time his hand pulled from between them, she was moving with him, urging him deeper. Compliant, eyes half-mast as he gripped her tight, Grant held her backside tight and thrust until he filled her completely. Pleasure speared her sharply and she bit down on her lip so hard Sheila swore she tasted her own blood. Chest rising and falling rapidly, Grant squeezed her tightly against him. Her body clenched around him, thrilling at the feel of his closeness, of his very possession.

"'Tis hard this," he murmured, his lips trailing down her neck. "I want to…"

"What?" she whispered, barely able to push the words past her lips.

"Take ye until ye cannae stand it," he rumbled against her chest, his lips clamping over a rock hard nipple.

When she cried out and her hips jerked, he pulled back just a bit then thrust deep.

Another small cry erupted and she wrapped her other leg around his backside, wanting more. As a deafening crack of thunder split overhead, he pulled back further then thrust harder.

Her throat seized and sound strangled in her chest as every nerve ending in her body ignited. Eyes as dark as the night rose to hers as Grant scooped his other arm under her leg then braced his hands around her ass. Pulled high and tight, imprisoned by nothing but the monsoon at her back and the storm at her front, Sheila wrapped her hands into his thick hair.

With a deep thrust, he wrangled yet another cry from her. He then lifted her, crawled onto the bed and brought her back up against one of the bed posts.

Eyes lethal with lust, he said, "Raise your arms and grab hold."

Up for the order, anything to feel him move inside her again, she complied, her body rippling against him. The moment her hands clasped around the cool wood, his hot hands covered hers and brought her legs impossibly high and him uncompromisingly close.

Caught in the scent of their musk, she struggled for breath when he started to move. Not fast and furious but in small, circular motions that sparked friction. Sweat slicked their bodies as he continued his calculated assault. The glint of the fire caught the gray depths of his eyes and pure lust cultivated the blue swirled within. Yet all she could see within his turbulent, determined gaze was how he saw her…beautiful, desirable, nearly unattainable…but his regardless.

Little flecks of light started to flash in the corner of her vision as his slow movements grew into more steady thrusts. Though trapped she had enough freedom to slide her hips forward, to meet his eagerness, to pull each movement deeper.

His jaw clenched, his brows lowered, but he never stopped watching her.

Encouraged by the need he showed her, she gripped the post and thrust harder, meeting him with a ferociousness she didn't know she possessed. With a near snarl, he no longer thrust but pounded into her, an old anger that didn't belong to her merging with a new desire that belonged to her entirely.

Both were angry, though not at each other, and they took it out now, here, with nothing but a highland storm beyond to witness. Rain gushed in through the window, splattering on the floor, as they fought one another with nothing but their limbs and their passion.

Sheila had no idea when she ended up beneath him on the bed. There was no need for him to hold her now. No, she wrapped her legs around his back and met him thrust for thrust, urging him on as more flecks filled her vision and the world fell away. Bodies drenched, they moved against one another in a near frenzy.

Powerful muscles sliding against her soft skin, Grant rode her every bit as much as she did him. Nails dug into the flex of his back muscles. She bucked and thrashed as he took and took. One second the thrusts were so very deep, the next not deep enough.

Until they were.

As if sensing victory, he ground so deep that her lungs seized and she ran her nails up his back, senseless. Scared. But needy. Unable to flee the near horrid pain pleasure he was forcing her to feel.

He pushed then pulled away, a wicked driving force.

Over and over and over.

Oh no, oh no....no...no....yessss Grant!

She hadn't meant to say anything at all but it'd slammed into her mind then right into his.

Always for ye, my geal.

His words within her mind were so incredibly full of passion and need for her that his next thrust pushed her right over a cliff. Flailing, flying, gone, she didn't just scream but wailed as a powerful orgasm tore through her so fast she lost all air. Her toes curled then every other muscle in her body from her thighs to her stomach to her upper arms.

Both pain and pleasure spliced her in half. From far, far away, she heard Grant's cry of release and God help her it sent her already lost body into yet another poignant climax that made her again cry out long and hard. Even when she thought the last had come from her throat, the long wail continued.

Though his breathing was harsh and his throb within her endless, Grant stilled.

Sheila felt his alarm and tried to stop screaming.

Still caught within the throes of pleasure it took her a few moments to realize she wasn't screaming anymore.

But somebody else was.

Trying to speak through the thunder of blood pounding through her veins, she said hoarsely, "Grant…that's not me, right?"

He kissed her and his tender eyes met hers one more time before he pulled away and sat up. "Nay, lass. The bairn comes."

Baby? What was he talking about? For a split second she nearly looked at her stomach in shock but soon realized that would be impossible. But in her defense, you just never knew what to expect when sleeping with a wizard. Insta-married and insta-pregnant might go hand in hand. And jeesh, everyone and their cousin seemed to be getting pregnant lately.

A whole new slew of emotions bombarded her at the thought of a child. That was about the last thing either of them needed right now. Not that she didn't want one eventually. But she'd had the birth control shot so no worries.

Another long wail filled the hallways of the MacLomain castle.

Completely disconcerted, she jumped from the bed, eyeing the chamber for a dagger so that she could go fight and defend whoever cried like that.

"'Tis a wee bairn coming, lass." Grant stood. "But we should go and see if Adlin needs comfort."

Adlin? Sheila frowned at him until his words sunk in. Baby? Adlin? "Holy crap! Meyla's having her baby."

Grant's lips curled up as he wrapped his plaid. "Aye."

"This is what you meant when you said 'another comes' when we were by the river," she said, amazed as she looked at him.

"Aye," he murmured, pulling on his boots.

"How powerful *are* you?" she muttered as she yanked on her dress. "Better yet, why didn't you just say as much before?"

"Because destiny isnae mine to share."

Sheila stopped and looked at him. Yes, he was as tousled and handsome as hell. Still. "You're as evasive as Adlin for sure."

"Do you think we enjoy being such?" he said as he pulled his tunic over his head.

"Hard to know," she said under her breath. But he'd likely never give a truthful answer to his own question. Not if he was anything like Adlin. And it seemed more and more like he was. But she loved them both so wouldn't get grouchy about it right now. Meyla was having a baby!

Sheila barely had her shoes on when Grant pulled her after him. All was silent in the MacLomain castle save Meyla's horrific wails.

It seemed even strong, war-faring Vikings didn't much like labor pains.

Thunder crashed, lightning slashed and rain drove across the wall walks as they continued down to the great hall. All had been cleared. Nobody remained but the chieftain as he paced in front of the fire.

Though Adlin made no acknowledgment that they'd joined him she knew he spoke to them as he eyed the Viking tapestry and muttered, "She willnae let me near her."

Mugs of whiskey had been left on the table and Grant handed one to Adlin. "Drink, my friend, for soon you will welcome in your future."

Adlin eyed the proffered mug for a few moments before he took it and drank deeply. Then, mug in hand, he continued to pace. Grant, meanwhile, sipped from his own mug and worked at idle chatter with the disgruntled laird.

Keeping her eyes *off* the faces carved into the mantle, Sheila sat nearby and watched the men. Adlin's pacing reminded her of Malcolm, and Grant's steady, calming presence reminded her of his father, William. One way or another, these MacLomain men all shared one mannerism or another. And, one way or another, all were part of Adlin himself and the child being born upstairs.

It was hard not to ache for Meyla as her long wails filled the hall. Sheila took a small sip of her whiskey then pushed it aside. Her friend needed to get his mind off this at least a little. Besides, Meyla didn't deserve to deal with a drunken Adlin after she went through hell to ensure his child made it into the world.

Eyes to the wall, she walked over and grabbed the smallest sword she could find. Even that was weighty but she didn't complain as she turned to the men. "I've learned quite a few things since traveling back to medieval Scotland but never how to swing a sword. How about you two set aside the booze and teach me now?"

Adlin's brow's lowered and he shook his head as Meyla released another long cry.

Grant's eyes went to Adlin then to her, a small smile ghosting his face. "I think she has the right o' it, my laird."

"Nay," Adlin admonished even as Grant took his mug and set their drinks aside.

"Aye." Grant nodded toward her. "'Tis a request well made. She's set to fight evil the likes of which ye've never known and doesnae know how to swing a blade to defend herself."

Sheila recognized that Grant had once more purposefully turned to his deep brogue, one that spoke to Scots on a deeper level. Or so it seemed based on the way Adlin eyed the sword in her hand.

Thankfully, they headed her way which made her all that more aware that both were young, large and always bloodthirsty. Though Adlin might be shorter at six foot five and a fraction less muscled than Grant, he was not the old man she'd met in the future but every inch a vibrant highland warrior.

Grant pulled a blade off the wall and tossed it to Adlin then grabbed another, held it out to her and took the one she had. "It might look larger but 'tis lighter and better suited to you. Normally you would train with a wooden sword but 'twill naught be but the basics learned amongst friends, aye?"

After he returned hers to the wall, he grabbed his own sword from the corner. It was hard not to smile when she saw it was the blade given to him by Meyla. He fisted its hilt as though he'd been remiss without it in hand.

There was plenty of space in front of the fire for the three of them to spar so Adlin took his stance first, eyes on her. "The first thing you should always remember when sword fighting is to never expose your back. Eyes on the enemy at all times."

Adlin turned in Grant's direction and held up his sword. "Elbows tucked to protect yourself, the sword should be held in front of you, right down the middle, with the point of the blade aimed at your enemy's head." He spread his legs slightly. "Legs like this, knees loose, you should lead with the same foot as your lead hand."

"While there are many ways to use a sword, 'tis best for you to lunge and thrust as it requires far less strength." Adlin executed the move a few times as Grant blocked. "The more you sword practice, the more you'll learn about the feint. This is when you make small maneuvers that lead your enemy to believe you'll be making one move when you make another altogether."

Adlin made a motion with his arm and shoulder to the right then came in at Grant quick from the left. Though Grant blocked, she got the gist.

"Never look directly in the enemy's eyes," Grant continued as they parried, implementing everything Adlin had told her. "Keep your attention on as much of their body as possible. 'Tis easier to fall victim to their feint if you lock eyes with them."

Adlin stepped away then turned to her. "Now you try."

Grant set aside his blade and stood behind her as she mimicked Adlin's stance. He made adjustments to her position, his soft words in her ear. "'Tis my greatest hope you never have to fight like this, lass."

Sheila couldn't agree more after having seen the way Scotsmen wielded a sword.

"Dinnae look him in the eye," Grant murmured and she tore her gaze from Adlin's as he held up his sword.

Grant positioned himself so that his hands closed over hers. It was a heady sensation having the man at her back and the sword at her front. Something about the sweet sting still lingering between her thighs from their lovemaking combined with the power of the blade gave her a rush. She inhaled deeply and her heartbeat slammed into her throat.

He clearly felt it as well because his aroused, gravelly voice rumbled against her. "You must try to focus on Adlin and nothing else."

"You don't make it easy," she muttered but nodded.

There was a small smile in his voice. "Let us focus on the thrust of the blade so that we might return to another type of thrusting altogether, aye?"

Sheila chuckled as he urged her to move the blade a few times. He even kept his hands over hers when Adlin's blade connected the first time. The vibration of the contact traveled through her arms down into the pit of her stomach. She grinned, surprisingly aroused at the sensation. That couldn't be good. Grant nodded and stepped away but she knew when his eyes met hers, that her reaction had not gone unnoticed.

"You've a natural draw to the sword," Grant commented. "Mayhap in time, 'twill be your weapon of choice."

Adlin made slow, measured thrusts and Sheila met his blade, adjusting to the feel of it. They'd just connected again when a long wail filled the castle.

This time it wasn't Meyla…

But a baby's.

Iain MacLomain's father had just been born.

Adlin blinked several times then pulled back, tossing aside his blade. Like a man racing to save his soul, he tore up the stairs.

"We will practice again another time," Grant said. He returned her and Adlin's blade to the wall and set aside his. They exchanged a smile as he grabbed a skin, sat before the fire and pulled her onto his lap. Both took a long swig before she rested her head against his chest. The need for words was absent as they soaked up the pleasure of a wondrous night at the MacLomain castle. A new baby had been born…one that would make her and Grant sitting here to begin with possible.

Exhausted, she closed her eyes and nuzzled close.

It took several long moments for a woman's words to break through her relaxation.

"Nay, nay, it cannae be….nay!"

Sheila cracked open her eyes only to find that dim daylight now filled the great hall and Kenzie her vision. Before she could speak, the woman pointed over her shoulder and said…

"It takes her! Right from her wee bairn's arms, it takes her!"

Chapter Eleven

Grant never slept.

He'd felt the storm surge grow stronger as a new day came. Low light filled the great hall as morn crept forward. Sheila slept on his lap and the fire was fed by servants. All the while he kept his cheek nestled against the top of her head, breathing in the sweet scent of her hair as he waited. This would be a sad day in MacLomain history and all that gave him comfort was the lass in his arms.

She was his hero.

Selfless, giving, everything he could hope for in another. It seemed never-ending how she gave. What she'd done for Adlin the eve before, distracting him as his lass suffered, was just one more attribute to her pure goodness. He ran his hand down her silky curls and again inhaled deeply. Aye, he might be married to her but he wanted so much more.

He wanted her heart.

Her soul.

Not to own but to share, to intertwine. As the Celts of his heritage intertwined all that they cared for, he wanted the same with Sheila and no other. When they'd lain together it had been so very different than the lasses he'd experienced before. So much bloody better. It had been something far deeper, something he had no understanding of.

Her body had hummed alongside his. They'd become one.

His groin tightened at the mere thought.

Bloody hell.

The great hall was still quiet when Bryce and Kenzie made their way down. Unlike most, they were accustomed to being up before the sun so he was surprised to see them a bit after. Joining Grant, they talked together in hushed tones. Though there was cause for celebration, his friends felt unrest as surely as he did. Could it be the unnatural storm badgering the castle? Aye. But it wasn't. Nay, it was something else altogether. The bairn had been long born now, enough time for Adlin and Meyla to have had time with him. Yet no celebration sounded as would befit the birth of the chieftain's son.

Though he couldn't see it, Grant knew the sun had just crested behind the raging storm when Adlin, Meyla and their baby came down. It wasn't long before the chieftain and his new family stood before the fire. Heads bowed, Kenzie and Bryce stepped aside. Eyes only for Meyla and the bairn she held, Adlin looked with adoration at both. Time passed as they stayed that way. Though pale from her exertions, his Viking seemed stronger than most would be after birthing a bairn.

Adlin looked into her eyes and whispered, "It doesnae need to be this way. You could stay."

Meyla cupped his cheek. "You know I cannot." Then her eyes dropped to the bairn, tears in her eyes. "Take good care of him, Adlin. Raise him to be strong and mighty, to honor his Viking blood."

"You already have proof of that," he murmured.

Her eyes skimmed over Grant then back to the bairn. "It seems I do."

Adlin's hand closed around the back of her neck and he gave her a long thorough kiss, babe tucked between them, before he pulled back. "You are always welcome here, lass. This is your home as much as 'tis mine."

Meyla, shoulders back and stance strong, nodded before her eyes turned to the Viking tapestry. Grant didn't watch as she walked toward it but kept his eyes on Adlin and the bairn. The MacLomain chieftain's emotions played over his face briefly then fell away.

The storm raged outside as it did within the Viking tapestry. Through magic, the two fronts had always been one and the same.

Kenzie's eyes widened as she watched Meyla. "Nay, nay, it cannae be....nay!"

Sheila stirred in his arms and must've looked at Kenzie because the lass pointed and said, "It takes her! Right from her wee bairn's arms, it takes her!"

But it had never been from her wee bairn's arms at all. That had simply been how Kenzie perceived it. When Sheila jumped to her feet and spun, Grant joined her.

The Viking in the tapestry had movement.

Before she could go too far, Grant wrapped an arm around Sheila's midsection and pulled her back while he put a staying arm out that Kenzie and Bryce not move. All remained still as Meyla walked closer to the tapestry.

Adlin, legs splayed, holding their child, watched with nothing less than respect.

Dark eyes shone through his helmet as the Viking looked down. Everything remained frozen around him in the tapestry save the raging ocean and storm. He stepped from the blade slicing through the man at his feet to hold his hand down. Meyla glanced back once at Adlin and their child, a look of not anguish on her face but rightness, before she ran and jumped at the tapestry.

The tall horned Viking caught her arm and pulled her toward him. Swirling, black, all faded into the raging ocean before everything once more appeared.

Just as it had been.

A depiction of a horned Viking driving a sword through the head of the man at his feet.

"Christ," Sheila whispered.

Adlin went up the stairs to hand the bairn to a nursemaid.

"Did I see that as I did?" Kenzie whispered.

Grant nodded and urged them to sit at the table so that they might break their fast. "Aye, we all did." After a servant left some mugs and food, he continued. "The Viking you see in that tapestry is none other than Meyla's Da, Naðr Véurr."

They glanced at the tapestry, surprised.

"How do you know that?" Sheila asked.

"Because I told him," Adlin said, returning. Back to the fire, the chieftain crossed his arms over his chest and stared at the fierce Viking. "Two winters ago Naðr sought my help through an ancient form of Norse magic. While I gave aid freely he wouldnae have me unrewarded. 'Twas his daughter, Meyla, who he offered."

Sheila gasped. "That's horrible."

"'Twas not as bad as it seems," Adlin said. "We'd formed a bond and she felt she owed me a debt as well for saving her life. Unlike many Vikings now scouring the seas, Naðr Véurr and his people hold fast to honor. Not only that but there is another, one amongst his enemies, that has long desired his daughter. Removing her from their village put her out of harm's way."

The laird paused for a moment before he continued. "Little did I know that Naðr cast a spell that our union might give us a bairn." Adlin's eyes drifted up to where he'd brought his little one. "Soon after she conceived we were visited by both a Celtic and a Norse god, Fionn Mac Cumhail and Freyja. It was then that we learned Meyla must return to her people once our bairn was born and that the bairn needed to stay here, that his destiny within the MacLomain clan was too great."

Sheila's eyes were round as she stared at Adlin. "I'm not familiar with Norse mythology. Who is Freyja?"

"She is known for many things," Adlin said. "But above all, love, fertility and even battle."

"Quite the mix." She cleared her throat and glanced at Grant. "But definitely plays in to everything I've learned about the MacLomain men."

He gave her credit for not dispelling Adlin's notion of other gods existing besides her own. It seemed showing her the lights in the forest had helped some. But then, Sheila was not the sort to argue with Adlin during such a difficult time.

"It had to be unbelievably hard for her to leave," Sheila said softly, eyes on Adlin. "While I'm happy for you, I'm also very sorry."

"Many thanks, lass and whilst 'twas sad for her, that tapestry," he glanced at it, "Is a means for her to return to visit if she so desires. Her Da wouldnae have it any other way so requested it be weaved and hung before the birth of the wee bairn."

"That's wonderful." Sheila's eyes flickered between the tapestry and Adlin. "But obviously you raise the child in a different century. Why?"

"'Twas how Fionn Mac Cumhail said it must be. He didnae give a reason and I dinnae question a god."

"So your future self must've raised him," she said, expression troubled, sad for him.

"Aye," Adlin murmured. "And the people of this clan will only think that both mother and bairn didnae survive the birth. When I take you to the Defiance I will bring him to the future where I eagerly await to be reunited with my bairn."

"Wow," Sheila said. "Won't the clan wonder where your newborn came from?"

"Nay, 'twill be plenty of time for me to prepare so that it might all seem natural indeed."

Grant was going to leave it be but couldn't help but ask. "What of you and Meyla ensuring that my magic was part of hanging the Viking tapestry. Dinnae say it was otherwise, shaman."

"I willnae, lad." Adlin appeared a tad bit too innocent. "But did I not already speak of this to you in the future?"

"You spoke that I might have Meyla's sword, that it was necessary to my endeavor but never of why you might need my magic."

"Ah, well then you have my apologies." Adlin clasped his hands behind his back. "You see it was less the magic you were born with but more the black magic that became part of you beneath Keir Hamilton's rule."

Sheila shivered next to him. "Why would black magic be needed when hanging a Viking tapestry?"

Before Adlin could respond, Grant narrowed his eyes. "To keep those with similar magic from passing through or mayhap even to imprison such within."

"That doesn't seem right." Sheila frowned. "I'm new to magic but wouldn't black magic attract and even help someone with similar magic to travel through that tapestry?"

"Not if it was interwoven correctly with another type of magic altogether," Grant said. "Mayhap that of an immortal wizard or a Viking with dragon magic at his disposal."

A heavy weight settled in Grant's chest as all the missing pieces fell into place.

Though Adlin from the future had explained much he hadn't explained everything.

"We will travel soon." Adlin redirected the conversation. "You must return to your war with Keir Hamilton."

Grant met Bryce and Kenzie's eyes. That was about the last thing either wanted to do. "My clan will need us. Colin will need us."

"Colin MacLeod you mean." Sheila frowned. "That's not gonna go over real well with the MacLomain men."

"Nay, 'tis not," Grant allowed but said nothing more about it. One way or another, he'd see Keir dead and his best friend alongside all the other prisoners freed. No matter if it meant forfeiting his own life in exchange.

"Horses are already provisioned," Adlin said. "We leave soon."

The chieftain returned above stairs and they continued to eat. When Sheila only nibbled, Grant frowned. "You need to eat, lass. Gain your strength for what lies ahead."

"I'm not hungry."

But when his frown deepened, she nibbled on some bannock. The coming days would see nothing but strife and hardship. Grant didn't want her to fall prey to something as simple as starvation. He knew all too well what that looked and felt like.

They had little time to talk further before hooded cloaks were handed to them and Adlin reappeared with his bairn. The weather had abated very little as they swung onto their mounts and left the castle. Driving rain and mud under hooves made the going slow. But Grant knew the MacLomain laird kept his precious cargo well covered against his chest.

The traveling was not long before they arrived at what had to be the most inconspicuous Defiance amongst them. No higher than his knee, it was naught but a leaf strewn jut of rock in the middle of the forest.

After they dismounted, Adlin clucked his tongue and the horses trotted back toward the castle. "They need not suffer this weather."

Before he could mutter another word, Sheila embraced both him and the child. "Thank you for having us...for allowing us to be part of such an important part of MacLomain history."

Adlin looked at her fondly. "The pleasure has been all mine, lass. I look forward to seeing you once more in the years to come."

Sheila eyed him. "Any chance you'll give me a hint in the future that we met here?"

"You already lived those moments." Adlin arched a brow. "So you have your answer."

"Hey, it was worth a shot." She gave him one more quick embrace then stepped away. "One more thing, Adlin."

"Aye, lass."

"We've seen you off and on in various points in the future but the one person who most wants to meet you has yet to. Maybe you could cross his path at some point? He's currently the chieftain, Iain's son, so your great-grandson."

"What name does he go by?" Adlin asked, contemplating. "And how fares he ruling my clan?"

"His name is Colin and honestly, though he hasn't been in charge long, I think he's doing a great job."

"Then mayhap I will try to seek him out." Adlin eyed her with a twinkle in his eye. "And mayhap I'll request that he's put in such a position to begin with."

Sheila's brows shot up in delight and she nodded. "Well wouldn't that make perfect sense."

Adlin only winked.

Kenzie and Bryce thanked him before Adlin's attention turned to Grant. Though he might garner some frustration with the arch wizard, they gripped arms, hand to elbow.

There was nothing but fondness in Adlin's eyes when he said, "'Twas an honor to meet you, my lad. Never forget that you above all of my kin most impacted this clan. Your sacrifice, however unwilling, ensures that all of what has passed and what will come is possible. You have my utmost respect and thanks."

Grant pushed past bitter emotions and nodded.

The truth was he'd do it all again if it ultimately led to what he and Adlin hoped for.

They squeezed arms one final time then pulled away. When Adlin started chanting, Grant did the same. He took Sheila's hand as the world spun away and burning sugar filled his nostrils. Driving rain soon turned to snow and they stood not in the heart of the enemy but the heart of the MacLomain war party.

Before any could move toward him, William was there, words commanding as his eyes narrowed on several MacLomain warriors with swords already drawn. "Stand down! My long lost bairn brings a Broun lass as did he ensure Torra was returned safely."

Colin MacLomain wasn't far behind, his eyes sweeping over his men. "Our kin escapes the enemy and seeks to lend aid. We willnae strike him down for it."

Though their blades had lowered some beneath William's sharp order they were withdrawn completely beneath Colin's.

The laird's eyes turned to Grant. "Torra and Bradon explained much about your disappearance at the castle. You need not fear the MacLomain blade."

Grant nodded, keen eyes watching closely where every weapon was sheathed.

Bradon and Sheila's cousin's appeared.

"Shay!" Cadence exclaimed.

"It's about time you returned," Leslie grumbled.

The women embraced for a long moment before Cadence looked her over. "How are you?"

Sheila squeezed their hands. "I'm good. No worries."

Leslie's gaze flickered from Grant to Sheila and she murmured, "I'd say more than good."

Grant recognized her abilities as an empath. She likely sensed quite a bit from them.

"Kenzie." Bradon's eyes narrowed. "Is that you, lass?"

Kenzie cocked her head at his cousin. "As I live and breathe, Bradon MacLomain?"

Bradon shook his head, grinning as he scooped her into a quick embrace. "The last I saw you we were but bairns and I'd just stolen your basket!"

Leslie's surprised eyes turned their way. "This is the girl you and Grant stole the basket from the day he was taken?"

"Aye." Bradon looked from Kenzie to her brother. "And Bryce is it not?"

Bryce nodded and shook his hand.

Bradon's smile soon dropped as he glanced at Grant then back to them. "Though 'tis good to see you, I dinnae ken why you're here."

"Though 'twas not the same day, I wasnae the only one taken during that time," Grant said. "There were others from allied clans including Kenzie and Bryce."

Coira and Malcolm had just appeared.

Grant kept his hand close to the hilt of his blade when his brother's eyes narrowed on him.

"Bloody hell, 'tis hard to hear," Bradon murmured, concerned as he looked at Kenzie. "How fare ye, lass?"

"Happy to be amongst friends once more," she said, mustering a smile.

"Come sit by the fire and warm yourselves," Coira said, wrapping her arm around Kenzie's shoulders. When Bryce and Grant made no movement, her eyes went to them as well. "Please, all of you."

Tension blanketed their surroundings as he and Bryce followed. The MacLomain clan might've heeded their chieftain's orders, but their distrust ran deep. Malcolm's narrowed eyes remained on him and his hand hovered dangerously close to his weapon. Grant was surprised his sword hadn't been taken immediately. It seemed Colin wanted to make a statement. Had their positions been reversed, he would not have done the same.

Grant ignored his brother and turned his attention to Bradon. "How fares Torra?"

"Well enough." He nodded toward a tent. "Resting."

"I wish to see her," Grant said.

"Soon enough," William said. "First, let us sit and share words."

Furs replaced their cloaks and whiskey was given to all. Skins had been strung high, protecting the fire from the bulk of the wind and snow. This would be their final encampment before they met the MacLeod's and Hamilton's in battle. Grant had already cast his magic to figure out their numbers and was shocked. More allied clans had joined the MacLomain's than Keir had expected. If it wasn't for Colin MacLeod and the many warriors enslaved by Hamilton, he might have found this news favorable.

Colin motioned to his warriors that it was to be a meeting between few and all left save immediate kin and the Broun lasses. Yet as he looked at each of the Brouns by their men, Grant realized they were as much a part of this clan as any. Kenzie and Bryce sat to his right and Sheila to his left. As far as he was concerned, these three, Torra and Colin MacLeod were his only true kin.

"Tell us what happened when you returned to Keir's army." Colin locked eyes with Grant. "And how you managed to leave with three when you arrived with only Sheila."

Malcolm grumbled but said nothing.

"I went not with the intention of leaving so soon but maintaining Keir's trust so that I might better assist my brother-in-arms, Colin MacLeod." He didn't bother looking at his blood brother but felt the turbulent emotions barely kept in check. "As it turned out my

141

master…Keir, soon thwarted my plans. My only choice at that point was to stay and aid Colin or flee with Sheila."

He clenched his jaw. "I wouldnae have her imprisoned in that castle at the disposal of the Hamilton. And I knew if I left Bryce and Kenzie behind they would suffer at Keir's hands for my betrayal."

"What of my lass?" came a deep voice moments before another man appeared.

Grant eyed his Sinclair colors. This could only be King Alexander.

"Believe it or not she seemed just fine," Sheila intercepted. "Worried about you mostly."

But Alexander's eyes never left Grant's. "What know you of Keir's plans for her?"

Grant proceeded to share what they'd learned traveling back in time to the MacLomain castle. As he spoke, Sheila's hand slipped into his. A comforting gesture meant to soothe beneath such varied expressions. When finished, silence settled over all and he took a swig of whiskey.

Colin looked at Coira and William. "Did you know such about the Viking tapestry?"

They shook their heads. Coira spoke. "Nay. It wasnae part of the information Adlin imparted to me before he left but," she pointed out, "I did once fly into that tapestry to visit Fionn Mac Cumhail. When I did that Viking pointed the way to Ireland."

"So you MacLomain men are all more Viking than you thought." Leslie glanced at Malcolm. "That certainly explains you a whole lot better."

Sheila and Cadence chuckled despite Malcolm's frown.

Colin asked several more questions about their time there and Grant answered to the best of his ability. At last the chieftain muttered, "'Tis good that Adlin helps us as he does. I hope someday to meet him."

"I'm sure you will," Sheila said. "After all, he seems to be popping up everywhere."

Grant squeezed her hand. Little did Colin know that her very words likely put him in his current esteemed position.

Leslie, chin propped on her fist, continued to eye Grant and Sheila. "So I totally followed everything that happened when you traveled back in time to Adlin but I'm still a little confused about some things."

"Oh?" Sheila said, not quite looking her cousin in the eye.

Cadence watched Sheila closely as well when Leslie's lip quirked. "What happened to get you thrown into the Hamilton dungeons?"

The becoming stain of pink he'd come to adore spread over Sheila's cheeks and she shrugged. "Some words were exchanged."

Grant perked a brow at her but kept his silence.

Cadence's eyes narrowed a fraction. "What sort of words?"

"Binding words. Forced words." Sheila's jaw jutted out ever-so-slightly as her glance slid over everyone present. Grant's heart sunk. Then she pulled his hand into her lap and continued, "But words I wouldn't want to take back."

"Out with it, lass," Malcolm said, eyes dark.

Sheila nodded once. "All right then. Keir had us married so that it might anger all of you."

"*Us?*" Malcolm said, incredulous. "Keir married you then threw you in his dungeons?"

"Nay." Grant met his brother's eyes. "Keir had Sheila married to *me* then threw her in his dungeons."

A thunderous darkness entered Malcolm's eyes.

"I'll be damned," Leslie muttered.

"So the rumors are true…at least partly," Colin said.

"What rumors?" Bradon and Malcolm said simultaneously.

"I only just received word. 'Tis said the enemy was married to one of our lasses but 'tis also said Grant still leads his armies." His lips curled up. "'Tis good that last part is not true."

It came as no surprise that Keir would say such. He'd not have his warriors appear weakened and without one of their leaders. Grant ground his jaw. Leaving as he did would not have made things easy for Colin MacLeod in more ways than one. But if anyone understood the bone-deep need to protect love it was the MacLeod chieftain.

Which brought his thoughts to Torra.

He needed to see her soon and know that she was well.

"So I heard Sheila's thoughts on being married to you," Leslie said, shrewd eyes on Grant. "What about your thoughts about being married to her?"

Grant found it amusing that his lass-loving cousin had ended up with this one. But then her confrontational personality would likely always work toward keeping Bradon entertained.

"I wish to keep her," he stated bluntly.

"*Keep* her?" Leslie's brows lowered sharply. "You don't *keep* someone you marry."

"Well, depends on how you look at it," Sheila began.

"It doesn't depend on that at—"

"I meant to say I favor the union," Grant cut her off. "I verra much desire that Sheila remain my wife."

Cadence amongst a few others wore a look of relief. Grant suspected it had more to do with intercepting the lasses from a good bicker than anything else.

"'Tis good then that you share an agreeable bond," Coira said, warmth in her eyes.

"Aye, indeed," William said.

Grant still had trouble being around his parents. Some might say it was because he'd so recently been part of a battle that intended their death. But he was not in a state of denial. He'd done such a thing and could look them in the eye over that. Things had to happen as they did for everything to work. Nay, what ate at him had done so for a long time…that they had not tried hard enough to save him. Though he knew they'd thought him dead, it would take time to move past his troubled emotions.

And now, in light of what he'd learned when with Adlin, it had to happen anyways.

"How did you manage to free four of you from Keir's grasp?" Alexander asked. "Is Keir not more powerful than the lot of us?"

He wondered how long it would take for someone to ask such.

"I've learned to harness the power of the Defiances therefore bringing Kenzie and Bryce to Sheila's cell was easy enough. From there I could take only three with me so I used the glow of Sheila's ring and my mark."

As he knew would be the case this got a reaction from many.

Bradon grinned.

Malcolm frowned.

His parents gave knowing looks.

Leslie and Cadence smirked.

Sheila blushed furiously.

But none of their reactions mattered as the king's eyes narrowed on him. "You had a choice and you left behind the lass who Keir needs to enslave Torra for good? *My* lass."

All expressions dropped beneath the Sinclair's glower.

"Iosbail will be saved before the solstice comes," Grant said, not threatened in the least by the swelling rage in Alexander's eyes. "Had I left Sheila, Keir would have torn her physical form to shreds and cast her soul into eternal damnation. Leaving her behind was not an option."

Sheila pulled the fur tighter around her shoulders and frowned. "I should have stopped you...would have." Her sad eyes turned his way. "And I never asked why. He's right, you should have taken Iosbail. She's far more important."

"Aye," Alexander ground out.

"I don't think so," Leslie said.

"Right," Cadence agreed and frowned at Sheila.

"I would do it again if put in the same position." Grant encased Sheila's hand in his as he looked at her. "None are as important as you. At least not to me."

When Alexander stood, enraged, so too did Grant. Colin put a staying hand on the Sinclair's arm. Sheila on Grant's arm.

Bryce stood; hand on the hilt of his weapon.

Malcolm did the same, eying him.

"Ye thought with yer cock, not your head," the king ground out.

"Nay." Grant's fists clenched. "I thought with my heart."

Alexander wore a look of disgust. "Ye cannae have a heart left after fourteen winters beneath Keir's heavy hand."

"Not that long ago I might have agreed with you," Grant said. "Before I discovered 'tis possible because of my wee geal."

"Your wee what?" Leslie said.

"Geal, it means light within darkness," Sheila said.

Cadence put a hand over her heart. "Awe, that's so romantic."

"It really is," Leslie agreed.

"Enough!" Alexander frowned at them.

Coira stood, sighed and placed a gentle hand on Alexander's arm. "We cannae undo what is done. 'Tis clear that Grant has been acting in our best interest from the beginning. While we might not ken his reasoning as of yet," she looked at him, "'tis safe to say he will soon reveal it."

Grant and Alexander eyed one another for several more moments before the Sinclair reluctantly sat. "Then have at it."

There was only so much Grant could share at this point. As Adlin always said, the less people knew the better. "What should be understood before all else, is the creation of the rings and the mark. For without them defeating Keir would be impossible."

His eyes met Colin's. "Which of course leads us back to the beginning. If you had never sought out Adlin in the future but instead turned your attentions to McKayla, every last one of you would already be dead."

Chapter Twelve

Sheila listened avidly as Grant shed some light on too much confusion.

"Though I traveled through the Defiance to see Adlin I also, unbeknownst to him, once encountered his sister, Iosbail." His eyes went to the king. "'Twas soon after she met you."

Alexander said nothing, only waited.

"She spoke of an enemy so great he rivaled Adlin in power at the verra least."

The Sinclair frowned. "Innis MacGilleEathain of the Hebrides?"

"Nay, 'twas not the name given." Grant stared into the fire. "Somehow through this evil enemy she knew the Viking dragon bloodline would be reignited in Torra. It was she who knew of our Broun lasses and that they had to unite with us MacLomains in order to defeat this new threat. If not, we would fall beneath Keir's tyranny."

"But how would she know I'd seek Adlin and become distracted by McKayla?" Colin asked.

"Every MacLomain descendant of Adlin's eventually seeks him. She just pushed you along," Grant said. "From there it wasnae hard for your eyes to fall on your one true love, aye?"

"How did she push me along?" Colin asked, amazed.

For the first time since they'd arrived, the king offered a small grin. "How does Iosbail push anyone along? 'Tis an aggressive magic my lass has."

"As she knew it would," Grant continued, "such actions drew the eyes of Keir who had long been executing his plans when he took me. He needed my powers and the skills I would develop as a warrior."

William cursed under his breath. "So he knew about Torra even fourteen winters ago?"

"Aye."

"Then why not take her right away?" Malcolm said.

"I dinnae know," Grant said. "I watched his dark magic progress over the years so mayhap he didnae have nearly the strength then that he does now."

Bradon remained focused on his earlier words. "So Keir's tied in with this evil enemy she knows of?"

"Aye," Grant murmured. "She even knew of Seth who would play such a vital part in the creation of the rings and their connection to Torra. 'Twas Calum's dark magic that needed to be part of that."

"What's this about Calum?"

Sheila looked over her shoulder, shocked when Devin and Malcolm's Dire wolf joined them. "Devin, you're here!"

Devin grinned. "Aye, I couldn't help but stick around. Seth got in on the last adventure and I wasn't about to miss out on another." He ruffled the wolf's head. "I mean after all, with a pooch like Kynan along we're bound to kick ass."

"You're pretty brave hanging out with him," she acknowledged, then smiled. "But I'm glad you're still here to help. Thanks."

"No problem." His gaze slid to Grant. "Again, what's this about Calum?"

Grant eyed Kynan and Sheila swore he shook his head to keep him away. When her eyes met his she understood. He had no intention of making Malcolm feel as if the wolf didn't belong with him.

"Calum descends from Iosbail. Thus 'twas her Celtic blood merged with the warlock's black magic that would lend the power of the ring and marks. Torra alone couldnae have created such magic." Grant stared into the fire. "Then it took the physical love of the MacLomain/Broun connection to ignite the rings and marks which in turn ignited a powerful magic as well as Torra's scales when in dragon form."

"Why would Iosbail never have spoken to me about any of this?" Alexander said.

"I know naught but she didnae speak to her brother, Adlin about it either. He learned of this when we traveled back to the ninth century," Grant said. "I cannae tell you if all has gone as Iosbail wished thus far but there cannae be any doubt that she intended to be captured and brought to Keir's castle."

Coira's eyes narrowed slightly, her soft words aimed at Grant. "You knew all along I would try to give you that dagger upon our first meeting. A dagger given to Caitlin by Iain's sister Muriel to defend against a MacLeod. Though it certainly possessed her magic, it had been given to her by Iosbail before that." Her eyes met his across the fire. "A gift I promised to give you when old enough."

"Aye," Grant said. "One I knew Keir would turn on you or," he seemed to struggle with the word but said, "Da, when you arrived at the Hamilton castle."

"You urged Keir to banish William and Coira to the Hebrides, didn't you?" Sheila asked, stunned.

"Aye," Grant admitted. "I knew Colin had convinced Keir to banish his sister, Nessa there. 'Twas then just a matter of reminding my mast...Keir, that I had the ability to get you all there, most especially the horse."

"Soul Reader. Iosbail." Leslie shook her head. "You trapped her!"

When she went to stand, furious, Bradon took her hand and pulled her down onto his lap. "Easy, lass. Hear the lad out, aye?"

Darkness had fallen and snow whipped and twirled under the skin then over the fire as Grant continued. "Iosbail told me she'd be in that horse. She somehow even enlisted clan Sinclair's help beforehand to make sure her journey north with the MacLomain's continued."

"Naturally," the king said but there was pride in his eyes.

"That's when Soul Reader...I mean Iosbail, was brought along when we merged with the Sinclair's en route to the Hamilton castle the first time," Leslie said. "Why didn't Keir just take her then?"

"Because he needed her incarnate free of that horse," he reminded. "You didnae see her again after arriving, aye?"

"Well no," Leslie said, voice taking on an edge of sarcasm. "But I was pretty caught up in learning you were alive and then there was the huge fire breathing dragon overhead."

"Iosbail only sought to see the castle, to eye the dark overlord before she fled to the Hebrides. 'Twas important that she be there to help save whoever fell to her own dagger," Grant said to Leslie. "And truthfully, she's quite fond of you, lass and wanted to see you safe even if it meant leading you into the heart of the enemy."

Leslie gave a slow nod. "Yeah, I can see that." Her eyes turned to Alexander. "Hell of a woman."

"Aye," the Sinclair agreed. "She is." Alexander sighed. "One who has now put herself in a position where her enemy wants to feed her to the serpents of hell so that he might possess Torra at her fullest."

Silence once more fell as Grant's information sunk in. Adlin hadn't been kidding in the least when he'd said his sister had been one step ahead of him the entire time. How such a thing was possible had yet to be discovered.

William at last spoke, eyes on them. "Are you hungry then? Game is roasting at the next fire."

They shook their heads no.

"Do you need a break from all this?" Sheila said into Grant's mind.

When he responded 'aye, please' she looked at Colin. "I can't speak for Kenzie and Bryce but Grant and I are pretty wiped. Any chance there's a spare tent?"

"Aye, of course," Colin said.

"Goodnight everyone," she said, following Colin and Grant.

"G'night *newlywed*," Leslie chimed from behind her.

Sheila rolled her eyes but grinned. She was surprised when Colin led them to a tent larger than most with a fire burning inside.

"Compliments of Euphemia." Colin ushered them in. "The moment she knew you'd arrived she had this set up." Colin's voice grew soft. "She said nothing but the best for the lass who fought by her side in battle and for the lad who sent Malcolm a great beastie Dire wolf."

Sheila's heart warmed at the little cook's generosity. It was Euphemia who had told Malcolm that Grant had sent Kynan the wolf to protect him. And after she'd seen how Grant looked at Kynan when at the MacLomain's she didn't doubt it for a second. Yet she knew full well it hadn't been discussed between the brothers. She supposed they'd get around to it when they were ready...or perhaps not at all.

"Kenzie and Bryce will be housed as comfortably," Colin assured, glancing around their tent. He was about to leave but paused, his eyes going to Grant. "Thank you for releasing Torra from her dragon form and I suspect much more that we dinnae yet know of." He nodded, mouth firm but emotion evident in his words. "'Tis good to have you back amongst your brethren, cousin. You were sorely missed."

Grant nodded, eying his cousin. "Might I have a word with you alone?"

Colin nodded and they stepped outside. Little time passed before Grant returned.

"Is everything okay?" she asked.

"Aye," he said. "I thought it time I share with Colin what I knew of Keir's armies, including their strength and numbers."

"I'm surprised he didn't ask right away."

"The MacLomain's have had scouts out for days and have a good idea of what to expect," Grant said. "Colin would have eventually asked but was giving me time, most likely to see if I would volunteer the information."

That made sense. "Good that you did then."

Grant grunted. "'Tis no easy task giving ammunition to those who mean to kill your friends."

She didn't suppose it was. What a difficult and sad position to be in. Sheila watched him as he sat, braced his arms on bent knees and stared at the fire. Though he might be the youngest of the MacLomain men, he'd certainly carried the heaviest burden.

Gaze still to the fire, hand held out to her, he murmured, "Come sit with me, lass. I've a need for the sweet easiness of your company."

Though that could be taken a few different ways she knew he meant it as a compliment. His was a genuine request that she help him out from beneath the heavy weight of the conversation left behind. Crossing her legs beneath her, she sunk down beside him.

"I'm so sorry about all that out there," she began.

His tired eyes shot to her. "Nay, 'tis nothing for you to be sorry for. They but desire the reason behind my actions and further insight into all they've been through. I expected nothing less."

Sheila sipped from her whiskey and eyed the skin set by his side, opting for what he'd desired...simple conversation. "You don't seem to drink as much whiskey as the other Scotsmen I've met here."

"'Tis not for lack of enjoying it," Grant said. "'Twas something given to us rarely and well imbibed then to be sure. Mayhap when all of this is over I'll enjoy a good round of drinking. Until then, 'tis best not to let my mind fog too much."

"Understandable," she allowed. "Heck, I'd never even tasted whiskey until I traveled back to this time period."

His eyes rounded at her and a grin swiped away any chance at a frown. "No whiskey? Mayhap my plight wasnae so bad when compared to yours."

Sheila offered a lopsided grin and shook her head, feeling almost giddy. Or at least she supposed that must be the lighthearted, almost goofy feeling of happiness that washed over her. It was new and she liked it.

One arm wrapped around her shoulders and he urged her to rest her head against his shoulder, his deep voice soothing. "We're quite the pair. With you never having tasted whiskey and me pushing it away when I'm now free to drink it."

Sheila smiled. "Well, it's right up there with marrying the enemy I suppose."

She flinched. Now why had she said that? Stupid.

A chuckle started in his chest but fell flat. He cupped her cheek and made her look at him. "What you said was humorous, lass. What you just thought? Nay." His lips pulled down. "I dinnae like this word stupid and I ken well enough its meaning. Know that you are anything but."

When she went to apologize, he put a finger to her lips and shook his head. "And no more apologies either. You've naught to be sorry for in any of this. I tend to think you've naught to be sorry for in anything you've done in life."

Sheila nodded and he pulled his finger away. "I'll work on it. Takes time I guess."

"Aye," he murmured. His gaze lingered on her lips before they rose to her eyes. "We'll get there together, aye?"

"So it seems," she whispered, caught up in the intense assurance in his beautiful eyes.

"Come, straddle me," he urged. "I wish to talk with you against me."

Sheila shot him a coy look. "And do you really think we'll do much talking with me in that position?"

Grant grinned as he pulled her over him, pushed up her skirts and lowered her. "I think it cannae hurt to try."

A breathy sigh escaped her lips when he wrapped his arms around her lower back and made a slow roam of her face with his hungry regard. The equally eager erection pressing between her thighs didn't help any either.

"You know of me as a bairn. What of you?" he asked.

"Actually, I don't know of you as a bairn," Sheila said softly but determined. "Not with the MacLomains or with the Hamiltons."

For a second she thought he'd detour from the question based on the shadow that passed over his features but he didn't. "I remember little of my time with the MacLomains. Keir worked hard at pushing those memories away," he said, the words catching in his throat. "But what I do remember was verra good."

Sensing he was about to focus more on his years with Keir, she said, "Tell me what you do remember."

Grant paused and considered. As he shared, his gaze became unfocused, looking over her shoulder at memories only he could see. "I remember sunlight." A small grin hovered. "Coira…Ma, had just walked me through the armory. She urged me to pick out my favorite dagger so I did. 'Twas bonnie and sharp. Then I followed her out to the gardens beyond the courtyard." His words grew softer. "Her yellow skirts dragged over flowers nearly the same color but not quite. Only because the fabric was dimmed by the dry dirt on the summer ground."

"Did that bother you so much?" Sheila murmured.

"Aye," he said. "My Ma should never be soiled by dirt and I told her as much."

"And what'd she say?"

"She crouched in front of me, all surrounded by flowers and said, "'Tis of the Earth, lad. I am no dirtier than any of us. Do you think me less vibrant for it?' Grant shook his head as if in answer to a long gone question. "Nay I told her. 'Twas then that I realized beauty could be found in anything. Not just the flowers or a clean dress but in the dirt and rocks beneath my feet."

Sheila couldn't help but think how well Coira had prepared Grant for years of captivity. Did he even realize it? Was there more to it?

"And what of the dagger?" she asked.

A genuine smile met not only his lips but his eyes. "A magical one. You could cut flowers to give a lass, cut herbs to give to the kitchen, but always the plant would remain alive, its bloom to regrow."

"Enchanting," Sheila said. "Not to sound like Leslie but…why harvest at all when such a blade was at the MacLomain's disposal? It sounds like it could keep an herb garden alive for years and with equipment to match, no seed for grain would ever need to be planted."

"If it were only that simple," he said. "But magic doesnae work that way. It can drain away like any living thing and be without life, much like the Defiances. Can it be manipulated as I did? Aye. But what sort of life is that for something born of the Earth." Grant shook his head. "'Tis always best to let ground feed mouth, not magic."

"So what came of this blade?" Sheila asked.

A cloud of emotion drifted over Grant's face. "Keir tried to kill my Da with it."

"Oh Jesus," Sheila whispered. "I'm so," she started but stopped when his stern eyes swung to hers. So she rephrased. "That's terrible. No good memory deserves to turn into such a bad one."

Grant cupped her cheek. "'Tis not so bad if I still remember the good behind it, aye?"

"No," she whispered.

His eyes stayed locked on hers. "I dinnae want you to think I control what you say, lass. 'Tis simply my hope you'll want to say things that dinnae put yourself in a negative light." His thumb brushed over her lower lip. "'Tis my hope you'll need not worry over it as you'll soon see yourself that way regardless."

She smiled, enjoying the way the movement of her mouth pulled his calloused thumb across her lip. In response to the way it felt, sensation drilled down to her core and she breathed harshly against his finger. Grant's pupils flared and he pulled her tighter against him. "Tell me of when you were a bairn."

Sheila leaned her cheek into his palm. "Not yet. First give me a memory you have of William."

Grant appeared surprised by the request but didn't say no. Instead, he seemed to mull it over. Where there was a distant look in his eyes when he spoke of his memory of Coira, a smile shimmied over his face when he spoke of his father. "Being laird at the time, Da always kept a stern way about him…or at least he tried."

Sheila continued smiling. "I can see that."

"There was a sword practice that I never forgot." Grant pulled a dagger from his waist and held it up between them. "'Twas about the size of this that he had me battle with."

"Did he hold a real sword?"

"Aye!"

"I don't get it."

Grant shook his head. "It'd been the Christmastide games." He nodded toward something she couldn't see. "Outside in the courtyard. Snow was falling much like it does this eve. I'd fought and beat all put against me until the last. Yet even he I could have taken."

Sheila cocked her head. "Then why didn't you?"

"Because I broke the rules," Grant gave. "I saw his weakness so took it."

A chill ran through her. "How so?"

"He was short of stature, his arms half my length, so 'twas easy enough to pin them while running my blade through his shoulder."

She cringed. "Not nice."

"Nay, not when a warrior is upon the battlefield. You use whatever God gave you to advantage."

"And William didn't like that?"

"Nay, not entirely," Grant said. "My Da tends to work on a different level of thinking than most."

"Which I assume led you to fighting him with a dagger."

"Aye," Grant said. "I still remember the bite of the wind that eve, but more so his words as he handed me a dagger then braced to fight with a sword. 'If you've the means to take advantage of a lad's difference in size then might you feel the same with your dagger against my sword, might you become more aware of being at a disadvantage yourself."

Another telling shiver rippled through her.

"And did you take anything from that lesson?"

"Aye," he murmured. "That oftentimes men are at a disadvantage against me but not because they choose it. While there are times 'tis best to take advantage there are times when 'tis better to look past the warrior and see the lad beneath his battle ridden eyes. Often time's lives can be saved in such a manner."

"So he taught you to turn your enemy to your ally rather than take his life?"

"That he did and 'tis a lesson that has served me well over the years. One that Keir never thought to teach."

Again, she couldn't help but think that his parents had trained him well for his unfortunate future. But both claimed to know nothing of it. Still, what were the odds?

Grant tossed the dagger aside and gripped her waist. "'Tis time to hear of you, lass."

Though tempted, Sheila decided against prying into his childhood with the Hamilton clan. Obviously, it wasn't good.

"There's little to hear," she admitted. "As it turns out, when compared to my cousins, my life wasn't all that bad."

"Nay?"

Sheila shook her head. "No. McKayla's parents split up. That was hard. Leslie and Cadence's parents were never around. That was hard. But me? No, my parents stayed together. Despite the fighting and the hard years they never gave up."

"'Tis good this," he murmured. "But what of the fighting and hard years?"

"We got through it," she replied, surprised at the defensiveness in her voice.

His thumbs massaged her hipbones, not to arouse but to comfort. "You speak of 'we' when you speak of your parents. How old were you when you made their battles your own?"

"Young. But I never got involved in their fights...for the most part. What does it matter?" Sheila shook her head and tried to shift away but he held tight.

"'Twas not a question meant to discomfort, lass," he said softly.

"But it did," she said without thinking.

"Why?"

Sheila breathed through her nose and searched for calm. For whatever reason this conversation was making her as upset as Leslie's had about her ex. "I never caused any problems. I was quiet, even quieter during the years they fought."

"You were compliant."

"How would you know such a word," she muttered, eager to turn the conversation away.

"I've been in your mind and Adlin's," Grant provided. "Through such I've learned certain words pertaining to you, though I might not ken many."

Sheila looked skyward. Of course. "Yes, I suppose you could say I grew compliant."

"But never insecure," Grant said.

"No, never that."

"Then why let another convince you that you were stupid or less than desirable?"

A knot lodged in her throat and she shook her head.

"You wanted your parents to stay together so never interceded," Grant said softly. "'Twas no hard thing for your *ex* to take advantage of your softness, your compliance and form it to what he needed it to be."

Her heart caught, hurt. "I'm not that simple."

Grant wrapped his hand around the back of her neck and put his forehead against hers. "You mistake my meaning. It takes a caring, kind, loving lass to put another's needs before her own. You couldnae fix those difficult years between your parents so tried to be less troublesome in your own relationship. My guess is that your lad didnae much like himself so sought to demean you so that he might feel superior."

Though she wanted to push away, she didn't. No, she'd ride this one out. Jaw clenched, she said, "I loved my parents."

"I didnae say otherwise," he whispered.

Sheila was appalled when a tear hit his plaid. Blinking, she tried to pull back but he kept her close. He put one arm tight around her waist and wrapped his other hand into her hair, pressing her cheek against his chest.

Squeezing her eyes shut, she tried to fight the emotion coursing through her but it was impossible. Not with him holding her. Not with her facing old memories...newer memories. With a quick thrust, she wrapped her arms around him and held on. If tears fell, she didn't feel them. All she felt was the warmth of his chest against her cheek and the strength of him around her.

Minutes, hours, days might have passed as she faced old demons.

It was impossible to say if his words made her feel better or worse...but they made her feel something. When he laid her down and curled against her back, Sheila stared at the fire. She blinked, not surprised to discover moisture leaked from her eyes. Hell. Eyes squeezed shut she relaxed into his easy embrace. Again, it was hard to tell how much time passed as she drifted. When next she awoke, the wind howled and the fire was low.

Rolling over in his arms, she cuddled against Grant's front. When his arm again snaked around her lower back and pulled her tight against him, she sighed into the nook between his chest and jaw. He smelled of spruce and spice, a heady masculine musk. With another deep inhale, she flicked out her tongue and tasted the warmth and salt of his skin.

In response his large hand cupped her backside and pulled her tighter against him. A slippery tingle speared her core when his leg pushed between her thighs and pressed deep. Though it could be taken as a cuddle, her body thought otherwise. With a deep-seated groan she didn't recognize as her own, she ran her hand up beneath his tunic, relishing the feel of rock hard muscles.

"Sheila," he groaned and brought his mouth beneath her jaw, tongue teasing just below her ear as she arched.

Her lips opened seeking his but they were nowhere to be found. No, they were still busy suckling at her neck. A deep growl came from his chest when he flipped her beneath him and yanked her dress down, imprisoning her arms by her side. Fast, furious, he pulled one nipple then the other into his mouth. When she arched in pleasure, he grinned softly against the tender area between her breasts.

Though she might have thought she had escaped, she didn't. His mouth once more clamped over a deserted nipple while his hand dusted then stroked the other. He was quick to unclothe them before returning to her breasts. Moving into his touch, she moaned and squirmed but when he placed a gentle hand against her upper stomach, she calmed.

Light kisses dropped along the way, he trailed his lips up her neck and pressed his chest against hers. The feel of his muscled body so close made her legs jerk up. He buried his hands in her hair and ran his tongue up her neck while grinding his pelvis hard against hers.

Startled both by his ferocity and dominance, she bucked. In answer, he swung around so that she straddled him once more…except this time it wasn't to promote just intimacy but pure, unadulterated lust.

With a quick thrust, he wrapped his elbows beneath her kneecaps and moved her until she sat over his throbbing arousal. Hands braced on his shoulders, she panted. There was no other way to describe the way air broke from her lungs in sharp little bursts.

"What will you have of me," he ground out, his deep voice steeped in desire.

For a split second she nearly asked the same until his turbulent, needy eyes met hers and his muscles tensed. He was a restrained beast held back by nothing but her next order, desire…need.

Emboldened by the feel of his strong body beneath hers, she leaned down and offered a delicate kiss against his chest before whispering against his pent up flesh, "Give me your all. Don't hold back." When his hands came to her sides, wavering, unsure, she said, *"Please."*

Before she could blink, Sheila was slammed to her back. Wide grin on her face she went to push him away knowing all the while he'd take her in a whole new way, one that she'd never escape from. When he held her tight and fell between her legs, she reared up as he manipulated her tender flesh with his lips, tongue and fingers.

A tsunami of chills and gooseflesh broke out over her skin as her muscles tightened further and further, bracing for impact. Her body reacted so strongly to the mounting sensations she actually felt a flash of fear.

Then everything exploded.

Her pleasured sounds turned to a strangled cry, blending with the howl of the wind badgering the tent. Blood rushed through her so quickly that her vision momentarily dimmed before a thousand flickers of bright light danced around her.

Pounding throbs expanded from her center to the tips of her toes and fingers. Shallow breath turned to rapid gulps of air. As both deep sensation and emotion bathed her in bliss, she was vaguely aware of Grant peppering her hipbones and belly with gentle kisses.

When he flipped her onto her stomach and crawled over, his front to her back, she bit the corner of her lower lip. Sheila pressed her cheek into the soft fur beneath, still basking in endless ripples of pleasure. Brushing aside her hair, he kissed then gently nipped the side of her neck. His body brushed against hers, igniting nerve endings she didn't know she had over her upper and lower back. In reflex, she lifted her backside and pressed against his erection.

Instead of taking advantage of her offering, he trailed his tongue down her back so excruciatingly slow that she nearly wept. On and on it went, his tongue, teeth and lips exploring every last inch. All the while, the lasting ripples from her previous climax turned into renewed throbs of overwhelming need.

This time when she pushed up against him he allowed it. Hands on her hips, he pulled her backside up until her knees braced against the fur. When he trailed a feather-light finger from the back of her neck down her tailbone while pressing into her, she about came undone. Still so highly sensitized from before, shivers raked her while a delicious burning accompanied his slow progression. In no rush he took his time, seemingly savoring his slow journey forward.

At last he filled her completely, curling over her protectively, his breath close to her ear, his baritone words hoarse. "I would stay this way always if I could, lass."

Sheila murmured her agreement, or at least some sound came from her mouth. But it soon turned to a groan when he started to move. She fisted her hands by her head when his nimble fingers slipped around to her front and worked at the swollen flesh between her thighs. A tremble started in her legs and vibrated throughout her limbs.

Her mouth fell open and her heart hammered as his movement increased. When his hips rotated a fraction with each measured thrust she instinctually moved her backside in a counter-rhythm. Sweat slicked their bodies and the musky scent of their desire perfumed the air. When the first roll of orgasm took her she clenched her teeth and moaned into the fur.

Though his body quaked against hers, Grant didn't let go but nibbled along her shoulder blade until her intense throbs lessened some but not fully. When he moved again, it was with far more aggression. With deep, determined thrusts, he rode her so quickly that Sheila was shocked to feel another orgasm building.

When he locked up tight and roared his release, she soon followed.

Something about his strong body sinking against hers and his heart pounding against her back made her own release the most powerful yet. Still tucked inside her, he leaned them onto their sides and spooned her. It took a long time for her to drift down from the high peaks he'd sent her to.

Eventually, she pried open her heavy lids and smiled softly at the stone in her ring. It was actually the first time she'd truly taken a moment to enjoy it. That she was now officially connected to Torra through such a thing was remarkable and humbling. "Such a beautiful shade of silver."

"Aye," he murmured.

Her eyes had just drifted shut when Torra's whisper brushed her ear. "Sheila."

When she opened her eyes, Iosbail crouched in front of her. "Is it just a tree?"

Confused, she could only stare at her.

Then suddenly she was no longer in Grant's tent but back in the small tent she'd spent a night in with Malcolm. Though before he'd remained sitting on the opposite side, now he crouched with Kynan beside him. Both looked at the little pine she didn't want killed.

"'Tis just a tree," Malcolm muttered.

"Is it then?" Iosbail asked over her shoulder.

When Sheila once more glanced at the little pine it was gone, in its place the baby oak on the mountain. Wind buffeted her as the tent, Malcolm and Kynan vanished. Again she was seeing what she had that night at the MacLomain castle.

A vision.

Yet how was she on the mountain and beside a raging ocean at the same time?

Again Iosbail's voice asked, "Where are you?"

But then it changed and became Torra's.

And the vision repeated itself.

"Just run already! What are you afraid of?"

I won't. I can't.

"Now. Go! I'll not say it again."

Sheila looked between the dark clouds and the cool welcoming water. No, she thought, I can't do this. If it meant saving herself or saving the tree...

"Sheila, you're living, breathing. The tree? There is naught but embers in the branches."

But the tree was more than that.

More than her.

Fire started to roll along the rock, the grass, until it snaked her way. Petrified, she watched, aware but unmoving. I won't leave the tree! Determined, she ran into the flames, felt the pain and screamed.

And screamed.

Over and over.

"Sheila, wake up, lass."

It took a long moment for the vision to abate and her screams to die away.

When they did, she was no longer in Grant's tent but kneeling in front of Torra.

Chapter Thirteen

Grant couldn't get to Sheila fast enough.

How had she managed to leave without him knowing?

Her screams led him amongst many others to Torra's tent. Heart in his throat, her wails had just died off when he entered. Grant dropped to his knees, pulled her into his arms and yanked a fur around her as Colin, Malcolm and Bradon entered, weapons drawn.

Torra shook her head in their direction and put a comforting hand on Sheila's arm. "'Tis all right. She was but having a vision."

Weapons sheathed, Bradon murmured to whoever was outside the tent.

"Let us by," Leslie said and entered with Cadence.

Malcolm tossed Grant a plaid and muttered, "Bloody hell, cover yourself."

Grant didn't care in the least that he wore no clothes. Still, he yanked it around him as best he could when Sheila's cousins crouched on either side, faces etched with concern.

"What happened, honey?" Leslie asked

Cadence stroked Sheila's hair. "It's okay, sweetie."

Though Sheila continued to tremble, her breathing had evened some as she stared at Torra. Voice wobbly, she recounted what she saw. "I don't understand what it means but I feel like it's meant more for you than me."

Torra appeared troubled. "'Tis an ill thing that tree burning."

Leslie frowned at Torra. "I told you about my experience inside Adlin MacLomain's mind. My vision of you and that tree except you were in dragon form and breathing fire down on it…and me. Sort of an odd coincidence, don't you think?"

Torra's eyes flitted over the men then back to Sheila. "I cannae tell you how sorry I am that you're seeing such." She released a heavy sigh. "I need to get to that tree."

"Nay." Colin shook his head. "We're on the brink of war. The solstice is tomorrow. We cannae risk you being beyond the safety of your clan."

"I willnae have Iosbail sacrificed so that Keir might have me," she whispered.

Grant narrowed his eyes. "Dinnae even think it, lass."

Sheila shook her head. "No, don't. Please."

"Think what?" Leslie asked.

"She means to bargain with Keir," Malcolm growled.

"Nay," Bradon said. "'Tis foolish that."

"Keir doesnae make bargains," Grant said. "'Twould mean death to both you and Iosbail."

When he saw the firm set of her jaw he shook his head. "She didnae put herself in such a position so that it might all be for naught. If Keir possesses the whole of you he will be nearly indestructible."

"Nearly," Torra said softly. "But not completely."

Grant had never been so upset. After all this his cousin thought to give Keir what he'd so long sought. If that wasn't heartbreaking enough, he cringed to think of how Colin MacLeod would suffer beneath such a thing. Though rumor had it that Colin was able to visit the other half of Torra's soul at the Hamilton castle, he knew better. Keir would never allow such a thing. Nobody could get near her.

"You are weakened," he murmured. "You are not thinking clearly."

"That is where you are wrong, cousin," Torra said. "I have never thought *more* clearly."

"What of Colin MacLeod then?" Leslie pressed the heel of her palm against her forehead. "I can feel your emotions, Torra. Is he really that important that you'd risk yourself to be near him again?"

Grim, Grant closed his eyes for a long moment then opened them to the torture flickering in Torra's luminescent eyes. "'Twill be no future for you and Colin if you go to Keir. 'Twould be a disservice to my friend if you do such."

"And how do you think Colin fares now?" she said, pained. "Though Keir doesnae suspect him of betrayal the overlord continues to work the dark magic in that tattoo on his arm. I feel the draw of it as surely as I feel my heart beat in my chest. And for all that it calls me to Colin it does tenfold for him." Her eyes glistened. "Things cannae go on like this anymore."

"And they willnae," Malcolm said. "We soon fight his armies then will take his castle and the man himself."

"Now that all rings and marks are ignited, we stand a verra good chance at victory." Grant's eyes pled with her. "And well you know it, lass."

"Aye," Colin agreed. "Meanwhile, you will stay safely in this encampment so that we might reunite your soul once the threat is extinguished."

When Torra made to reply, he shook his head sharply. "That is not a request, sister, but an order." Then his expression softened. "I will always be partly to blame for this and after having left you for three winters I intend to make things right, to be the brother who vowed to protect you."

Colin nodded for Malcolm and Bradon to follow and left.

Leslie and Cadence continued to look at Sheila concerned.

"Are you okay now?" Cadence asked.

Sheila nodded. "Yeah, I'm good. Go get some rest."

"No need. It's morning," Leslie said.

"Wow, really?" Sheila shifted on Grant's lap. "I'd swear I just drifted off when this happened."

Leslie squeezed her hand with a quirk of her lip. "Sometimes the night can get away from us."

Grant didn't need to see Sheila's face to know she blushed.

"Come on, Les," Cadence said. "There's a lot to do."

When alone with Sheila and Torra, he once more focused on his cousin. "We both know you've the power to do what you wish. None here could stop you. I beg once more that you lose this foolish line of thinking. 'Twas never our plan that you might do such."

"Nor was it my plan to love Colin so deeply," she said softly. Her eyes went from Sheila's to his. "What might you be capable of doing for love?"

Anything.

Everything.

But his cousin was far too important and had been through so much already. "I owe you my freedom and quite possibly my life, Torra. If you remain determined to do this thing I will see you to the tree and even back into the heart of the beast. But I would wish against it. Whilst you think to save Iosbail and once again be near Colin, you sacrifice many more than that. If you do this, Keir will be more mighty than he already is and any hope that all the warriors and those enslaved beneath his rule will ever see freedom becomes naught. They'd but see endless cruelty freed only by death."

Torra's eyes dropped and her lips drew down further.

Sheila took her hand. "We're going to wipe out Keir. Don't doubt it for a second. Before all of this is said and done, you and Colin will be together."

Torra's sad gaze rose to Sheila. "Many thanks, lass. Might the gods see it such."

"They will," Sheila assured, saying nothing about the one God. "There's too much goodness surrounding the MacLomain clan for it to be any other way."

A small smile met Torra's lips but not her eyes. "Aye, lass. There is indeed." Her eyes went to his. "Go get dressed. I will meet you at the fire to break our fast."

Grant knew she would. And if she didn't he'd follow her to hell and back.

After he helped Sheila to her feet, he wrapped his plaid then pulled the fur more securely around her. Crouching once more, he cupped Torra's cheek and met her eyes. "I will see you at the fire then I will see Keir defeated, aye?"

Torra put her hand over his, voice tender. "Aye, cousin."

Yet he felt the unrest in what remained of her soul and could only imagine what the part imprisoned by Keir felt. Grant pressed his lips against her forehead then stood. When Sheila made to leave the tent he shook his head and lifted her into his arms.

"I can walk just fine," she said.

"Through the snow with no boots? Nay," he scoffed.

"What about you then?" She peered down. "You've barely a thing on."

"Och, I'm a highlander. Born for such weather."

By the time he set her down in their tent a light layer of snow covered them both. He made a project of dusting it off, taking his time touching her. Carnal thoughts of the eve before surfaced and burned a path down to his groin. Soft, willing, she'd laid herself out for him. Her silky skin had tasted so good, warm, pliant, and sweet.

If there was a Heaven on Earth, he'd found it in her arms.

166

"I'm worried about her," Sheila murmured, her eyelids drifting as his hands skimmed the sides of her fur covered breasts.

"You'll never meet a stronger lass," he said. "She just wars with her heart right now."

"And that's what worries me the most."

His eyes met hers. "Why?"

Sheila placed her hand over his heart, bonnie blue eyes serious. "Because while we think with our heads, our hearts always win. If you imagine for a second hers won't, you're wrong."

Grant put his hand over hers. "Might it be that her heart wins then," he whispered. But he understood her greater distress. "Between the MacLomains and me, and most especially Colin MacLeod, we'll see her freed from all of this."

Though his lass nodded he felt her doubt. He cupped her cheeks and kept his eyes locked with hers. "We *will* see this through and triumph."

"If she ends up fleeing for the tree or even if you escort her there you better bring me." Her hand curled as if she sought to hold his heart. "Promise me, Grant."

He'd never leave her behind if he didn't have to. As to a journey to the tree, aye, he could oblige such. But as to where the tree might lead beyond that she would not go. "I promise, lass."

Yet his guileless, trusting Sheila was gone. In her place, a lass who clearly saw what lacked in her question to begin with. "Anywhere you go, take me. Let me help."

"I will take you so far as I know the outcome and no further," he said. "Though I'll admit there is uncertainty around the tree, there exists absolute certainty if you once more end up in Keir's hands 'twill not end well."

"No more than it will for you," she countered and frowned. "Don't go back to that castle while Keir's still alive."

"Nay," he murmured and brushed his lips over hers. "I willnae lest alongside my kin in battle."

Her lips pressed against his, then she whispered, "You lie. You'd do anything to save Torra, Colin and those enslaved by Keir." Sheila sat and pulled him down with her. "I want to know what happened to you when you were with Keir."

When he shook his head, she gripped his cheeks. "Not all, just some."

Coldness settled over him. "Nay, lass."

"Aye," she murmured in the way of the Scots. "Please."

He'd not said a word but already his heart pounded. While bits and pieces of freedom had slowly drizzled around him since leaving Keir, he'd not dared to put into words how he felt. He couldn't help but think that if he did it would bring the blade down upon his neck and somehow make all of this a dream.

"Please," she prompted softly.

Grant swallowed, eyes vacant as he finally relented to sharing some of his shaded past. "The first few years I didnae see beyond the dungeons. On rare occasion, a storm would shift wind and come in from the east. Those were the best days." He closed his eyes. "I would build my muscles hours on end so that when the winds came I could jump and hold myself up to the bars if only to feel the salted wind upon my face." He licked his lips. "The taste." He inhaled. "The scent... 'twas like nothing else."

With a deep release of breath he said, "Long after the storm had passed and the disagreeable wind was once more westbound, I'd give into my shaking limbs and sink to the dirt."

Sheila's eyes stayed true on his. Though there was compassion there was also strength. "Then what?"

"Then I grew angry," he admitted. "Each and every time it happened and all the in-betweens I never once let go of my wrath. I would *not* become what Keir wanted. I would *not* grow weak."

Sheila waited patiently as he sifted through old memories.

"I was thirteen winters of age when my bars first opened, when I was walked up to the courtyard for the first time." He closed his eyes. "Though I might have hated Keir, I never loved a courtyard more. It was my first taste of freedom in far too long."

Grant tilted back his head, remembering. "There is nothing like the sun on your face when too long absent. Whilst I might have thought God abandoned me I knew 'twas not the case when those first few heated rays met my skin. Nay, he'd always been there just...as lost as I, both of us unable to find one another."

Grant hesitated but a moment. "Once I felt the strength of Him fill me, I knew all would be well." His gaze fell to the small embers left by the fire. "To this day I dinnae know the methods behind Keir giving me such freedom but he gained favor when he did. I never wanted to go so long without the sun on my face again. So while I detested him for all he'd done I also strove to prove worthy of him."

He paused, remembering, before he continued. "The lessons he started to teach me were a far cry from those Da tried to impart. Where William taught mercy, Keir taught the opposite. Dinnae hold back. If ye see a weakness, grab hold and defeat. No battle is won by softness, only by ridding oneself of emotion and winning." A metallic taste filled his mouth, one he recognized too well. "If ye cannae taste the blood on yer tongue then dinnae bother holding the blade in yer hand. Kill or be killed. Always defeat those who stand in yer way or try to take yer life because they are unworthy."

Sheila said nothing but held his hand, urging him to continue.

And for some reason he did.

"So I became everything Keir wanted. Cold, bloodthirsty and through his praise, I strove for greatness. My world became my master and how I might please him. The only thing that spoke to me of hardship was Kenzie, a girl caught in a memory of good times and a simple basket." Grant felt strengthened by thought. "And her brother, Bryce. Though of Malcolm's age it didnae much matter. When thrust together we became brothers. I trained him in warfare and through such we moved forward, both finding our places in Keir's armies, friends always."

"And what of Colin MacLeod?" Sheila said.

It felt as though the weight of a pine tree had been placed on his chest at the question. "I never hated a lad so much upon first sight."

Again, Sheila gave no response but her hand remained in his.

"I first met him four winters ago. After years of training beneath Keir's guidance I had finally earned the prestigious title of first-in-command of his armies. What I didnae realize is that he didnae intend me to lead his armies but have another do such…Colin."

Grant ground his jaw, immersed in old bitterness. "I'll never forget the first time I saw him. Angered and defiant as I once was with Keir, this highlander enjoyed the freedom of no shackles. Nay, he walked into our encampment in a clean MacLeod tartan with nothing but fire in his eyes."

Grant shook his head. "I nearly said, "What foolery is this?" but bit my tongue. After all I was but a slave given rule over his armies. Nothing more. While Keir might have enjoyed my defiance it might have also gone the opposite way." Grant clenched his fists, eyes narrowed on the past. "So I said nothing as Colin roared and seethed at all that he might lead us, that none knew warfare as he did." Grant gripped Sheila's hand and spoke through his teeth. "But like me he was pent up, furious, lost, ripped from all that he knew, made to betray his clan."

"I know," she said softly. "I know, Grant."

But her words were far away as he reflected.

"'Twas a long time before I finally spoke to Colin without Keir overseeing and even then it was strained. We hated each other for the positions we were thrust into, more so because we knew there was greater comfort in being favored by our master. So we fought and battled over the next year, his position always greater than mine," Grant said. "Until the day it wasnae."

Sheila looked into his eyes but he only saw that day so long ago.

"We were sparring. The sun was nearly set and at a good angle to use against one's enemies. Colin was a strong fighter, the best, but not as good as me. Or at least I thought as much. 'Tis hard to know." Grant's lips curled up. "We'd been made to spar against one another once more. Yet this time was different."

"Why?" she asked.

Grant grinned, remembering. "There was a new fire in his eyes, not one made of magic but something else entirely. He was so enraged I was forced to battle as I never have. 'Tis no easy thing to fight the MacLeod when he's upset." He chuckled. "But fight him I did. There was a new heaviness in the slash of his blade. One I thought nothing of as we gave all a good show."

"No doubt," she muttered. "I've seen you both fight. I can only imagine how intense it'd be if against one another."

Grant again grinned beneath the memory. "'Twas not a thing for me to be defeated, even during swordplay. I'd come too far and sacrificed too much."

Eyes closed, he felt the crash of their blades. Opening his eyes, he bared teeth. "I would see Colin defeated as easily as any other. *I* had been trained beneath Keir. *He* had not. And for some reason, with his added fury coming at me, I was determined that would be the day I'd show all which of us was better."

Sweat once more beaded on his brow and Grant couldn't help but relish a fight long past. "'Twas a battle well fought and mine to own." Grant clenched his fist as though his blade were still in hand.

"I fought him until his blade was against my neck and his words venomous and close to my ear."

"And what did he say?"

Grant looked to the past then to her, a grin still on his face. "That he would see every Hamilton dead so that Torra might one day be his."

She swallowed hard, the movement of her delicate throat muscles drawing his eyes. Grant longed to once more put his lips against her skin.

"And how did you respond?"

Grant shrugged, just as he had when Colin's sword was at his throat. "I told him he was a bloody fool and if he went near my kin I'd see him done for."

"I'll bet," she murmured. "So did he tell you he'd been traveling through the Defiance to see her?"

"Not right then, nay," Grant said. "But because of his words I managed to flip him and deal the final blow. Never was there a better win. Yet soon after I sought him out so that I might further ken his knowledge of Torra. 'Twas that eve that I learned that another lad existed within the warrior I'd come to think of as my enemy."

Grant threaded their fingers together as he continued. "Colin told me of Keir's part in his wounded fate and how he only sought to protect Torra. How much he loved her. 'Twas he who first showed me the Defiance. One that he could no longer travel through but mayhap I could."

"But didn't Keir follow all of this through his mental connection with you?"

"Nay," he said, fingering the pentacle around his neck. "For Adlin had ensured I received this via Colin. Until your mental connection with me I thought its sole power lie in speaking with Colin undetected and traveling back in time to see Adlin himself. 'Tis uncanny still that Keir didnae see the pentacle as a threat. It says much of Adlin's powers."

"Tricky wizard." She shook her head. "But if you had the ability to travel through the Defiance why not travel to the MacLomains? Why not escape?"

"Because I wouldnae leave my friends behind," he reminded. "And as I learned more about Torra and why Keir truly wanted her it became clear that I would better serve my kin if I stayed amongst the enemy."

"Crazy," she whispered but squeezed his hand. "But amazing of you." Sheila pursed her lips. "It was pretty intense being there the first time Torra and Colin met. Did he ever tell you *how* he came to be there?"

"Nay, never. I assumed they'd first come together at the MacLomain castle."

"Well, nothing says it still wasn't that way," she said. "Seeing how he can manipulate fire and be just about anywhere he wants."

"To an extent," he murmured, stroking her cheek, caught as always by its soft texture. Tired of talk, Grant ended the conversation when he kissed her long and thoroughly.

Caught in the feel of her body, aware that there stood a good chance he'd not have her like this again, he brought her to the furs. He didn't care if the others ate by the fire or even if Torra fled, he'd feel the pleasure of his lass one more time. Wasting no time, he pushed the fur up and his plaid aside and pressed between her spread thighs.

Sheila gasped against his lips.

There was nothing easy or slow about his taking of her this time. Arms braced on either side of her head he thrust deep, fast, his lust consuming. Her chest arched and her head fell back. Just as ambitious, she met his thrusts and rolled her hips. Growling deep in his chest, he nipped her lower lip on one thrust then the side of her neck with the next.

When her legs wrapped high and tight around his back, his thrusts became frantic, nearly involuntary. He could barely remember ever having taken a woman simply for his pleasure alone but now found himself in just such a position. Hungry, ravenous, he took and took and took, driving against her.

Sheila might've gasped, moaned or even cried out but he heard nothing but the slam of his heartbeat in his ears and the unabashed need to free himself within her. When he felt the sharp pull in his groin and the whiplash of his muscles, he buried his face in her neck and cried out. She whimpered and her delicate body shuddered beneath his.

Her muscles clamped him so tightly that the last of his breath escaped. *Bloody hell.* Pressing his cheek against hers, he reveled in the feel of what she'd given him and whispered, "If ever you find me not by your side know that I'll once more find you."

Rolling her against his side, he stroked her hair, more content than he'd ever been. Grant thought of how she'd pulled from him old abandoned memories of his time with his parents. She'd made him recall things well worth remembering. Somehow, through those memories, he found not necessarily forgiveness but mayhap the start of it.

There had been a time when he was happy.

Now, through her, he'd found such again.

If so much uncertainty didn't lay in their future, he'd revel in it. But it did. So he couldn't...at least not for long. When she kissed him softly, he smiled. Another thing he'd not done much of in the past fourteen winters. Smiled. For that alone he wished he had the power to give her everything she ever could desire.

"We should join everyone for breakfast," she murmured into his neck.

"Aye," he said though it was the last thing he wanted to do.

Nay, if he had his way, they'd make this tent their home and be done with all else. But Sheila soon stood and commenced dressing. All the while he watched her. He liked her slender back and the way her small waist flared out to the heart shape of her arse. Though not muscular, her legs were trim. But most especially, he liked how freckles managed to scatter here and there over her body. Her cheeks, arms, upper chest, even some points on her thighs. If he could lick them off, he knew they'd melt on his tongue.

"C'mon," she murmured, her knowing eyes crawling down the length of him as she secured her dress. "Time to join the others."

Grant sat up, grabbed her hand and pulled her down for another long kiss. Yet before either could sink too far into rekindled passion, he stood and brought her up with him. Pulling on a tunic, he said, "'Tis a shame. I'd rather stay here with you than eat."

As she helped him rewrap his plaid, her humored words warmed him. "I couldn't agree more but you're needed and where you go I go."

When both were ready he again cupped her cheeks. Touching her face was at the top of his most favored things to do. "All of this will end well, Sheila and if it doesnae know—"

Finger to his lips, she shook her head. "Don't even. This *will* go well and we'll have our HEA."

He frowned. "I dinnae ken."

Sheila gave a small smile. "Sorry, too much time spent around writers and such." She brushed her warm lips over his. "It means, happily ever after."

"After what?"

"This." She chuckled. "After all the bad things that happen in a story, things usually turn out all right, setting aside Romeo and Juliet and a slew of others."

He'd been in her mind but knew nothing of this. "Are these friends of yours who need saving? Mayhap after we've defeated Keir, I'll set to task."

She again chuckled. "There's no saving Romeo and Juliet, sweetie. They're fictional characters."

"With a bad ending," he confirmed.

"The worst," she assured. "But let it go. We're *so* not that tale."

"Nay," he said. "'Twill be no bad ending for us."

Or at least he prayed as much.

They pulled on boots, drew furs over their shoulders and stepped out. Morning light was dim as snow continued to fall coating the woodland in pale gray and dull white. Even the pines slumped beneath the cumbersome weight. Heavy, wet, this snow would make battling especially difficult.

"Well, look at that. Yet another MacLomain!"

Grant didn't recognize the tall, red-headed lass who stood when they approached the fire.

Head shaking, she planted her hands on her hips. "Ye dinnae recognize me, Grant?" She strode around the fire and came face to face. "Who first put a blade in yer hand, lad? And me, from the future such as I was!"

As if it were yesterday, he remembered a girl a few inches taller than him pressing a dagger into his hand and challenging him to use it. As fierce at ten winters as she was now, it could be none other. "Ilisa?"

A grin crawled onto her face and she notched her chin. "Aye! 'Tis me, lad."

Grant had seen her at the Hamilton castle, had fought against her, so couldn't imagine why she put on such a display of affection.

174

Guarded, he kept his voice low. "Aye, I see that now. But last we met 'twas on different terms, was it not?"

"Aye, different." Her clever regard sized him up. "But rumor has it ye've a grand plan and all happened as it should have." Her eyes narrowed. "If I've the wrong o' it say it now so that all might hear."

Though loud spoken at ten winters of age he understood why she was especially so at this moment. She meant to carve a path for him within the clan. He'd liked her then when gangly and rebellious and liked her more so now. But then, some things didn't change.

"Ye've the right o' it, lass, I've a grand plan with nothing but my clan, the MacLomains seeing favor from it," he said.

"Aye." Her eyes locked on his. "It could be no other way."

Before he could utter another word, she flung her arm around his shoulders and turned him toward the fire, toward all who were his immediate kin. But her gesture and words were seen by men huddled at nearby fires so that their observations might spread far and wide. "My cousin has returned. Fierce as a bairn," she patted his abdomen, the core of his strength, "and just as fierce full grown. With him by our side, with his knowledge of the soon defeated enemy, we cannae see anything but victory!"

Though those around their campfire remained silent, men beyond murmured then hollered, "Aye!" and "Bloody hell, right!" through the forest, the sound echoing until the cries were too far off to hear.

Colin raised his skin and roared. "Again to victory!"

All raised their skins and yelled the same. Slowly but surely, men around campfires followed suit, the sound carrying on and on. Ilisa banged her dagger against her shield and laughed. Sure as could be, the sound was hammered fire by fire until the forest of MacLomains and allied clans did the same.

Ilisa, wide grin on her face, plunked down next to a dark haired man and knocked shoulders with him. "This is my lad, Shamus." She nodded at the fire. "Come, sit, join us before we go to war."

Grant nodded his thanks and was about to sit when two more men appeared.

One he recognized as Ilisa's Da, Arthur. The other took longer to place but was no doubt immediate brethren based not only on appearance but the tightly restrained magic fluctuating around him. Magic much like Colin MacLeod's.

This could only be Ferchar.

Arthur didn't greet Grant as exuberantly as his daughter but he patted him on the shoulder and nodded. "'Tis good to have you on the right side of this war, lad."

It didn't overly surprise him that Ferchar merely eyed him. Though he remembered him vaguely he didn't stand out in Grant's memory as Arthur did. Both lived in the future now but had visited often in his youth. While Arthur had typically been boisterous and smiling, Ferchar had been a different sort altogether. However, having befriended Colin MacLeod for years he could better ken his brethren's cool indifference. Not only was it of his nature but of his magic.

The men shook hands with the others then joined them by the fire.

All were here but Malcolm. Grant suspected his brother had not changed in his pre-battle habits. Even when young he'd separated himself from the crowd so that he might better eye the oncoming threats.

Grant was relieved to see Torra. Her eyes met his and she nodded. At least for now she would not flee.

Coira handed him and Sheila some meat. "Please. Eat."

Grant took the meat from her and for the first time in far too long locked eyes with his Ma. His thoughts went instantly to when he was a bairn. How she crouched before him in the flowers. He was surprised to suddenly feel a genuine spark of tenderness toward her. It was an odd, jarring feeling and he knew she felt it by the way her startled eyes met his.

"Grant. My wee bairn."

He nearly pulled his hand back but Sheila's grip came around his wrist, her words soft within his mind. *"Take the food, sweetie. It's a good first step."*

Though he hesitated, in the end he would always be unable to deny Sheila anything. Taking the food, he nodded his thanks before turning his gaze to the fire.

But just beyond that fire were William's eyes. Though he struggled to do otherwise, his gaze and turbulent emotions soon traveled beyond the flames and entangled with his Da's. In his eyes he found sternness at the front but so much more beneath.

Regret.

Need for redemption.

Love.

Grant quickly returned his attention to the fire, set aside his drink and ate. He wasn't a fan of the weighty emotions determined to push past his long erected mental wall. Honestly, such sentiment had no part in any of this. Nothing but defeating Keir and saving the others should weigh on his mind. To allow weaker thoughts right now was dangerous. As if to confirm such, a fiery arrowed whizzed through the stormy twilight and thunked against the tree just above King Alexander's head.

Nobody overreacted. Nay, this arrow had traveled far via magic.

With a flick of the Sinclair's hand the fire doused.

His eyes narrowed.

Something was attached.

Pulling the long swath of bloody hair free, Alexander's expression turned thunderous.

"Bloody hell, 'tis Iosbail's!"

Chapter Fourteen

Sheila fully expected the forest to break into pandemonium.

But it didn't.

Instead, Alexander tossed the arrow into the fire with a look of disgust then tucked Iosbail's hair into his plaid. His eyes shot to Colin, voice surprisingly calm. "'Tis time then."

Malcolm, Devin and the wolf appeared. It seemed since her warlock friend had traveled back in time, he'd spent the majority of his time with Kynan.

"They initiate war as we knew they would," Malcolm said with a thin grin of malice. "A few wizards and warriors at the front. The bulk of the army not far behind."

"What of our men?" Colin said.

"All in position." Malcolm glanced at his wolf. "Kynan and Devin leave now. We should do the same."

The downfall to having been with Grant was that she knew nothing of what the MacLomain's had planned. Yet whatever it was had been well thought out or so said the organized, unrushed movements of the clan.

"I'll see that Grant stays by my side," Torra said. "If and when Colin MacLeod comes 'twould be best that someone who kens his training protects me."

"Aye," the MacLomain laird agreed. "And I'll have you both in the center of the clan. While some of our warriors seek to flank them I dinnae doubt they attempt to do the same to us."

Sheila didn't miss the look exchanged between Grant and Torra. The conversation only she'd been privileged to was worrisome. Would Torra ultimately try to go to the tree to save Iosbail? To say she wasn't tempted to forewarn the MacLomains would be a lie. They had already gone to hell and back to try to ensure Torra's freedom. The thought that it might all be pointless in the end didn't seem fair to any party involved.

Yet she hadn't said a word.

The truth was though he'd not asked it of her, she wouldn't betray Grant. He'd sacrificed so much and she had full faith that he would always put the MacLomains first. If he chose not to tell them about this new development then neither would she. But that wasn't the only reason she remained silent. No, not at all. Sheila wasn't such a fool that she didn't recognize that there was another whole reason entirely.

She was falling in love.

Or at least she suspected that's what this feeling was. Deep and consuming, it was so entirely different than anything she'd ever felt. An easy happiness was developing despite their unfortunate circumstances. Even within the darkness of their slowly unraveling shaded pasts, she felt snippets of joy surface. As she glanced at Grant, Sheila couldn't help but wonder if he felt it too.

Colin and the others stood. The chieftain managed to lock eyes with all as he spoke. "'Tis time that we put our plan in motion. Stay strong and fight well. Might it be that when we next meet 'twill be over the dead bodies of our enemies."

Then he walked in a circle around the fire, eyes to the warriors far beyond and sword thrust in the air as he cried, "*Ne parkas nec spemas!*"

Grant's voice entered her mind. "*'Tis the clan's war cry. Neither spare nor dispose.*"

As far as the eye could see, warrior's thrust their blades into the air and repeated, "*Ne parkas nec spemas!*"

Then most mounted their horses and raced north.

The next generation of MacLomain men strapped on their weapons, eyes eager for battle.

Devin grinned and winked at Sheila. "See you after the war."

Then he and Kynan were off.

"Where are they going?" Sheila asked Malcolm but he'd already turned his attention to Cadence. Not about to interrupt their intimate exchange, her eyes went to Grant in question.

Grant's eyes only narrowed on Devin's retreating form. "He chooses to fight both as warlock and wolf."

"Huh? I don't get it. Wolf?"

"There's a curse about him," Grant said softly. "Or so some might call it. But not your warlock. He embraces such."

Sheila frowned and shook her head. "A curse that…makes him a wolf…" The words died on her lips. She'd learned since becoming a witch that she was amongst many supernatural creatures. Mouth dry, she whispered. "A werewolf?"

But Grant gave no answer, his attention on what was happening around them. "I wish to speak with my cousins before they depart." He looked at her. "Go with your family and gather daggers. You should be well-armed."

Oh, she knew the name of this game. "Will do."

Like it'd done before previous battles, her heart started to slam a little bit harder. Leslie and Cadence soon pulled away from their men and joined her.

"Any sign of Euphemia?" Leslie asked.

"I've barely seen her since yesterday," Cadence said. "Malcolm said she was helping to oversee the allied clans cooking but my guess is she's been hovering near Ceard."

Leslie grinned. "Ah, her new love interest."

Sheila well remembered meeting him. Determined to protect them in a recent skirmish against the enemy, he'd nearly met his own death if Euphemia's dagger hadn't saved him. It'd been love at first sight.

Cadence nodded toward her tent. "Come on ladies. Malcolm's got a ton of daggers for us to choose from."

"He would," Sheila said but was grateful. She knew damn well Grant had little in the way of weaponry outside of the sword Adlin had given him. Hopefully, his clan would hook him up.

Leslie frowned. "I wish to hell we were going with them."

"I still don't know why they're splitting up like this," Cadence muttered.

"Splitting up?" Sheila asked, aggravated. "I'm totally out of the loop. Care to share?"

"Colin's determined to take a small band north to Keir's castle," Leslie informed. "Hamilton has grown cocky and keeps few warriors left to defend it."

"So he's hoping to save Iosbail while the war's raging to the south." Cadence shook her head. "But something feels off about it to me."

"Everything that's happened since this war started with Keir has felt off," Sheila said. "But when I was at the castle it did seem pretty abandoned so maybe it isn't such a bad idea."

Leslie scowled. "I dunno. It makes no good sense that Keir would go through all of this to get Torra and then leave half her soul and Iosbail so vulnerable."

"No it doesn't," Cadence said. "But the MacLomains know what they're doing. If they see logic in this move there must be something to it."

"Easy for you to say," Leslie quipped. "Your man isn't going."

"Who is then?" Sheila asked.

"Colin, Alexander, Bradon and Ferchar I believe," Cadence said. "Malcolm tried like hell to be included but Colin would have none of it. He wants him close to his brother."

Sheila's eyes narrowed. "Why?"

Cadence and Leslie's eyes met briefly before Cadence looked at Sheila. "He wants Malcolm, Coira and William to stick close in case something goes wrong."

Sheila offered a sour expression as she received a few daggers. "What, like betrayal?"

Leslie's lips thinned. "Don't sound so irritated, sweetie. All these guys have come a long way in a very short time with Grant. They're giving him a lot of trust leaving him alone with Torra, never mind us. It couldn't hurt to have some immediate family around in case he turns reluctant against swinging his blade against warriors who served under him for so long."

"And then there's Colin MacLeod," Cadence reminded. "His best friend."

"They're just being cautious and I don't blame them," Leslie said. "You shouldn't either after everything we've been through."

Sheila knew they were right but it was still hard to swallow.

Cadence put a comforting hand on her arm. "I see the love between you and Grant so I know how hard this must be."

"Love," she muttered and shook her head.

"Felt by both of you I'll bet," Leslie said. "Your highlander has a way of looking at you that's pretty damn hot."

"Lust will do that," Sheila said, ignoring the burn beneath her skin.

"Heck yeah." Cadence grinned. "Especially when combined with love."

"Great combo." Leslie winked. "But I suppose you're both at the point where you're *thinking* love but not *saying* it."

"Doubtful," Sheila said. "Seeing how we've only known each other a few days."

"That's all it takes," Cadence said.

"Yup," Leslie agreed. "Maybe it's the magic or maybe love at first sight really exists, but falling in love with these guys is pretty damn immediate."

Eager to lose this conversation, she glanced at Cadence. "Speaking of love and all things related I'm shocked to see you here. I figured for sure Malcolm would chain you to the MacLomain castle."

Cadence grinned. "I didn't have long to convince Colin when he came back to the castle but managed. After all, I'm the only one who hears Adlin MacLomain from beyond the grave. That's too important of a gift to be left behind."

"Malcolm must've been furious," Sheila said.

"At first," Cadence conceded, a slow smile crawling onto her face. "But I put my all into helping him see the good sense in it."

Leslie snorted. "They're the only ones not married and I swear they're putting the rest of us to shame."

"Speak for yourself," Sheila murmured.

Cadence chuckled. "Les ended up with Bradon. That says it all. Good thing they intend to live in the future. The whole of Scotland will need a peaceful night's rest after they leave."

Leslie was about to respond when Torra's soft words drew their attention. "The lads are leaving."

Plenty of daggers on hand, they nodded, gave each other one more group hug and left the tent. As before, Sheila despised watching those she'd come to care about mount for war. She hated the unpredictability of Keir Hamilton. His dark methods and manipulations seemed forever beyond their grasp.

Grant exited a tent with more braids than usual interwoven in his hair and far more weapons strapped to his body. His face was carved into granite and his smoky blue eyes as dark as the storm bearing down. He spoke once more with the men before returning to her side, his tone ominous. "The Hamilton and MacLeod's second-in-commands as well as many allied leaders are at the front. Colin MacLeod has not been seen." A muscle ticked in his cheek. "Colin and I always lead the armies. Something is amiss that he is not there."

"Something is already amiss that *you're* not there," Sheila pointed out. "Keir's bound to play things differently this time."

"Aye, mayhap," Grant murmured but he by no means sounded convinced.

Kenzie and Bryce joined them.

Like him, Bryce was heavily armed and his expression grim. "Will they be leaving us horses?"

"Aye," Grant said. "But not many."

Sheila was surprised to see Kenzie with a sword at her side. When the other woman caught the look she offered a little shrug. "I learned a few things spending so much time with warriors."

Sheila bet she had. "I'm interested in swordplay. Maybe when this is all over you can show me a few tricks."

"'Twould be my honor, m'lady."

Sheila shook her head at the title, an unsettling sensation rippling over her as the others left. The fires had been doused far and wide as their surroundings quieted save for the sound of distant fighting. Unlike last time, she and the girls weren't left alone eager to follow and help. No, this time the fighting was closer and by the sounds of it, far more vicious. Or most likely that was merely the sound of so many more men fighting.

Coira, William and Malcolm weren't in their immediate vicinity but close enough that they could make out their forms through the driving snow.

"They are our last line of defense," Grant muttered, eying his family as he paced.

"Couldn't get much better," Leslie said. "Save for Bradon and Colin being there as well."

Though Leslie was about as tough as they came, she sensed her cousin's distress and squeezed her shoulder. "Bradon will be okay. Don't forget he's got Ferchar with him, one of the four original MacLomain wizards. We've seen him in action. Pretty darn powerful."

"Mmm hmm." But a heavy frown had settled on Leslie's face. "Yet two of the original wizards are *here*." She glanced at Grant. "And another who I'm thinking should be considered one as well."

Suddenly, Grant stilled in front of Torra and slowly unsheathed his blade, order low. "Silence. Eyes to the forest. Weapons ready."

As far as she could tell, nothing had changed. Wind still blew snow and flashes of light lit the woods from the yawning darkness. Grant narrowed his eyes, hand firm on his sword. Though she couldn't see it, Sheila knew he was using magic. Bow and arrows in hand, Torra turned slowly, her eyes scanning the forest.

Nearly back to back, there was something mystical and frightening about them.

Meanwhile, Bryce angled himself closer to the Brouns.

Sheila barely breathed as she peered through the trees. No longer able to see Grant's family, she did what was taught to her when sword fighting when with Adlin. She didn't focus on one area but let her vision see the bigger picture.

Whiz. Whiz. Whiz.

She saw three arrows seconds before she heard them and ducked. *Thunk.* One hit the tree at her back. *Thunk. Thunk.* The second and third came dangerously close to Leslie. Luckily, her cousin dodged out of the way. Or at least she thought so until she saw a small bloom of blood on her upper arm. The arrow must've grazed her. When Sheila frowned, Leslie shook her head sharply and nodded toward the forest.

The sound of clashing swords met her ears moments before a loud whistling. Grant spun and leapt, his blade deflecting a spear moments before it hit Cadence square in the chest. Meanwhile, Bryce deflected another coming from the opposite direction. Torra had apparently focused on something because she began to unleash arrow after arrow. Men cried out in pain.

Then silence fell again.

Too much silence.

The calm before the storm.

Fire erupted in the distance and Sheila's blood went cold. *Oh no.*

"He comes," Torra said. Already, the woman sounded weakened. No shocker there. She was functioning with half a soul!

Grant's eyes flew to the Brouns. "Go back to back. Fight as a team. Now!"

He unleashed a mighty roar as ten warriors rushed at them from all directions. Wide eyed, she was ensnared by the power of Grant's attack. What he'd dished out at the MacLomain castle during swordplay was one thing. What she saw now, another altogether. *Slash. Slash.* Two were down before they'd barely swung their weapons.

Fear flashed on several faces as three others saw the savage intent in their former commander's eyes. That brief hesitation was their downfall when his blade gutted one then slit the throats of the others. Even as his blade chopped off another's hand, he whipped two daggers and more men fell. Blood began to stain the snow around them, the circle growing wider and wider.

Bryce and Kenzie fought magnificently, downing warrior after warrior. With Bryce she'd expected it but Kenzie really wowed her. The woman could fight!

The Brouns barely had to do a thing yet but she knew that wouldn't last long. Far too many warriors kept coming. Sheila glanced at Torra. Her arms shook as she tried to hold the bow steady and Grant was deep in the throes of battle lust as he fought.

"I'm gonna go cover Torra," Sheila warned her cousins and rushed over until she stood in front of the MacLomain woman, muttering, "Why don't they use their magic and down the bastards."

"Because of the MacLeod," Torra rasped.

Good thing she'd come over. Torra was already slipping down the tree she'd been leaning against. Sheila held two daggers up, eyes on everything at once.

Grant slashed and thrust, his blade tearing through flesh. When another large group rushed him she heard another roar as Malcolm thundered through the trees on his horse, swinging his axe like a mad man.

Sheila couldn't help but flinch as he decapitated one MacLeod then slid down from his mount and ran his blade across the chest of another. Though she never thought she'd see the day, Grant and Malcolm fought alongside one another. Brutal, beyond ferocious, they made a formidable team as more men than she could count fell. And even though they'd likely not battled together since they were kids, they soon developed a rhythmic system. While one took down three or four at once, it gave the other a slight reprieve to down two or three.

Meantime, Cadence and Leslie were well into the fighting. They'd had practice battling with daggers before and it showed. Working as one, they'd managed to stab a few men already. Even William and Coira had joined in, a vicious team on horseback as they circled around their sons.

Two low growls rent the air moments before Kynan and another wolf joined the fighting. Nearly as large as the Dire wolf, this new beast had a dark brown pelt with a hint of auburn. Her eyes rounded. It couldn't be. But certainty settled over her as she watched the two rip through warriors.

That was Devin.

She didn't have long to process the revelation or admire his fighting before her attention snapped forward. As she figured would happen eventually, a warrior slipped by all, intent on her and Torra. Revved by the activity around her, Sheila realized she wasn't frightened in the least.

Adrenaline rushing, she grinned at the grimy warrior. Yet another MacLeod. Issuing a near toothless grin in return, he eyed her up and down. Not long ago she'd been in a similar position with a Hamilton warrior. If not for Cadence that might have ended poorly.

No chance of it this time. Even if her cousin were in any position to help, she'd not need it. Nope. She was out for blood.

"Och, lassie, ye dinnae have a chance." The warrior wiggled his sword a little to make obvious the size difference in their weapons.

Sheila said nothing but kept her elbows tucked, chin down and daggers steady. The days of men thinking they controlled her outcome were officially over. Naturally, he underestimated her resolve and thrust hard. Fully aware of exactly where Torra was, Sheila evaded. The second his sword hit the tree, she crouched and thrust a dagger as hard as she could into his groin. There might've been a zillion cries of men meeting their deaths but none as loud as the wail her guy released.

When he buckled over she utilized Cadence's trick and drove another dagger up under his chin. Done with him, she kicked hard. No sooner had he fallen dead to his back than another was heading her way. Bring it on! Pulling free two more daggers, she waited.

Thwak. An arrow pierced the center of his throat. He gurgled then dropped at her feet.

When she glanced behind her it was to see Torra's arms falling limply to her side. With a slight shrug, she cocked a crooked grin at Sheila. "Sorry, I couldn't help myself," she said. "Besides, 'tis best to regain your focus before rushing back into battle."

When a harsh cry rent the air, she looked to her right. Her heart lodged in her throat.

"Kenzie!" she cried. "*No!*"

A warrior had just thrust a blade through her lower abdomen, an evil, righteous grin on his face as he drove the blade deeper.

A blasphemous sound penetrated the air as Bryce spun and swiped his blade across the man's back. When the enemy fell to his knees in shock, he was dragged back. With a sharp thrust, Bryce drove his blade through the man's mouth out of the back of his head. Then, without missing a beat, he pulled the blade free from his sister.

Heart seized in her chest, Sheila had no time to see what happened next before Cadence and Leslie's angry curses caught her attention. Both had been scooped onto horseback by the enemy and were being taken in opposite directions. Refusing to leave Torra, she watched Malcolm pursue Cadence and William, Leslie. No sooner had relief flooded than she realized the men who had taken her cousins appeared to be fleeing far faster than possible.

Magic.

The endless fighting seemed to fade away and a ripple of warning straightened her spine. He'd clearly felt the unexplainable change in their surroundings because Grant's position had shifted. He now battled directly in front of her and Torra. With a quick parry, he drove forward a few steps then back as fire unfurled toward them, stopping within mere feet.

Colin MacLeod.

Sheila had become all too familiar with his particular brand of arrival. He'd no sooner appeared out of the fire when Grant began to chant. "*Per aerem, et ut orarent, ego autem quatuor circumdabit.* With the air to implore, I surround but four."

She didn't know what to focus on first. Coira's scream of rage as she and many others hit an unseen wall just beyond them or Colin's narrowed eyes. It was hard to relate the man she'd seen but a few days ago with the tyrannical highlander leering at Grant. No, this version of the MacLeod laird reminded her more of the man she'd seen when they'd first fought him at the Hamilton castle.

If not worse.

"'Tis piss poor this," Colin said through clenched teeth, murderous eyes on Grant, "that you turn on your brethren."

Sheila had never witnessed such fury as these two men striking swords against one another. Sparks flew as their blades crashed in rapid succession off one another's. "Ye act before ye think," Grant hissed. "Have I not got the lass then?"

Another round of chills broke out over her skin.

Was she hearing what she thought she was hearing? Please God no.

Despite his words, Colin kept driving at him. It was clear they'd trained often together so similar was their method of attack. Last time she'd witnessed Colin fight it had been from far away and through driving rain. Now the man was but a few feet away and terrifying. Though by no means unhandsome, his fierceness made it impossible to see him as anything but a monster. Slightly taller than Grant, his mouth forever in an uncompromising slash, he truly petrified her.

"I didnae betray ye," Grant ground out. "Keir needs to know that." They slashed blades three more times. "Come. Let us take her to him together."

Her heart sunk. She couldn't be hearing correctly.

Had Grant manipulated them all? Had he manipulated her?

It seemed impossible to believe.

"Nay, I dinnae trust ye," Colin roared and slashed down hard.

Grant deflected the blade then drove his shoulder into the MacLeod's midsection. With a heavy thump, they landed on the ground. If there was a 'Highland Warrior Hall of Fame' Grant's next move would've earned him a top spot in it. Moments before they started to roll, he tossed his sword in the air. Once, twice, then three times they rolled, the sword flipped up then down before Grant caught it and pressed it tight against Colin's windpipe.

Surprised, enraged, the MacLeod froze, his eyes narrowing to furious slits.

"Ye would already be dead if I meant to kill ye, brother," Grant growled. "But I dinnae. Nay, I mean to see Keir to greatness and us as his leaders in limitless glory."

Hell. She'd been duped. Pushing past the tight squeeze in her chest she clenched her jaw. Infuriated, Sheila glanced down at Torra only to see her half-mast eyes locked on Colin. She was fast fading with nobody left to protect her but a twenty-first century woman.

But how to do that against tyrants like these?

Impossible.

Or was it?

She looked to the fighting beyond Grant's magical wall. Though it blasted on, Coira was still there as were Kynan and now Devin not as a wolf but as a warlock. Regrettably the magic they threw at the wall did little but spit, fizzle and die away.

Devin's frustrated eyes met hers and he shook his head. Still, he didn't give up as he threw black whips of magic even as he fought oncoming warriors. Meanwhile, Coira had never looked so infuriated. But above all, there was incomparable sadness in her eyes. It seemed she'd trusted her son as much as Sheila and felt more the fool for it.

"Ye *have* to trust me," Grant was saying, his blade still against Colin's neck.

A long stretch passed as they glared at one another. Finally, Colin said, "It doesnae seem I've much choice, aye?"

Grant shook his head. "Nay."

Colin gripped his arm. "Know this. If ye betray I will hunt ye down from the afterlife and promise a slow death to any ye might care for."

"I care for none but my master and clan." Grant stood and held out his hand. "Come, brother. Let us give Keir all that he desires."

The MacLeod chieftain eyed him another long second before he took the proffered grip and stood. When they turned in her direction, Sheila already had her daggers in position. *"Tell me this is all some sort of joke and that you've got a plan up your sleeve,"* she said into Grant's mind.

His hard eyes met hers, his words in her mind harder. *"You've been too trusting, lass. Toss aside the blades and I might offer you a swift death."*

Sheila flinched but didn't back down. Eyes locked on Grant's, she seethed, "You lying, traitorous asshole. I'll die before you take Torra."

Colin cocked a brow at him. "Though I dinnae doubt you bedded her it seems ye've yet to tame the wench."

Her heart might've slammed so hard it hurt. Her palms might've been slicker on her grip than she would've liked but Sheila didn't hesitate to look at Colin and say, "Go to hell."

Yeah, she wasn't overly huge on cursing but if she was going down against these two, they'd not get sweet words from her in the process.

They chuckled as they slowly approached. Sheila tuned out the fact both were splattered in blood and likely twice her size. Nothing mattered now but protecting Torra. Both eyed her daggers and stance, gauging just how dangerous she might be. Sure she was nothing but a woman with a few small daggers but she'd never been so mad.

But how best to do this? Think, Sheila, think.

First, focus on the bigger picture.

Where Grant easily fought with both hands, Colin seemed to favor his right hand. Where Colin moved lightning fast on his feet, Grant took his time about rushing anything below his waist. Nope, that area of his body was slow and calculating until it was whiplash fast. Sheila almost snorted. Funny, what held true on the battlefield held true in bed. An idea blossomed. Maybe, just maybe, she could use that to her advantage. After all, she didn't wear pants but a dress loosened from fighting.

That they hadn't already ended her with magic was a Godsend.

Not wasting another moment on talk, she implemented what she'd been taught and thrust a dagger at Colin's sword hand. The infamous *feint*. As she did, Sheila yanked down the front of her dress.

Four things happened according to plan.

Colin blocked with his sword and her bared chest slowed whatever move Grant was about to make. Sheila took advantage and thrust her dagger where intended, toward Colin's left side while simultaneously whipping her other dagger at Grant.

Unbelievably, she grazed both.

Clearly surprised by her attack, the men took a step back. For a split second, Sheila felt the thrill of a small victory before unadulterated fury metastasized on Grant's face. Growling a healthy stream of Latin, he flung out his hands, his last English words devouring and ripping at the world around her.

"Ye'll not die here, lass. Nay, 'twill be far sweeter to watch my laird have you!"

Chapter Fifteen

Sheila flailed at the feeling of magic surrounding her.

While traveling this way always felt helpless, now it was suffocating and endless. Nothing but doom, despair and Keir Hamilton existed on the other side. Gone were her chances of a Broun/MacLomain connection. In its place, a terrible end.

But nothing felt as awful as Grant's ultimate betrayal.

So when the jarring feeling of being magically transported against her will faded, she lashed out. Sure, she could barely see and sure she was dizzy but she fought nonetheless. And as she figured would be the case, it was against hot, hard male flesh. It didn't matter if it was Grant or Colin who tried to seize her, she wouldn't go down without a fight.

"Easy, lass," Grant's words came against her ear. "'Tis over now. Easy."

"Screw that," she muttered against his chest and continued to punch and kick.

But he was far stronger and she was without a dagger. When he pinned her down with his body, hands against the side of her head, his eyes came into focus. Concerned, his gaze remained locked with hers. "'Twas all a ruse that the enemy might better believe," he said. "You havnae been brought to Keir Hamilton but to the baby oak."

Heart thundering, Sheila was about to spit another round of words at him but stopped. She blinked, breath coming in harsh gasps. Slowly but surely reality surfaced. Not the baby oak, but the mother oak in the cave below it now towered overhead. She'd know it anywhere. It was the most impressive tree she'd ever seen, its aged top wrapping and twisting into a cave while its trunk grew up the side of a mountain. Warm sunlight dappled its bright green leaves and speckled Grant's face.

"No Keir," she whispered.

"Nay," he said softly, vehemently. Releasing her wrist, he cupped her cheek. "No Keir."

Sheila swallowed. While her mind was accepting his words, her body remained tense and she clenched her fists. "You were convincing."

"I had to be." He stroked her cheek. "I'm so verra sorry, lass."

But her mind was still on the battle she'd recently been surrounded with. Her stomach clenched and she whispered painfully, "Kenzie."

Grant's eyes darkened and his lips pulled down. "I saw it happen. I can only hope they are able to get her to your cousin, McKayla in time."

Right, McKayla was a healer. Sheila pushed past the knot in her throat. "God I hope so."

She again focused on the tree branches. While grateful that it had all been some sort of magical, whirlwind lie, her thoughts went instantly to his cousin. Panicked, she said, "Is Torra all right? Where is she?"

"She's here. Safe."

When Sheila went to sit up, Grant helped her but not before he yanked up her dress. It didn't take long for her to locate the other woman. Sound asleep, she rested in Colin MacLeod's arms. "Holy hell!"

Before she could jump to her feet, Grant caught her around the waist. "Nay, lass. He means no harm."

"No harm?" she said, incredulous. "You've got to be kidding me."

Colin didn't bother looking her way but rested his cheek on the top of Torra's head, eyes closed. Still, she knew he heard.

"*Think*," Grant said. "Think of all you learned before what you just witnessed during war."

"That's a tall order, all things considered." But as reality slowly settled around her, the anger started to dissipate.

When Torra murmured something indiscernible they looked in her direction.

Grant was soon at her side, crouched, eyes tender. "How fare ye, cousin?"

Confused but soon at ease, Torra's gaze fluttered from Grant's to Colin's where they stilled. Sheila stopped breathing when the woman's shaky hand rose to his face and she whispered, "Tell me I'm not dreaming this time."

A heavy tear rolled down the MacLeod's cheek. "Not this time, my lass."

It was nothing less than surreal to see such a violent man this emotional. As if it'd happened a moment ago, Sheila was once more watching Torra and Colin meet for the first time. How they'd frozen when they'd nearly bumped into one another in the Highland Defiance's courtyard. It'd been made of magic…indisputably the spark of true love.

Yet to this day little was known of their courtship.

Torra's eyes covered his face along with her fingers. "Look at ye."

"Far fiercer," he murmured. "Not the lad you once knew."

Surprised by her emotional response, Sheila brushed away her own tear. Maybe it was because she was coming down from being thrust into pure hell moments before, but she doubted it as she watched the touching exchange. This was the first time they were together beyond the fire in Torra's hearth since he'd gone to Keir. Four years!

"Never so fierce as that," Torra whispered in response to Colin's admission.

The hint of a smile swept across Colin's lips but he said nothing as his eyes remained locked with hers. Overly aware that they intruded on a private moment, Sheila stood and cleared her throat. "I think I'm going to head up to the younger tree."

As if suddenly aware she was there, Torra's eyes tore from Colin's and she looked at Sheila. "Wait, please."

Desperate, she tried to move but it was clear how weak she was.

"No, please relax." Sheila knelt in front of her. "Don't try to move. Stay here. I only thought to give you some privacy."

Sheila was shocked when Torra, still in Colin's lap, wrapped her arms around her shoulders and pulled her close for a hug. Though there wasn't much strength in the embrace, Sheila knew the MacLomain woman meant such as she murmured, "Thank you so much, lass. Many times over you would have died for me. Such a thing…" her words faded before once more strengthening. "You are my sister now in all ways."

Giving her a tight hug, Sheila nodded. "You bet I am."

When her weak arms fell away, Sheila helped ease her back against Colin.

Torra turned her eyes to the MacLeod chieftain. "Lay me down here. I need rest." When he went to argue she said, "I am safe within the oak. Go talk with Grant. Make sure your next move is planned well."

Sheila stood and turned away, determined to give them a few moments alone. When Grant joined her she nodded upward. "Let's go see the baby oak."

"Are you sure?" he said softly. "We can always go down into the cave, down to the Defiance."

"No," she said. "Up. To the baby tree. I've never seen it."

"But your visions."

She shook her head. "Up, Grant."

His gaze lingered on hers for a good ten seconds before he nodded. "Aye then."

While Sheila thought the oak below was a wonder, nature's pure perfection, she'd never been so wrong. The minute Grant hoisted her up and she locked eyes on the baby oak for the first time, emotion threatened to bring her to her knees. She might have approached a newborn baby struggling to survive so profound was the feeling.

Every color existing in a rainbow sliced across the mountaintop as a sunset burst over the young tree. She'd heard its tale. It'd started growing when Alan Stewart and Caitriona had coupled beneath its mother's branches. Some said the very moment the infamous original Claddagh rings were created then handed over to a Celtic god to oversee the great MacLomain/Broun romances.

Where rumors spoke of it being a sign of great things, Sheila saw it for what it was...

Survival.

"Where did its mother tree come from?" she murmured, still in awe at seeing something she'd only ever dreamt of.

Grant's hand slid into hers. "I dinnae know, lass."

"Yes you do," she whispered then looked at him. "You must. All MacLomains must."

Confused, he shook his head but clearly reconsidered something because he said, "I cannae speak for their knowledge but 'tis clear this tree's origin should not be kept secret from you."

When she continued to stare at the tree only tall enough for a child to walk beneath, Grant tilted her chin and made her eyes meet his. "'Tis at the root of everything, aye?"

"Since the beginning," she whispered, not sure in the least why she said as much.

"What know you of the MacLomain's Irish history, of Chiomara the Druidess and King Erc of the DalRaida?" he murmured before pulling away. He crouched by a small puddle and splashed water over his face several times to wash away the blood.

"Next to nothing," she allowed as Grant sat and pulled her onto his lap, his back against a boulder as they faced the tree. "Cadence likely knows more than me as she's read up on MacLomain history and is in touch with Adlin."

"Mayhap but doubtful. While she might know of the druidess and her king, she could never know of this tree. None but Torra and I ken her beginning."

"And how is that?"

Grant was about to respond when Colin appeared. If his presence alone didn't freeze her thoughts in process, the way he stopped and stared at the baby oak surely did. His hard eyes once more softened and instead of sadness there was nothing but happiness. Sheila nearly relaxed under his appraisal until he turned it their way.

Instantly stiff, she clenched her teeth.

If there was a dagger in her hand, she'd feel far safer.

When Grant stood abruptly and set her aside, Sheila stepped back in fear. But his sudden action had nothing to do with her. No, apparently it had to do with comradery. Eyes locked, hand to elbow, the men shook hands. Then they both clenched their jaw and shook their heads before yanking close and patting one another on the back.

After a good long moment they pulled apart. Eyes narrowed, Colin clamped his hands on either side of Grant's head, a wry grin curving his lips. "I've thought a lot of things about ye over the years, MacLomain, but never that ye were capable of what ye pulled off today!"

Grant grinned. "I told ye to have faith, my friend, did I not?"

Again they stared at each other for a long moment, caught in an exchange Sheila couldn't define other than to say they'd traveled far and were happy for it. Then, as if the respite hadn't happened, Colin put his arm around Grant's neck, ducked and yanked hard flipping and throwing him over his shoulder. Sheila was about to dart forward when Grant hit the rock hard but stopped when he rebounded quick, swooped around and knocked Colin off his feet.

She jumped back, uncertain what was going on when both lay on the rock, eyes to the sky, laughing. Not just your normal laugher but full bodied, joyous laughter. It was then that Sheila realized she was simply watching the roughhousing freedom of a friendship out from beneath evil for the first time. Not that she was entirely convinced Colin didn't have his own brand of evil within. Regardless, right now the highlander seemed pretty damn civil.

When at last Grant sat up, he held out a hand to Colin. They again shook hands as Colin sat up as well. Both continued to sit on the rock, arms draped over bent knees as they gazed at the baby oak.

Despite what she'd seen of him with Torra, Sheila remained uncomfortable anywhere near Colin MacLeod so she slid down against a nearby rock and watched him warily. When Colin's deep voice spoke of her, she pulled her knees close to her chest.

"I dinnae think yer lass is ever going to see me as you do, Grant," Colin said. Then, as if eager to put his words in her face, he tossed a glance in her direction. "No matter how willing she is to bare her breasts."

Mortified but equally miffed she shot back. "And what are you willing to do to protect someone?"

Colin's brow lifted then lowered slowly in her direction. "If I might champion Torra nearly as well as you, lass, she'll always be well protected." He nodded. "You've my thanks from this life straight into the next."

Sheila could only stare at him. Had Colin MacLeod just *thanked* her?

When she gave no response, the MacLeod looked to Grant. "'Tis good I didnae go to embrace her with thanks, aye? She might have taken to the cliff."

"Not likely," she finally managed. Sure enough that her voice wouldn't wobble, she said, "You've been nothing but a tyrant. Every reaction I've had to you has been justified."

When Colin's eyes once more went to her, Sheila nearly looked away. If ever there was a man used to controlling all around them it was him. The MacLeod's eyes bore through her and as they did every time she was around this man, shivers raked through her body. He might've shed a tear for Torra but that was a moment owned by them. She wasn't such a fool to think he was a sentimental man by nature.

Even as she locked onto the molten silver of Colin's direct regard, she felt barred off from his time with Torra. Somehow, within magic or simply because he was inherently overwhelming, she knew Colin was severely overprotective of her. If Sheila didn't know better she'd swear there was a soft growl in the polite way he once more said, "Again, thank you for protecting my lass. I willnae forget it."

Images once more flashed before her. The Hamilton castle when she'd first seen him. Torra as a dragon. Fire reigning down. The way his destructive magic, his fire, had fought hers. It'd been powerful, intense, beyond reason.

Yet now she knew they loved one another immensely.

And if she knew nothing else it was that Colin MacLeod didn't like anyone being privy to it.

He tolerated her because Grant cared for her and because she'd protected Torra. Simple as that. Colin's desire for Torra was singular and he'd let nobody close to his emotions save maybe Grant. But she didn't need a warm, fuzzy moment with the MacLeod chieftain so gave no response. Instead, she redirected her eyes to the tree.

Colin's attention once more turned to Grant and he scowled. "Torra's determined to give herself to Keir." Black storm clouds all but gathered over the MacLeod's face. "You cannae let it happen."

Sheila thought it was interesting how like the MacLomain men his way of speech changed around her. She couldn't help but wonder if it was simple adaption due to their magic so that she might better understand them.

"Torra's magic is strong, my friend," Grant said. "If she wishes such I willnae be able to stop her." He glanced at Colin. "Nor will you."

Colin shook his head. "I have had enough of using my magic to battle with her. I dinnae want to do such anymore."

Grant frowned. "We both did what we had to so that Keir would never suspect our lack of loyalty."

"And now with any luck he will once more think you loyal…mayhap," Colin said.

"What happened after I left with Sheila, Bryce and Kenzie?" he asked.

Colin's lips thinned. "Nothing good. I returned to the castle with him that he might seek answers from me."

Grant's brows drew together and he rested his forehead in his palm. "Bloody hell, I'm sorry. I know better than most how the Hamilton seeks answers."

"He got nothing from me he didnae already know because you had shared nothing." Colin clasped him on the shoulder. "Dinnae worry, friend, I know 'twas not your desire to put me in such a position. The need to protect our lasses will always rule our actions."

"If I could have brought you with me I would have," Grant said.

"Och, nay, dinnae fib now when we have come so far." Colin shook his head. "Though you meant to see me safe eventually, 'twas always your intention that I remain and mayhap persuade Keir to your cause. That though you broke the mental connection he had over you then fled with Bryce and the others, surely you had a devious plan that would aid his cause from behind enemy lines."

Grant sighed. "Aye, mayhap."

"Again, I dinnae fault you for such. Besides, had I been given the chance to flee I wouldnae have taken it, not with half of Torra's soul still imprisoned by the bastard." Colin's voice deepened. "I will have her entire soul safely beyond his control before ever fleeing the Hamilton."

"Aye," Grant said. "And then we will both see him dead."

"I want no easy death for such evil," Colin bit out. "He must suffer."

"With the MacLomains backing us, you cannae doubt such will happen," Grant assured.

"And the whole of the MacLeod clan as well," Colin promised. "If I defect they will follow."

"'Tis good this," Grant said softly. "But what of the Hamilton clan?"

"I believe you would find them quick to follow you, brother. Where the MacLeod's are mine, the Hamilton's have long turned kinder eyes to you than their own chieftain. 'Tis not respect but dark magic he wields over them."

Sheila thought back to what Kenzie had said when she'd shared the same belief.

A flash of pain flickered in Grant's eyes. She knew he cared for the Hamilton clan equally and longed to see them out from beneath such heavy oppression.

"Do you know where Keir is keeping the other half of Torra's soul?" Grant said.

"Aye," Colin said. "In one of his chambers."

Grant's eyes clouded. "Aye, I know which one. 'Tis at the heart of his black magic."

Colin's eyes narrowed on him. "So 'tis clear enough when you brought Torra and me here that you intend to return to Keir. Please dinnae tell me 'tis because of Torra's foolhardy desire to save the MacLomain lass."

"I'm afraid I cannae tell you otherwise," Grant said. "I know 'twill be impossible to stop her so thought this the best way of going about it. As least now I've hopefully gained myself time against Keir to free both Iosbail and Torra."

Sheila felt sick to her stomach.

Damn him and his need to save all at risk.

Colin considered this for a few long moments. "'Tis hard to know what we will walk into at the Hamilton castle."

"'Tis," Grant allowed. "That is why when we arrive you will remain Keir's faithful servant until we know if we can free Torra. She cannae be left there alone if things dinnae work out as I hope they will."

"I will always stay close to her." Colin cast a worried glance in the direction of the entrance to the larger oak, to where Torra slept. "She cannae remain like this for much longer."

"Nay," Grant agreed. "And though I know you are part of the reason she needs to go to Keir, her soul is inexplicably drawn to its other half."

"Aye, 'tis no sense in having me here when half of her remains there." Colin rubbed the tattoo on his arm and stood, words heavy as he left. "I will go be with her until she is ready."

Grant nodded and returned to Sheila's side.

The whole time she'd been listening to him she'd been festering with both sadness and aggravation. Not just at everything they'd all been put through but because of what Grant was about to do. Of all the crazy things that'd happened since arriving in Scotland, this sounded like the most dangerous.

Even as Grant slid down next to her and took her hand, she didn't look at him but stared at the tree. A long time passed before he finally said, "You are angry."

She gave no response. Grant didn't deserve her aggravation. He had enough on his plate.

"Sheila."

His soft plea made her shut her eyes.

"If you dinnae know," Grant whispered. "I love you."

That was about the last thing she expected to hear and despite the thrill it sent through her she remained upset. Mostly because she suspected he said it because there wasn't much time left to say such before he likely got himself killed. So instead of returning the words she flailed against them. Maybe if she could somehow make them untrue then he'd be forced to live and say them again. "How do you *know* that for sure." She looked at him. "Neither of us know enough about love to declare it."

He cupped her cheek, eyes intense. "I know that I'd die for you." He shook his head, a small smile curving his lips. "Better yet, I'd live for you...that I find all of this...life, better for it."

Sheila searched his eyes, heard his answer, but still felt so afraid, not ready. "I'd like to think you'll live but you're walking into pure hell willingly."

"But 'tis a hell I know verra well," he supplied. "I dinnae go into this at a complete disadvantage."

"Don't you?" she said, voice strained and emotional. "Because I'm feeling like this," she pointed from him to her, "is smacking of our last moments together."

A pained look crossed his face as he pulled her onto his lap. "My life has been nothing but risk for the past fourteen winters. You must remember that I was mainly raised by this monster and inside his mind. I know how he thinks and what his next actions will be sometimes before he knows them himself." Grant caressed her cheek. "And though I'll see my own death before that of Torra and Iosbail's, I have more to live for than ever before. Your love has given me more strength than I ever could have imagined. Dinnae doubt this, lass."

"I never said I loved you," she murmured.

"You didnae need to, 'tis in your eyes when you look at me." He entwined his fingers with hers. "In your hands when you touch me." He touched the area above her heart. "And here in all the kindness you showed me when no one else would."

Sheila refused to push the words past her lips. Not yet. Mostly because if she did she'd no doubt seal his fate. Instead, she brushed her lips over his and said, "You've done an awful lot for me too." She knew full well love was in her eyes when she looked at him. "I think it's safe to say my moments of happiness are no longer forced."

This time he brushed his lips over hers but instead of pulling away he deepened the kiss. Long, drawn out, she relished the sweet exchange and prayed that it wouldn't be their last. When their lips finally parted, she rested her head against his chest.

"We've traveled back in time to a few weeks before you first came to Scotland," he murmured.

Sheila wasn't surprised in the least by that news. "Why?"

"To give Colin and Torra time."

Lifting her head, she once more met his amazing eyes. "Won't Keir know?"

Grant offered a small smile. "Nay. I slipped the pentacle over Colin's neck moments before we came here."

"Impossible!"

"Is it?" he said softly, a grin in his voice. "As I recall you were busy whipping daggers and showing off your—"

Quick, she pressed a palm over his mouth. "Shh, I don't need my unique battle strategies to somehow make it to my cousin's ears."

"'Tis likely too late." He grinned. "All had returned before we vanished."

"Ugh." She rolled her eyes. "Great."

"I thought your actions quite clever." His grin grew into a full smile. "Search out the enemy's weaknesses then attack."

Sheila liked how he smiled more and more despite what lay ahead. She imagined she was grinning just as much. Until, that is, Torra and Colin reappeared.

Oh no. Not yet.

Torra leaned against Colin but at least she was standing. She grasped his hand as her eyes went to the tree and dampened. What exactly did it mean to the two of them? Frustrated, she realized that she'd completely forgotten to get the whole story on the tree's beginnings. But based on Torra's expression she knew now was not the time.

"The solstice comes," Torra murmured. "I must go to Keir so that no harm comes to Iosbail."

Heaviness settled in her chest as they stood. As he seemed to like to do, Grant cupped Sheila's cheeks, eyes intense. "I will see you returned to the MacLomain castle where you will be safe. Keir will be told that the MacLomain's magic managed to pull you away."

Like hell she'd leave his side. But Sheila had expected he'd pull this so she nodded her compliance and kept her fingers crossed that her own little side plan worked. Her heart clenched not only at what was about to happen but because of the tender embrace exchanged between Torra and Colin. She wasn't sure if she'd ever seen such passion. In fact, she had to look away. The moment was so totally theirs alone.

When at last the other couple joined them by the smaller tree, Grant murmured something and the blood he'd washed off reappeared. Sheila frowned and he explained, "As far as Keir knows we disappeared from the battle and went directly to him."

Ah, that made sense.

She glanced at the baby oak. "I thought time travel only worked at the big oak."

"This tree is part of me, lass," Torra said softly. "I can travel anywhere through it."

Sheila was about to respond when reality seemed to shift around her. Again the same vision she'd been having flared around her. Except this time she could clearly see Grant, Torra and Colin standing within it.

"Oh no," she whispered and held onto Grant's arm.

"What is it?" he asked, alarmed.

Wind buffeted her as she stared between the tree and the raging ocean. "Now I recognize where I am. How did I not see it right away?" she murmured. "It's the ocean beside the Hamilton castle!"

She looked at Grant. "Can't you hear Iosbail saying, "Where are you?""

"She's seeking us," Torra said softly.

Sheila nodded. That's why Torra's voice came to her in the vision. Iosbail's magic was calling her.

Like before, Iosbail shouted, "Just run already! What are you afraid of? Now. Go! I'll not say it again."

Sheila looked between the dark clouds and the cool welcoming water. No, she thought, I can't do this. If it meant saving herself or saving the tree...

"Sheila, you're living, breathing. The tree? There is naught but embers in the branches."

But the tree was more than that.

More than her.

"It's all happening like before." Sheila shook her head. "The fire. My need to save the tree." She gripped Grant harshly as the fire didn't just roll toward her but became something else. Fear like she'd never felt before cut through her as she pointed. "Fiery serpents!" She continued shaking her head, voice strangled. "They're heading for the tree!"

Torra went deadly calm, her words the last Sheila heard before all faded away. "'Twas always a vision meant to warn. Keir already has Iosbail between Heaven and Hell."

Chapter Sixteen

When the lull of darkness that had encaged her lifted, Sheila realized everything once more spun around her. Time travel. Pressing her hand against the stone in her ring, she chanted words that would hopefully bring her to the Hamilton castle. As the sensation of free falling and the smell of burning sugar faded, she breathed a sigh of relief.

Then she nearly screamed when Kier Hamilton spun and locked narrowed eyes on her.

He appeared nothing less than demon spawn eager for a taste of her soul.

Oh God. Had she traveled here alone?

But his eyes soon fell beyond and a slow grin slithered onto his face. Wide-eyed she looked over her shoulder to see Colin MacLeod nodding to Keir and Grant yanking Torra forward.

Oh God, she didn't want Grant or Torra anywhere near such pure, unrelenting evil.

Sheila tried to jump forward to protect but Colin grabbed her arm harshly.

"Nay, wench," the MacLeod chieftain seethed. "Ye wait yer turn to be had by my master."

Grant offered an evil grin and nod of approval in Colin's direction as he held on tight to Torra. Frankly, she was again amazed at how convincing a part he played.

Yet her attention was soon drawn to something far different and so terrifying her legs started to liquefy. If Colin MacLeod, of all people, wasn't holding her up she knew she'd hit the floor. While yes, the room reeked of burning flesh, that wasn't what turned her blood to ice.

Nope, it was the unbelievable altar that back dropped Keir Hamilton.

Oozing with the same black oily slickness he'd once unleashed at the MacLomain castle, Iosbail was nearly frozen, somehow half in and half out of the cavernous hole at the center. Inside the black abyss of a window, fiery serpents slithered, eager.

Sheila couldn't help it.

She started praying.

"Gracious Heavenly Father, in Jesus Christ's name, I approach Your throne of grace and ask for your help in my time of need. Help fight this evil. Protect me and mine and deliver us, Lord, from every evil spirit and evil influence afflicting our life."

Keir's horrid grin widened and he palmed the unusual pentacle criss-crossed with black leather at his neck. Even as she prayed her eyes widened as the air seemed to fluctuate and wail. It almost sounded like…

Torra?

She blinked several times and knew with certainty.

The other half of Torra's soul was trapped inside that pentacle.

As if he didn't have a care in the world, as if a lonely, scared soul didn't scream within something so casually hung around his neck, Hamilton peered darkly at Grant. "Ye've been busy."

There was no way to interpret what Keir meant by that. But she applauded Grant's cool indifference when he responded. "'Twas best handled this way if I was to get her to you."

Keir's jaw twitched as he searched Grant's eyes. "You have done well…but," his tone and eyes darkened, "expect severe punishment for putting me through such uncertainty."

Grant lowered his head in submission. "Aye, my laird."

Sheila remembered too well being inside Grant's mind when this bastard hit him and she clenched her fists. What she wouldn't do to whack that condescending look right off Keir's face. She could tell by Torra's expression she felt the same way.

But it didn't seem to matter as Keir's eyes left Grant and settled on what mattered most.

Torra.

While fiery serpents might hunger just over his shoulder, Sheila swore black, disease-ridden worms snaked eagerly through Keir's eyes as they roamed Torra's face with appreciation. "At long last, my sweet. Such beauty. And finally all mine." He licked his thin lips. "Both the lass *and* the dragon."

Sheila shivered at the dark promise in the Hamilton's voice.

How had they ended up right where he wanted them?

She'd no sooner thought it when Keir grabbed Torra's arm...

And all hell broke loose.

In a lightning fast graceful movement, Torra ripped Grant's sword from his sheath, spun from Keir's grasp and thrust the blade into the serpents behind him.

The dark overlord roared and flung up his hands.

Like before everyone was caught in his supernatural ability to slow down time.

And unlike before, even Torra was ensnared.

But whatever the Viking blade did when it entered that fiery hole had the creatures retracting and squealing in pain. She'd never heard a more God awful sound. Like a rabid animal being put through a meat grinder.

Spat out of the creepy place she'd been, Iosbail spun away from Keir's desperate grasp.

A healthy stream of curses came from the MacLomain wizard's mouth as she flung up her hands and Hamilton stumbled back a few feet. "Bloody bastard of a warlock," she muttered.

All were shocked, even Iosbail it seemed, when Torra ripped herself free of Keir's magic.

Her soft words hit the air. "Forgive me."

With a quick lash of her tongue she said, "*Cognati mei secundum carnem, non ad pugnam, iam extra muros procul haec fortuna '*. My kin not here to fight, now outside these walls beyond this plight."

Sheila's eyes widened as the same white fog she'd seen Torra release at the Hamilton castle once more crawled in her direction. As before, it quickly wrapped around its prey. This time that meant Sheila, Grant and Iosbail.

The MacLomain woman appeared stunned that she couldn't push away the magic.

Sheila only had a short second to see the fury on Keir's face before everything swirled around her then sharply resurfaced. Except now she stood on the outer fields beyond the castle thrust into what seemed the end of a great battle. More bodies than she could count littered the ground.

What, why, how?

Totally caught by the harsh shift of one pitiful scenario to another, her stomach coiled into her throat. Truly though, there was little difference in the sensation of going from Keir's presence to so much death surrounding her. If all of the carnage at her feet wasn't enough, Malcolm had just locked eyes on Grant with nothing but loathing.

"Bloody hell," Grant muttered. He crouched fast and grabbed a blade from a warrior who clearly no longer had use for it. Seconds before Malcolm's axe came down he blocked and metal clanged against metal.

"Malcolm, stop, he's not the enemy!" she cried.

"Nay, lassie." Iosbail pulled her back. "'Tis a battle that needs to happen."

"No it doesn't." She frowned and shook her head. Though she tried to pull away, the woman was surprisingly strong despite the fact they'd just been magically thrust from within the castle. "They'll kill each other!"

Iosbail watched them spar with a critical eye then nodded. "Aye, mayhap they will."

Fast, furious, wicked, every slash Malcolm dealt, Grant evaded and vice versa.

Where Grant and Colin MacLeod were a well matched pair, Malcolm and his brother were almost more so. There was a frightening beauty about how they fought. And even though her heart was in her throat, Sheila couldn't help but notice how they developed a certain rhythm much like they had when fighting alongside one another.

Yet Grant must've seen opportunity because he spun and slashed fast, knocking Malcolm's axe from his hand. But the older brother didn't miss a beat and grabbed a nearby sword. Now she knew Grant had the advantage.

But Malcolm was by no means backing down.

On and on it went, a ridiculous battle between two who should be allies.

"This is insane," Sheila cried and looked at Iosbail. "How can you be so calm?" She flicked a hand at the castle. "Especially after that."

Grant had no sooner driven Malcolm forward when his brother pushed him back.

Iosbail cocked an amused brow at her. "Live a thousand years or so then ask me again."

Sheila blinked at her. Shoot. She made a good point. Still!

"Och is that you my lass?"

A wide grin split Iosbail's face seconds before she was swept off her feet into Alexander's arms. Both laughed before he kissed her vigorously. Sheila watched the striking pair reunite before her irritated attention was once more returned to the heavy clang of swords.

About to try to stop them again, Colin MacLomain grabbed her arm and shook his head. "Nay, let them fight it out lass. 'Tis always the best way for Malcolm to work through such things."

"What about Grant?" she said. "He seriously doesn't need this."

"'Tis hard to know what he needs." Colin nodded at them. "I dinnae see him trying to explain things to his brother. Nay, he seems just as eager to cross blades."

Perplexed, she watched. He certainly did. Maybe he was using this opportunity to vent the last of his frustration. When she glanced beyond Colin she realized William and Coira watched their sons as well, not trying in the least to stop them.

Worried, she asked, "Does everyone know that Grant is not the enemy? I know what they saw but—"

"Aye," Colin cut her off. "We've the right of it now. Iosbail is strong in her magic. The minute you were freed from Keir, she made sure all knew telepathically that Grant acted once more on behalf of the MacLomain clan."

"Um, did the mental memo not reach Malcolm?"

"Most likely," Colin said. "But this has naught to do with that." Colin's eyes were sterner than she'd ever seen when they met hers. "Tell me what happened after you left with Torra, Colin and Grant."

Not a question but an order. She didn't blame him in the least.

Sheila sighed. If Colin wasn't freaked about Malcolm and Grant she supposed there must be something to that. Or at least she hoped so or things would go real wrong real soon between her and her cousin's husband. But as she eyed Colin, she sensed he was desperate for answers. Her gut told her Grant would want her to be honest, to provide any information that might prove helpful.

So she shared everything no matter how hard it was to think clearly while watching the men fight. The MacLomain laird listened intently, his frown deepening as he looked at the castle. Malcolm and Grant were breathing harder as they thrust and grunted, at times just plain old punching one another.

Sheila again glanced around. "Is it safe to assume we won most of the war?"

A mix of sadness and resolve settled on Colin's face. "'Tis down to a siege of the castle. Their allied clans have fled and those that are not within the castle walls are dead or now held captive by us."

"How many are on the inside?"

"More than I'd like," Colin said. "With enough supplies to risk our own lives through what will likely be a long drawn out affair during winter." His eyes scaled the castle's two outer walls. "Positions such as this can be as dangerous for those beyond as it is for those who wait within."

"And now he has Torra."

Colin sighed, anger flaring in his eyes. "Aye, so it seems."

"But Torra has Colin MacLeod," Sheila said softly. "Trust me, that will mean something."

The MacLomain chieftain scowled but gave no response. She sensed his mixed emotions. There were still too many unanswered questions about his sister and her love, who he'd long considered the enemy.

Sheila's heart fell into her stomach when Malcolm managed a thrust that nearly sliced into Grant's side. Clouds rolled away and a heavy moon promised bright light once the sun was fully set. Despite the distress she knew Colin felt she had to ask. "How are my cousins? Better yet, how is Kenzie?"

"Grant's lass?" Colin sighed. "I dinnae know. Coira took her back to the castle in hope that McKayla might save her but," he shook his head, "she was eager to get back and be here in case Grant returned. She said nothing more than that 'twas unlikely the lass will make it."

When tears welled in her eyes, Colin put his hand on her shoulder. "I'm so verra sorry, lass. But know this, if any can save her 'tis my wife."

They stood that way for a few minutes, his touch of support unwavering. Since she'd first ventured back in time to medieval

Scotland she hadn't officially lost anyone she'd come to care about. She prayed that it wouldn't happen now.

Colin eventually nodded behind her and answered another question she'd asked. "As to how your cousins fare, ask for yourself."

Sheila spun. Oh, thank God!

She'd never been so happy to see them.

Despite her concern for the men fighting, she caught them in a group hug and held on tight, mumbling, "I'm so glad you're okay."

"Oh, sure." Leslie grinned. "What are a few hundred medieval warriors when you're fighting alongside kick-ass Broun women?"

"Right," Cadence said then shook her head at Malcolm's determination to fight with Grant. "He just can't help himself."

"So it seems," Sheila muttered, attention back on the warring brothers.

For some reason, she felt relieved that neither of her cousins seemed all that alarmed. That said a lot about just how far they thought this fight might go. As it was, the men *had* to be getting exhausted. Sure they might be able to battle the enemy for hours but she knew those men didn't have a quarter of the talent these two possessed.

Still, it was getting old.

All she wanted to do was wrap her arms around Grant and revel in the fact they'd at least escaped death…for the time being. But then who knew after this mini war pitting brother against brother.

Leslie arched a brow at Sheila. "While I know Cadence and I totally rocked fighting earlier gotta say you get a gold star for the most inventive way to distract a highland warrior."

Cadence snorted, chuckled then winked. "Even Adlin thought that was rather clever of you."

Right, because her cousin heard him from beyond the grave. Sheila's face enflamed. "Ugh, I hope he didn't actually *see* me."

"He obviously did." Cadence outright laughed. "But I'm pretty sure you don't need to worry about stuff like that with a ghost, hon."

"What's so funny?" Devin asked, joining them.

Thrilled to see him as well, she gave Devin a big hug, forgetting for a moment that he was a werewolf. But even when she did remember, she certainly didn't mention it or hold it against him.

Rather, she held him at arm's length and grinned. "Good to see you made it, my friend."

Devin grinned as well. "I don't think I've had so much fun in my life. Well, maybe when I met my wife at the Georgian but it's a close call."

Sheila shook her head. "I see why you and Seth get along so well. Nobody in their right mind should find war fun."

"Not so much the war but the killing the enemy part." He clucked her under the chin. "Besides, I was referring more to the adventure of traveling back to medieval Scotland and spending time with Kynan."

Sheila had no sooner asked where the wolf was when a low growl met the air.

Kynan, hackles raised, had just managed to position himself between Malcolm and Grant.

Both stopped, panting in exhaustion, eyes flitting between the wolf and each other.

"Say what you will but never once did you search for me," Grant muttered in aggravation.

"Every day for five winters," Malcolm bit back.

Only then did she realize they'd been crossing not only swords but words telepathically. When she glanced at William and Coira there were tears in their eyes.

Sheila swallowed hard.

Every day for five years?

"I dinnae believe it," Grant grunted.

"Then dinnae," Malcolm countered, pain in his voice. "But I did and would have continued. I never believed you dead. Not my brother."

Grant narrowed his eyes. "Why would you stop?"

"Because I made him," William said softly.

Though their weapons were still raised, neither brother made a move with Kynan between them. Grant's tortured eyes went to his father. "Why?"

"Because 'twas slowly killing your brother." William ground his jaw as though defying old memories but his sad eyes gave him away. "As it was killing your Ma and me to watch such a thing." He clenched his fists. "We had already lost one beloved son. I'd not see another waste away in front of our verra eyes."

Grant's eyes flickered to Malcolm then to his parents, unsure. "So then you all gave up on me."

"Not once," Coira said, voice hoarse. "*Never.*"

"We never gave up hope, son. *Never.*" William said. "Every week thereafter either your Ma or I searched. We've scoured the whole of Scotland looking for you but Keir had you well hidden. Despite your elevated position within the Hamilton clan, never was there a whisper that 'twas you…our *son.*"

Malcolm seemed as surprised as Grant by this news.

When Grant lowered his blade a fraction so did his brother.

Grant glanced at the castle. "Keir watches."

"Nay," Coira said. "He sees nothing beyond my magic, nothing but his fallen warriors."

But it was still a long moment before Grant's eyes returned to Malcolm and he lowered his blade completely. "I'm done warring with you, brother. I told you everything that happened. If still you dinnae believe then take your blade to me and be done with it."

Malcolm looked at him long and hard, a mixture of emotions crossing his face, before at last he shook his head and tossed aside the blade. "Nay." When he moved toward Grant, Kynan stepped away. Raw feelings thickened his voice as he held out his hand to shake. "I willnae have my brother so far gone from me again."

Silence fell as Grant eyed his hand then met Malcolm's gaze. Time seemed to slow as they looked at one another. Sheila didn't dare breathe. Would the struggle between them finally be put to rest? Would forgiveness at last be found?

Finally, thankfully, Grant took his arm, hand to elbow and offered one heartfelt word. "Brother."

Malcolm grasped his arm tightly and it seemed the years peeled away in an instant as their eyes held. Though it was likely right away, it seemed a lifetime before he finally said the same, voice hoarse. "Brother."

Then when Malcolm suddenly yanked Grant into an embrace, more than just one tear slid down her cheek. And she wasn't alone. Their parents and her cousins were equally touched. All had tears in their eyes.

Cadence and Leslie wrapped their arms around her lower back from either side, smiling.

"Thank the gods for Kynan," Cadence said, chuckling through evident emotion.

"No doubt about it," Leslie agreed.

"'Tis verra good this," Bradon said, appearing beside Leslie with a wide smile on his face.

Leslie took his hand and nodded. "Sure is."

And only made better when Grant and Malcolm finally fell apart so that Grant might be pulled into first his father's arms, then his mother's where he stayed for a long minute. Sheila brushed away another tear as she watched them. When the four of them began talking amongst themselves, smiling, happy, reunited, she turned away to give them privacy.

But it seemed Grant had other plans because she'd no sooner started to speak to Cadence when a warm hand came around her wrist and she was whipped back around straight into his arms. Cadence and Leslie stepped back, grinning, as he pulled her close and buried his face in her neck, murmuring, "'Tis good to reunite as I should with my kin but first I'll feel against me what might have been lost."

Without a moment's hesitation, Sheila wrapped her arms around him, swamped in yet more emotion as she whispered, "But not lost at all."

"Nay." He held tight, his hand threading into her hair. "Thank God."

She thought of the Viking sword and both the Norse and Celtic gods. "And perhaps some other gods as well."

Grant pulled back, his gaze tender. "Aye, mayhap but 'twas our God you called upon when facing Keir so I tend to believe he answered."

"I think you're right," she whispered.

When his lips met hers she melted.

And when they pulled away for the umpteenth time hours later, Sheila cuddled into his side. Grant had spent a long time with his brother and parents reconnecting. Despite the heartache behind and strife that lay ahead, an important part of the MacLomain clan's very strength had been reborn in the reunion with his family.

Meanwhile, Coira with her magical ability of turning deceased bodies to dust had disposed away with the carnage surrounding the castle. But she'd left the blood stains so that Keir might peer down from his battlements and remember that war had been waged...and that it hadn't left his front door.

Oddly enough, Sheila and Grant had been given the cottage she, Leslie, Bradon and Malcolm had been given the first time they'd stayed at the Hamilton's. Now they stood out front, Grant's arm around her lower back, Kynan by his side.

Her eyes drifted from the wolf to him. "How exactly did you come by an extinct wolf anyways?"

A small smile met his lips. "'Twas more like he came by me." His hand rested on the wolf's head, voice a little distant. "I'd only been free of Hamilton's dungeon for a year or so and was finally allowed beyond the gates for the first time. 'Twas also the first time I'd hunted."

It saddened her to think he'd been kept within the castle walls so long after the dungeons. But Grant sounded not bitter but nostalgic as he continued.

"Even though Kier was still mentally connected to me, I still so clearly recall the feeling of freedom when I got separated from the others I hunted with. It wasn't for long but enough," Grant murmured, his low tone lightening. "I was even lucky enough to come across a large buck."

"Did you kill it?"

"Nay." He shook his head. "But I did have my arrow aimed and if not for the feeling of eyes upon me 'twould have likely been a successful kill."

"Eyes?"

"Aye." A small grin met his lips. "Right beside me at that." He glanced down at Kynan. "I'll never forget the hairs on the back of my neck standing nor the terror I felt when I turned my head and came eye to eye with the wolf."

"Whoa, I can only imagine." Sheila again looked at Kynan and thought for a moment he looked right back. "What happened then?"

"Nothing." Grant shrugged. "He but stared at me and as he did everything else faded away. Long moments passed as we watched one another before he finally disappeared once more into the forest. I remember thinking it strange how many animals were about in light of such an animal. Degu's, birds, several more bucks... 'twas odd."

"Hmm." Sheila eyed Kynan. "I've heard it said that sort of thing happens when the Celtic god, Fionn Mac Cumhail is around. And interestingly enough, he apparently made sure Kynan got to your brother."

"Aye," Grant said softly. "I saw Kynan often over the years but somehow Keir never knew of him. 'Twas the wolf's companionship that made things easier."

"Yet you still parted with him."

"Aye, though I might've harbored anger and mayhap some resentment toward Malcolm, I wouldnae have him without the wolf's protection during this war," Grant said. "So I sent him into the forest one day with orders to seek out my brother, to watch over him. It seems a Celtic god indeed helped him along."

Grant ruffled Kynan's head then nodded toward Malcolm's cottage. "Off you go then, lad."

Kynan gave his hand a quick lick then trotted off.

She felt a small ache in her chest. No doubt, Grant had given away his best friend. As much as any wild animal, especially a wolf like Kynan, could be given away.

Sheila put her hand on Grant's shoulder. "Malcolm's lucky to have you for a brother." She was about to say more when young Euphemia the cook happened by, a gangly MacLomain warrior on her arm. She nodded at the cottage with a grin on her face. "I had 'em clean it just for ye two. How fares it?" Her eyes narrowed. "It best fare well."

Sheila grinned. "It looks amazing. All cleaned up with a warm fire lit. Thank you so much, Euphemia."

The tiny cook nodded then eyed Grant up and down before muttering, "Aye, me Malcolm's brother will do just fine with me Sheila he will."

Grant had no chance to say anything before Euphemia sauntered off, sparse brows fluttering up at her MacLomain. Ceard, meanwhile, looked back at her with absolute adoration.

"I dinnae know the lass but 'tis safe to say she's something, aye?" Grant murmured.

Sheila shook her head. "You have no idea."

But no sooner did she find happiness in once more seeing Euphemia than her thoughts turned elsewhere. Or better yet, where they'd been for hours now. "I hate that Torra is still with Keir. In fact, it petrifies me." Staring up at the castle basked in moonlight, she shivered. "There are a lot of warriors on those battlements. Do you think Colin MacLeod is one of them?"

Grant paused for a long moment, his profile hard and unyielding as he gazed up. "I dinnae know, lass. I can only hope."

"Right, because if he is then Keir still considers him an ally and he remains close to Torra…as close as Keir will allow that is." She shook her head. "I know the MacLomains are doing well in this war but I worry what it means that Hamilton has a dragon at his disposal now."

"We dinnae know what he does and does not have yet," Grant said. "'Tis my hope that Torra knew what she was doing when she took my sword and set us free."

Sheila shook her head but before something negative came out of her mouth, she stopped. Right now, there was no place for anything but optimism. "Well, if I've learned nothing else it's that Torra always seems to have a trick up her sleeve." She arched a brow at him. "Has anyone been able to question Iosbail yet on what she knows?"

Grant shook his head, the corner of his lip pulling up. "Nay, she and King Alexander vanished into a cottage and none have heard a thing more." He made a throaty sound that struck her as both a mix of discomfort and amusement. "Outside of their passion of course. 'Tis likely when she's ready she'll share all."

It was hard not to smile. If nothing else good came of this, Alexander once again had Iosbail in his arms. Sheila shook her head. "I still feel like you keep secrets, Grant. You seemed surprised that Torra did what she did; that the sword Adlin and Meyla gave you had that sort of power…but were you? Did you know what Torra was going to do?"

"A sword that is no longer in my possession," he reminded. "Nay, I didnae know of her plans. 'Twas supposed to go another way entirely. I'd put your ring to my mark and she'd use her power to see us *all* free and hopefully Keir dead."

"Which might've worked," she said. "Then why didn't she do it?"

"I dinnae know," he reported. "I can only guess that she learned something new when we arrived in Keir's chamber. Whatever it was, she had good reason for her actions."

"With thought to freeing us all of course." Sheila frowned. "If she loves Colin MacLeod so much why wouldn't she have sent him away as well?"

"Again, I dinnae know," he murmured. "But whatever the cause of her actions, 'twould be to protect him."

It was hard to imagine that keeping Colin at Keir's side was good in any way but she wouldn't press the issue. Who knows, maybe she was wrong. After all, she'd seen the intense feelings between Torra and Colin. There could be no doubt Colin would defend her with his last dying breath. But when against Keir she suspected that'd all it'd be…a last dying breath.

Sheila tried hard not to sigh. Having both his cousin and best friend behind enemy lines had to be excruciating on Grant.

So much of what had transpired had to be hurting him.

She continued to eye the castle, her thoughts on all that had happened to bring them to this moment. With those thoughts again came who they might have lost in all this and sadness overwhelmed her. "I'm so sorry about Kenzie," she said softly, offering again nothing but positive thoughts though she brought up anything but. "Yet I tend to think she'll pull through."

"Aye," Grant whispered. "If any can 'tis her."

"McKayla will heal her. I just know it."

Grant said nothing but pulled her back against his front and wrapped his arms around her.

Not necessarily to change the subject but to lighten it she said, "It seems that McKayla has not only been managing the castle alongside Torra's parents but she's been busy working on revisions for the story she wrote."

"Aye, I learned of her writing when we were connected through the pentacle." She heard the frown in his voice. "How is it possible she writes now? Is her story not in the twenty-first century?"

Sheila made a 'meh' sound out of the corner of her lips. "She might have retrieved it but don't tell Colin. God knows he'd freak out if he knew she time traveled again."

"'Tis dangerous at such a time," he conceded.

"Yeah, yeah," she muttered. "But it's done so no worries. Anyways, it seems she's now got the hero and heroine imprisoned together. There's still plenty of time travel and magic but the plot had a major overhaul. Now it involves not only the original couple but several others."

"It sounds like a long story indeed," he said.

Sheila looked over her shoulder at him. "Yep, one full of intrigue, war and most especially passion."

His warm eyes dropped to hers, full of desire. "'Tis a good tale that."

Though desire spiked through her, she returned her gaze to their surroundings. Highland warriors and weapons abound. "Without doubt," she murmured. "And she's decided to go with her original title."

"And what was that?"

"Plight of the Highlander."

"Odd sound to it," he said. "Why did she do such a thing?"

"I'm not sure." She again gazed at the Hamilton castle and thought of Colin MacLeod. "As she was convinced all along, she seems to think the hero is facing one heck of a plight."

Grant was silent for a long moment before he softly said, "I'm sure he is."

Her eyes fell once more to the fields beyond the castle. Bonfires had been lit to warm the warriors and make visible just a tenth of what lay beyond Keir's gates. Sheila stared at one bonfire in particular. "It wasn't all that long ago that I stood in a crowd around that fire and saw you for the first time."

She still remembered how fierce Grant looked, how breathtakingly handsome she thought him despite how much she denied it at the time. There was nothing like the cursed feeling of desiring the enemy.

But enemy no more.

Grant pulled her tighter against him, his words against her ear. "Your ring was but a confusing bright flicker in my eyes that night. 'Twas the beginning of my journey back to life."

"So you *did* see it."

"Aye," he murmured. "I saw it."

Sheila tilted her head and once more met his eyes. "Though a spark started in front of that bonfire it was your words that carried us so far."

His gaze devoured hers as he whispered those very words. "Have *faith* in me, lass."

"I did…have faith."

"As did I," he said softly. "In you."

Soft but desperate, his lips closed over hers. More eager than ever, she turned and wrapped her arms around his neck. Passion flared stronger than ever as he lifted her into his arms and kneed the door open.

A castle lay under siege.

The war was not nearly won.

But enemies had become allies and old bonds reforged.

Yet as the door slammed shut and her highlander laid her down, little else mattered.

They had pushed beyond their abused hearts and conquered their pasts.

"I love you," she whispered.

"Aye, my wee geal," he whispered back, lips hovering over hers. "But 'tis good to finally hear you say such."

"You knew I would," she murmured, smiling as his lips brushed over hers.

"Nay, I but guessed." He dropped several more small kisses then grinned as his loving eyes glittered through the darkness, his last words lingering in the air long after he swooped down…

"But never once did I lose faith that I'd hear such."

The End

Finish off the series with Torra's story, *Plight of the Highlander*, coming soon. Or start at the beginning in *Mark of the Highlander*, book one.

Interested in learning more about Devin and his curse? Check out *The Georgian Embrace*. Or join him and his cousins in the *Calum's Curse Series Boxed Set*.

Read about how another couple began. Follow King Alexander and Iosbail MacLomain's romance in *Highland Persuasion* or enjoy their complete tale in *The MacLomain Series-Early Years Boxed Set* which precedes the original *MacLomain Series*.

PREVIOUS RELEASES

~The MacLomain Series- Early Years~

Highland Defiance- Book One
Highland Persuasion- Book Two
Highland Mystic- Book Three

~The MacLomain Series~

The King's Druidess- Prelude
Fate's Monolith- Book One
Destiny's Denial- Book Two
Sylvan Mist- Book Three

The MacLomain Series Boxed Set is also available.

~The MacLomain Series- Next Generation~

Mark of the Highlander- Book One
Vow of the Highlander- Book Two
Wrath of the Highlander- Book Three
Faith of the Highlander- Book Four
Plight of the Highlander- Book Five

~Calum's Curse Series~

The Victorian Lure- Book One
The Georgian Embrace- Book Two
The Tudor Revival- Book Three

The Calum's Curse Boxed Set is also available.

~Forsaken Brethren Series~

Darkest Memory- Book One
Heart of Vesuvius- Book Two

Also available in the Forsaken Brethren Series Twinpack.

~Song of the Muses Series~

Highland Muse

About the Author

Sky Purington is the best-selling author of thirteen novels and several novellas. A New Englander born and bred, Sky was raised hearing stories of folklore, myth and legend. When combined with a love for nature, romance and time-travel, elements from the stories of her youth found release in her books.

Purington loves to hear from readers and can be contacted at Sky@SkyPurington.com. Interested in keeping up with Sky's latest news and releases? Visit Sky's website, www.skypurington.com to download her free App on iTunes and Android or sign up for her quarterly newsletter. Love social networking? Find Sky on Facebook and Twitter.

Made in the USA
Las Vegas, NV
03 March 2022

44964974R00125